SING A SONG OF EVIL

Midway through the song, Billie Lee Kidd began to feel strange. She felt a stab of fear. She lifted her head to the amphitheater's open roof. She stared at the night sky, horrified and fascinated at once.

The sky was changing. Stars snapped free of their moorings. Constellations spun giddily and fell like crystal chandeliers to smash in glittering shards. Fragments of starstuff sprayed the earth. The oceans erupted in a blue-green spray. The continents crumbled. In the depths of the starless sky, a door swung open. A river of darkness spilled out and became a whirlpool, a vortex, a spiral of chaos reaching out with octopus arms to swallow up the universe.

Billie Lee kept on singing her song. She never noticed that the words had changed to—words of a language dead for centuries. But they suited the melody. They made her song complete. . . .

DEATHSONG

DEATHSONG

Douglas Borton

AN ONYX BOOK

NEW AMERICAN LIBRARY

A DIVISION OF PENGUIN BOOKS USA INC.

PUBLISHER'S NOTE

This book is a work of fiction. Names, characters, places, and incidents either are the product of the author's imagination or are used fictitiously, and any resemblance to actual persons, living or dead, events, or locales is entirely coincidental.

NAL BOOKS ARE AVAILABLE AT QUANTITY DISCOUNTS WHEN USED TO PROMOTE PRODUCTS OR SERVICES. FOR INFORMATION PLEASE WRITE TO PREMIUM MARKETING DIVISION, NEW AMERICAN LIBRARY, 1633 BROADWAY, NEW YORK, NEW YORK 10019.

ONYX TRADEMARK REG. U.S. PAT OFF AND FOREIGN COUNTRIES REGISTERED TRADEMARK—MARCA REGISTRADA
HECHO EN CHICAGO U.S

SIGNET, SIGNET CLASSIC, MENTOR, ONYX, PLUME, MERIDIAN and NAL BOOKS are published by New American Library, a division of Penguin books USA Inc., 1633 Broadway, New York, New York 10019.

First Printing, October, 1989

1 2 3 4 5 6 7 8 9

PRINTED IN THE UNITED STATES OF AMERICA

For my grandmother
ANN DORIS KLEEN
with love

Author's Note

Grateful acknowledgments are due to my agent, Jane Dystel, who sold this novel for me; my editor, Kevin Mulroy, whose comments and suggestions helped to shape the story; Kevin's assistant, Elizabeth Martin, who also contributed several useful ideas; and my mother and father, for their support and encouragement.

D.B.

Prologue

He stole the child at dawn.

The marketplace was crowded with vendors and their customers, haggling noisily, exchanging coins and wares. The clear sky stretched like a canopy of blue over stalls gleaming with bananas and oranges, melons and dates, jars of sorghum and sacks of wheat—all the abundance of the verdant fields of Ur. In the haze of distance loomed the ziggurat of the moon god Nannar, a tiered tower of baked brick rising eighty feet above the dusty plain to touch the roof of heaven, its terraces planted with gardens, its three great staircases climbing toward the shrine at its summit.

Kuruk made his way through the marketplace, elbowing other men rudely out of his way, ignoring their muffled curses. He had no fear of these people. He towered over them, just as the ziggurat towered over the city; he stood fully two heads taller than the tallest of those around him. And he was strong, strong of body and will, while the people of Sumer were weak, fat, lazy, drunk on beer and flabby with affluence. Theirs had once been a mighty empire; now it had lapsed into decadence.

He swept his eyes over the crowd, noting with scorn the women's glittering jewelry, their wigs and headdresses bedecked with ropes of pearls and artificial flowers of lapis-lazuli, their summer gowns of red and yellow fabric, tissue-thin, their olive-skinned bodies smelling of oil and perfume, their broad faces painted in eye shadow and lip rouge. And he heard their laughter, bright and musical, mingling with the voices of the men in the crowd, bearded men with hawk noses and black hair, men who worked perhaps as artisans or boatmen or scribes. Men who had built this city and this world, and who were proud of it, pleased with what they had done.

Kuruk pursed his lips tight. There was happiness here, on this summer morning. Happiness and abundance, prosperity and pride. But soon—he thought, with the first hint of a smile—soon, there would be nothing of it left. Nothing at all.

He would see to that. He, and the gods he served.

He walked on. His gaze was drawn briefly to three naked children squatting near a booth, playing with a dead mouse. He passed them by. He needed a younger child, an infant. One whose mind had yet to be sullied by the least impurity of thought.

Ahead, a woman was arguing amiably with one merchant about the freshness of a cucumber. At her feet, momentarily forgotten, lay a baby in wicker basket. The creature was perhaps six months old. Still helpless without its mother's teat. Still as innocent, thought Kuruk, as when it was plucked from the womb.

This, then, was his quarry. His sacrifice.

He approached the woman from behind, walking swiftly but not furtively, his head high and shoulders straight. From his robe he produced a sheepskin sack. In one swift motion he knelt, picked up the child, and thrust it into the sack. The infant howled. The sack squirmed and writhed like a bag of eels.

He rose, turned, and began to walk away. The whole matter had taken less than a second.

Behind him, he heard a bewildered murmur from the mother, then her outraged scream.

Kuruk did not run. He never ran. It was unseemly, not to mention unnecessary, for the high priest of lost Antarok to flee from any man—much less a woman. Women were weak, fit only to be slaves, concubines, and bearers of children. No woman could ever threaten him.

The crowd shifted in confusion. Faces turned to-

ward him, then turned away. The men—small, soft,
weak—did not care to challenge one of his size and
strength. And perhaps some of them had heard the
whispered rumors about this man called Kuruk, this
stranger clad in black robes who had come to the city
from afar, who consorted with criminals and half-mad
beggars, who was said to worship other gods, dark
gods which had granted him dark powers.

Then one of the vendors, a fine young fool anxious
to prove his manhood, leapt out from behind his stall
and seized Kuruk's arm.

"Give back the child," said the boy in a voice that
was almost steady. "In the name of Enlil, king of all
the gods—give it back."

Kuruk smiled, most pleasantly, and hummed a little
tune. Just a brief snatch of melody, strangely haunting.

The boy stiffened up. Suddenly his skin was as hard
and inflexible as baked brick. His muscles were rigid,
corpselike. Only his eyes were still alive. They gazed
up at Kuruk, living eyes in a dead man's face, eyes
wide with terror and silent pleading.

The boy's hand, immobile, still clutched Kuruk's
arm. Kuruk closed his fist over the hand and squeezed.
The frozen fingers cracked and splintered like brittle
clay. Kuruk released his grip and the remains of the
hand disintegrated in a cloud of talcum.

Lightly he tapped the boy's shoulder, pushing him
off-balance. The boy teetered, a statue knocked off its
pedestal, then toppled over on his back. He hit the
ground with a dull thud. A webwork of cracks shot
through his body. A small sound, perhaps a muffled
sob or a cry of pain, escaped his unmoving lips in the
instant before he crumbled to dust.

Kuruk took another step, and then the mother thrust
herself in front of him, blocking his path. Single-
minded in her pursuit, she had not even noticed the
incident of a moment ago. But the crowd had seen it.
They drew back, forming a wide circle around the pair,

They, at least, understand my power, thought Kuruk with satisfaction.

The mother understood nothing. She glared up at him, her wide face flushed red, shrieking pleas to Nannar and Anu and Enki, gods of moon and sky and water, to strike down this thief who had dared to steal her son.

So it was a boy, then. Kuruk had not been certain. It was hard to tell when they were very young and clad in swaddling clothes, as this creature was. Well, a boy would serve.

He fixed his eyes on the woman. She paused for breath, oblivious of his gaze, then opened her mouth to speak again.

Kuruk sang. Three crisp notes rose in the sudden stillness like a burst of birdsong.

The woman hiccuped. A hoptoad shot out of her mouth. She stared at it, astonished. She hiccuped a second time, then again and again. Each time, a new toad popped out, arcing to the ground like a shooting star.

There were screams from the crowd. Kuruk smiled. He heard no laughter anymore.

The woman pressed her hands to her mouth, moaning in terror, trying to hold back the gruesome tide. It was no use. She made a choking sound. She vomited up a stream of tadpoles. They tumbled down the front of her gown, leaving crisscrossing trails of slime. Their tiny greenish bodies wriggled damply in the dirt at her feet. She doubled over, retching. A nest of scorpions exploded from her lips, scurrying over her face like a living mask. Earthworms crawled out of her nostrils. Rats scurried in her hair, their pink noses sniffing at her ears. She fell on her knees, sobbing, her child forgotten, as a viper slid out of her mouth like a swollen tongue.

Kuruk walked on. The crowd parted hastily. He encountered no more obstacles.

Inside the sheepskin sack, the infant boy kicked and squealed.

The child cried unceasingly throughout the day. No doubt it was hungry. Kuruk did not care. He paced the small courtyard of his house, watching the shadows lengthen as the sun swam slowly through the cloudless sky.

No soldiers came to arrest him. He had expected none. The authorities, even King Gimil-Sin himself, surely knew of his powers. They would not care to invite the wrath of a sorcerer, not even had the king's own son been taken.

At dusk, he placed the child in the sack once more and left the house with the sack slung over his shoulder. He walked swiftly through the maze of narrow, winding streets, avoiding the blind alleys which sprang up at every turn. He lived in the poorest part of the city; prostitutes and thieves were his neighbors. The din of drunken shouting, mingled with the wails of women beaten by their husbands, reached his ears from the doorways of the houses passing by. He barely noticed. He was utterly indifferent to his surroundings. He had never been concerned with wealth and luxury. Let the rich merchants and the court officials enjoy their three-story homes, their jeweled women, their banquets of salmon and roast pig and goat's-milk cheese. Let them revel. Let them laugh. He need only sing.

And tonight he would learn his greatest song, the song of songs, a song fit for the high priest of Antarok. And the rich and the proud would laugh no more.

His route took him past the temple of the water god, Enki. Its side wall was a sheet of bronze, catching his reflection in the sun's dying rays. He studied himself, noting with impersonal satisfaction the broad shoulders and massive chest barely concealed under his long black robe. Black ropes of beard framed his high cheekbones and jutting lower lip. A long, jagged scar, white as alabaster against his dark skin, ran down the left side of his face from his eyelid to his mouth. To the eye, he was no older than thirty; in truth, he had seen twice that many years.

He reached the city gates. The great wall extended on both sides, an immense elevation of mud-brick, embracing the city, protective as a mother's arms. From this impregnable battlement Gimil-Sin's archers had only recently repelled an invasion of the Amorites, barbaric nomads from the western desert.

The city stables were close by. From the liveryman Kuruk obtained his stallion. He swung up onto its back and rode through the gates, leaving the city behind. Hooves pounded the unpaved road. The horse galloped swiftly, passing riders on donkeys and farmers driving ox-drawn carts. The plain stretched to the dimming embers of the horizon. To the west, the Euphrates wound like a gleaming serpent past the city wall; sailboats and cargo ships dotted its wide expanse. A network of irrigation canals extended from the river, crisscrossing the fields of crops fed by the lifegiving water. Vineyards, wheat fields, and pomegranate orchards glided by. A few farmers and their slaves still worked the fields in the fading light.

A mile from the city Kuruk reined in his horse and looked back. Ur was alive with the glow of torchlight, flickering like the first faint stars. The wind, tinged with moisture from the river and canals, was cool on his face.

He spurred his horse off the road, into a weed-strewn field, and rode toward the ruins of a farmhouse. He reached the house as the last traces of daylight abandoned the sky. He dismounted and entered.

The moon was rising, low over the horizon; moonbeams slanted through the collapsed roof, washing the bare brick walls and dirt floor of a single featureless room. The room was empty save for a single clay tablet, twelve inches square, which lay in the middle of the floor.

Kuruk put down the squirming sack, then sat against a wall, his face upturned to heaven, waiting. The stars shimmered. The moon glowered down at him, its light cold and watchful. Perhaps the great Nannar suspected what he was up to. Kuruk chuckled at this thought.

The gods of Sumer were a lie, he knew, a fable impressed on childish minds, as were the gods of neighboring Akkad and Elam. Only once in mankind's history had a city-state arisen with knowledge of the true gods—of Ragnaaroth, the Spider King, and Beth-shul, the Screaming Woman, and Toth, the Wind That Hungers, and all the others in their legions.

He knew them well, because it had been his mission to serve them. He was the last in the line of Antarok's high priests, and the greatest of them all. He alone had come within reach of the dark gods' final secret, the most sacred of the songs of power, the song to end all songs.

In the temple of the Spider King, thirty years ago, he had stood with his head bowed over a pool of blood from a sacrificed child, ringed by disciples chanting their obeisance to the dark gods. As their mingled voices rose on clouds of incense, he had called upon the gods to reveal their last secret, so jealousy guarded. The song—and the power, the ultimate power—had nearly been his. He had come close, so tantalizingly close.

But it was not to be. The dark gods' still more ancient but ageless enemies—those nameless, antediluvian forces that did not seek power or make war, that found no joy in pain and no glory in destruction—had risen up to stop the gods of Antarok from imparting this deadliest of all secrets to man; and in the war that followed, the elder gods had triumphed over the Spider King and his legions, and had banished them to exile in another world.

Their downfall had brought low the great city-state of Antarok. In a single night of fiery chaos, its statues of limestone and marble were reduced to dust; its towers, greater than any ziggurat, were felled like mighty trees; its fortress walls were leveled. The city had been wiped from the face of the earth. Shifting sand dunes were now its only grave markers; jackals prowled among the litter of crumbled statuary and bleached bones. Nothing remained of Antarok save the underground chambers of tombs, where the corpses of the high priests who had gone before him lay sleepless in their caskets, demanding vengeance.

Kuruk, alone among the hundred thousand of the city, had escaped, taking with him nothing but his life.

For twenty years he had wandered the desert in exile, a sojourner in an alien land, stopping for a time at Lagash, at Kish, at Erech, and finally at Ur, the greatest of Sumer's teeming cities. Here he had settled; and here, for ten years, he had lived, schemed, waited for this night.

For on this night, he would try again.

Marching footsteps interrupted his thoughts. His followers, approaching.

They entered silently, a dozen men in all. They ringed the room. Torches blazed in their right hands.

Kuruk moved to the center of the room. He studied them. Hoods obscured their faces. They were men of all ages, races, and trades, men sought out in eating places and alleyways, in gambling halls and dungeons, men bound to him forever by an oath of blood and by the bracelets on their left wrists. Each bracelet was made of chain links holding a pearl-blue stone, a small and delicate stone that had been washed in Kuruk's own blood. Once clasped on a man's wrist, this stone—the Bloodstone—became one with its wearer; it was joined with him, body and soul; it could be removed only under penalty of instant death, a death too horrible to contemplate.

A girl stepped through the doorway and undressed Kuruk silently. She was Duanna, a female slave owned by his disciples. Ordinarily Kuruk would never have permitted an outsider to witness their secret rites or to

hear the mystic songs they sang. It would be too easy
for others to learn the secrets of his mystic powers,
then turn his own magic against him. But of Duanna
he had no fear. He had cut out her tongue. She could
not sing a note.

His robe fell to his feet. He kicked it aside. He stood
naked save for the Bloodstone glittering on his own
left wrist, the stone that he had worn since his initiation into the priesthood as a trembling young boy.

His body was a study in corded muscle. He had
huge hands, laced with blue veins, and massive legs
seemingly as thick and round as columns. There was
not a single hair anywhere on his chest or groin.

Duanna anointed him with palm oil. She knelt before him, rubbing the oil into his thighs and groin,
then rose and spread the last of the oil over his pectorals, neck, and face. She stepped back. He looked
down at his glistening nakedness. He nodded. She retreated to the corner and turned her back. She knew
she was not to see what took place next.

Kuruk knelt. Wordlessly he removed the child from
the sack.

It had wriggled free of its swaddling clothes and was
naked also. It kicked its stubby legs. Kuruk placed it
gently on the floor. He reached under the tablet and
drew out a bronze dagger with a hilt of gold.

The child stopped crying. It gazed, fascinated, at
the shiny blade, sparkling in the moonlight. Kuruk
moved the dagger from side to side. The child followed the motion with its eyes. It giggled. The knife
was a toy. The child reached up, wanting to play. Kuruk smiled, caressing the child's small, hairless head,
while very gently he slid the dagger into its groin.

At first there was no blood, no pain. The blade vanished into the soft flesh without a trace. Then Kuruk
tightened his grip on the dagger and drew it up slowly,
splitting the child open from loin to chin. Blood
foamed out from the parted skin flaps. The infant
wailed in sudden agony and incomprehension.

Kuruk put down the knife. He plunged his fist through the open wound, into the child's chest. His hand closed over its heart, still beating fitfully, tiny as a jewel. He wrenched it free.

The child's death cry was abruptly cut off.

Kuruk paused, listening. There was little chance that the killing had been overheard. Not here, so far from the city, in the night darkness when the fields were empty. Still, he listened. The years had taught him caution.

After a moment, he raised his free hand, fingers spread, as a signal to his flock. Around him rose a chant, low and breathless, building in intensity and volume. The Song of the Prophecy. The song he had taught his faithful. A powerful song, but not the equal of the song he was now to learn.

He squeezed the heart like a sponge. Blood dribbled onto the tablet. The chanting grew louder. The blood welled up in pools, then flowed across the clay in living rivulets, forming patterns, words.

Words.

Kuruk frowned. It was not musical notation he was seeing, not the pictographs of Antarok which recorded tones and meter, not a song at all. Always before, a song of power in bloody symbol had crawled across the tablet's face, the unsung glyphs pulsing with the promise of evil. But now, instead, a list of prophecies took shape before him, writing the history of generations yet unborn.

He cast his eyes over the neat rows of cuneiform script. He read of the end of Sumer, its conquest by the restless Amorites who even now were marshalling their forces against the empire. He read of a greater power which, in turn, would crush the Amorites under its heel. He read of the rise and fall of empires yet unborn, of wars that would drown the earth in blood. He read of the day when the last of the prophecies would come to pass. On that day, and not before, would the sacred song be sung.

Kuruk looked up from the tablet to the sky, the constellations wheeling in the heavens, performing their ageless dance. For the first time in his life, he knew sadness. He had waited so long. He had served his gods well. But, it seemed, he was not to be rewarded. He was not to sing the song. He was not to have the power. It was to be given to another. To one outside the ranks of his chosen ones. An unknown, a stranger in a distant land and time. A stranger selected, not by the Spider King and his hosts, but by the very forces that had defeated them. A stranger who would be—must be—their enemy.

So it was written. These, then, were the terms of armistice, the conditions forced on his gods by their bitter nemeses. It was a hard settlement, promising a long exile for the gods he served. Two hundred generations of men might pass away before the last of the prophecies could be fulfilled. Such a very long time.

He shook his head, dispelling sadness. He had work to do. He had been given a mission. What was prophesied here, he knew, was not what must happen, but only what might happen. Like a river, history's course was ever-shifting; it was up to him, and to those who would follow him, to channel and redirect it as his gods had willed. This he must do, if the song of songs were ever to be sung, and the dark gods' long exile ended.

He would leave Ur. He would travel the earth. He would gather followers from all the lands where men were found. He would train them in the mystic arts. He would teach them to infiltrate the ranks of the powerful, bend minds and wills, shape and direct events, and thereby bring to pass each of the prophecies in turn. His chosen ones, his army of spies, his secret brotherhood, would use their deadly gifts to write the future history of this world as it had been written on this tablet—in blood.

Above all, he would teach them to listen, always listen. Listen—to every melody whistled in the street, to every pipe of the flute and pluck of the lyre, to every stirring of the crickets and whisper of the wind. Listen—for the Deathsong.

And when, at last, that song was sung . . . they would strike.

1

Billie Lee Kidd stood in center stage, looking past the footlights at the encircling tiers of faces and clapping hands, and finished the lead vocal on the first chorus of "Even Cowgirls Get the Blues." Behind her, the band took over on the instrumental. Gary provided a flourish of drums and cowbells, Bobby Joe got in some hot licks on the bass, and K.C. was jamming on the acoustic piano. Billie danced away from the microphone, high-stepping in her white cowboy boots, her fingers plucking guitar strings rapid-fire, gliding effortlessly over the frets. She did a little spontaneous do-si-do with Bobby Joe while the audience hooted wildly, then twirled and jitterbugged back to the mike in time to sing the second stanza. Her strong, throaty voice surged with amazing power through dozens of speakers, splitting the stillness of a hot August night, rising through the amphitheater's open roof to the stars.

She had spent the last eight weeks crisscrossing the Sun Belt, playing Houston and Atlanta and Nashville and Phoenix and now, finally, L.A. It had been fun— a regular shit-kicker, Gary had said, using one of those trucker expressions she hated—but still, she didn't much mind being at the end of this tour. Tonight she could sleep in her own bed and listen to the surf caress the Malibu beach. When she got to sleep. Which wouldn't be for a while yet, because there would be the wrap party, of course, and because this pretty blond-maned boy in the first row had been smiling up at her for the past two and a half hours, and during the intermission Billie had asked one of her people backstage to slip him a note.

The song ended with a ruffle of drums and guitar chords, all but drowned out in the thunder of beating hands and cowboy hollers. Half the crowd was on its feet. She glanced over her shoulder and flashed a smile at her band. Gary tipped his hat to her. She bowed to him, then to the audience. The crowd responded with raucous yahoos. Nearly everyone was standing now. But not the pretty blond boy. He just smiled at her and held up a square of folded paper. So he knew the score. And he was like the song said, willin'. Good. She didn't care for lengthy courtships.

It was nearly midnight and she had exhausted her routine twenty minutes ago, but she wasn't ready to quit. She was high on adrenaline, breathing in the adulation of six thousand fans. Her heart slamdanced in her chest. Her face was flushed. Her legs trembled weakly. It was the kind of feeling she got only from a good show and from sex, the feeling that still kept her out on the road eight months out of the year. She loved this life. She loved the applause and the wolf whistles and the worshipful eyes. Maybe it was wrong, superficial, to care about all that, but she did. She loved her crowd and they loved her, and tonight she wanted to do something special for them.

But I can't fuck 'em all, she thought wryly.

Still, there was an alternative.

She pressed her mouth close to the microphone. "You are one hell of a crowd," she said in her New Mexico twang.

Waves of applause answered her. She raised her voice over the noise.

"And because you've been so darn nice to me, I thought I'd do you all a little favor." Lewd but well-meant shouts greeted this remark. "I've got a new song here I just wrote a couple of weeks ago. Never played it before, except for myself, and I'd like to debut it tonight. If that's okay with you folks.'' A rolling thunderclap of approval. ''I call it 'Dark Waters.' ''

She took a breath. It was a slight risk, playing a song she had not properly rehearsed. But she had tried it out during the sound check in Phoenix. Anyway, it was a simple tune, and her own arrangement permitted her to sing it solo, with only her own guitar as accompaniment.

She began to play. The crowd quieted, understanding that this would not be another foot-stomper. No, sir. This song was slow, sad, and haunting. Not really a country song at all.

Kenneth Blane watched Billie Lee Kidd, fascinated. He had never been so close to her—only a few yards away, in the third row of the orchestra section.

Beside him, Sharon listened patiently. He knew she would have preferred an evening of John Williams doing his movie themes. But she was a good wife. She indulged her husband's whims. She never questioned where he went on those nights when he was mysteriously called away, or why his clothes smelled of incense afterward. She never even asked him if he sometimes thought of Billie, instead of her, when they were in bed. Which, in both cases, was really just as well.

Kenneth had been a big fan of Billie's ever since her first hit album, *Lovers' Leap*, four years ago. Everybody said she was the best thing to happen to country since the Grand Ole Opry. She had shot out of obscurity to become an overnight sensation, sweeping every other country sweetheart into second place. In retrospect, she seemed destined to do it. She had the kind of restless, nervous energy that overflowed her five-foot frame and made her bigger than life. The press called her an auburn-haired fireball, a freckle-faced dynamo, the spunky kid sister who grew up to be prom queen.

She didn't dress like a prom queen, though. Tonight she wore white cowboy boots, stone-washed jeans with a hole in one knee, and a Farm-Aid T-shirt. She had started the show with a ten-gallon hat, but flipped it cheerfully into the audience after the last rousing chorus of ''Thank God I'm a Country Girl.'' People scrambled for it like baseball fans in the bleachers scrapping for a World Series ball.

Viewed with an objective eye, Billie was not beautiful, but she had charm, the earthy charm of a girl you could get drunk with. Her green eyes were mischievous, catlike. Her grin had been described as impish. It lit up her face like a flashlight in a jack-o'-lantern.

It occurred to Kenneth, as he watched her now, that the key to Billie's appeal was not her looks, not even her voice, but simply that magical quality she projected, the quality of being so very much alive.

Then, in the next moment, he stiffened in his seat, his mind focused with suddenly painful intensity on the song Billie Lee Kidd was singing. The song he had been trained to hear. The song for which the world had waited, through the slow crawl of the centuries, in an agony of suspense. The song at last given voice.

The Deathsong.

Midway through the first stanza, Billie began to feel strange.

Nothing like this had ever happened to her before. It was almost like one of those out-of-body experiences her New Age friends were always chattering about. She had never believed in that stuff. But now she had to wonder. Because suddenly she felt herself floating free of her body, looking down at the tiny figure spotlighted in center stage.

The song went on. Her song. But it was not her song, was it? Only the words were hers.

And the words were wrong. They made it a song about lost love. But the melody carried its own meaning, a meaning deeper than words, deeper even than conscious thought. A meaning that was only now becoming clear to her. Now—when it was too late.

She looked down at the crowd ringed in concentric circles around the stage. They still watched the figure strumming the guitar, unaware that the spotlight illuminated only an empty vessel, a form without essence.

She felt a stab of fear. She lifted her head to the sky, impelled by an instinct she could not name. She stared, horrified and fascinated at once.

The sky was shifting, changing. Stars snapped free of their moorings. Constellations shuddered, spun giddily, then fell like crystal chandeliers to smash in glittering shards. Fragments of starstuff sprayed the earth. A webwork of cracks shot through it. Oceans erupted in a blue-green spray. The continents crumbled, their wreckage flung wide. Only the lighted stage and the rows of seats remained, suspended in space like an asteroid. The performance went on. Billie watched helplessly. She moaned.

In the depths of the starless sky, a door swung open. A door vaster than a million galaxies. A door without shape or substance. Darkness spilled out, a river of darkness deeper than night, black currents swirling and eddying, an opaque stream which became a whirlpool, a vortex, a spiral of chaos reaching out with octopus arms to swallow up the universe.

Below, the distant mannequin figure still sang. But the words had changed. They were not Billie's words any longer. They were words musty with age, unknown to modern ears, words of a language dead for centuries. They were the right words. They suited the melody. They made the song complete.

The audience stirred restlessly. The members of the band exchanged bewildered glances. They had not seen the cataclysm. But they had heard the change in the song.

Billie noticed none of it. She was far away. She was floating through space.

She flew higher, toward the door. She did not wish to. She had no choice. Her only hope was to stop the singing. To silence this song which seemed to sing itself. But her body was not hers any longer. She could not dictate its actions. She could not stop. Dimly she understood that it did not matter, because the damage was done.

Maybe—she thought distantly—maybe it had been done anyway, not tonight, but two weeks ago, in a chartered plane skimming the Utah desert, and in a dream.

2

Two weeks earlier, Billie Lee Kidd and her backup band were doing a fleahop run from one concert stop to the next, flying in a chartered Piper Navajo with coffee stains on the seats and a lingering odor of cigar smoke in the ventilation system. She didn't mind. Her whole attention was focused on the low, comforting drone of the engines, lulling her to sleep. She needed sleep so badly, needed to restore her flagging energy, rekindle that inner fire in time to burn herself out again in another three-night gig in the latest city on their cross-country tour, whichever the hell city it was. Austin? Atlanta? She couldn't remember. And frankly, my dear—she told herself with a weary smile—I don't give a shit.

She put her seat back and closed her eyes, blanking her mind of thought, letting the engines carry her into the clouds.

She did not dream of the song right away. That came

later. First there were memories. Vivid as life, which was appropriate, because it was her life she was seeing, all twenty-nine misspent years of it, swimming before her closed eyelids like that total recall which, some say, is the prelude to death.

A summer day in the desert. She was ten years old, riding the bay mare her parents had given her on her birthday. The sky was a sheet of white fire. The air was furnace-hot. She had ridden miles from home, into the wilderness where no sign of human habitation broke the expanse of mesas, cacti, and yucca plants.

She was rounding a bend in the trail, challenging the stillness with her young, high voice raised in a refrain of ''The Streets of Laredo''—when suddenly the horse reared up, snorting and whinnying. She was pitched to the ground on hands and knees. She rolled over on her side, instinctively putting distance between herself and the kicking hooves, and came face-to-face with a rattler.

It lay in the dirt, two feet of mottled yellow and pink tapering to the triangular head and hissing tongue. It coiled and writhed, its tail shaking ominously, body ripping in multicolored bands like a barber-shop pole.

The mare, still spooked, spun and galloped away down the trail in the direction they had come, leaving Billie behind.

She hitched in a breath. She told herself to get away, crawl backward, now, dammit, *now.* She could not move. Her legs and arms were numb, useless. She stared into the sidewinder's black-resin eyes. They stared back, dark and chilly as night. Then with a snap of its head, the snake whipped sideways and sank its fangs into her right forearm.

She screamed. She hurtled back, away from the snake, which was already withdrawing, hissing in triumph.

She knew about rattlers. She'd had a dog once, a collie named Ranchero, who'd been bitten by one. He must have killed the snake in the next instant, then tried to carry the carcass home in his mouth. He never made it. She found him, stiff and dead, in the dirt a half-mile from the ranch. The ruined snake lay nearby. Later she looked up rattlesnakes in her father's medical book. She read the symptoms. Rapid onset of swelling and severe pain. Amputation of affected limb often necessary. Mortality rate: low. She asked her father why Ranchero had died if the mortality rate was low. He explained that a small animal, like a dog, was more susceptible to the rattler's venom. Ranchero had weighed eighty pounds. Billie, age ten, weighed sixty-nine pounds.

And she was miles from home, with no horse.

She got unsteadily to her feet. She began to walk the trail, forcing herself not to run, not to panic. She would make it. She would survive. Her father kept vials of antivenin at the ranch. She only had to get there. That was all.

She did not know how much time had passed before she became aware of the steady, throbbing pain in her right arm. It's starting, she thought with a stab of fear. Oh, Jesus.

She sucked in a deep breath. She walked faster.

The sun beat down. Clouds of dust rose from the trail. Her vision blurred. She felt feverish. She did not remember fever as one of the symptoms. It was her imagination, that was all. Probably the snake was not even a rattler. Probably it was just some harmless kind with similar markings. Sure.

The pain was bad now. Really bad. The whole right side of her body was on fire. Her forearm was puffing up. She was right-handed, too. If they amputated her right arm, she would have to learn how to write all over again. She had wanted to play the guitar, like Loretta Lynn. She couldn't play with one hand, could she? Could she even dress herself? Would people stare at her? Of course they would stare. Everybody would stare at a little girl with a stump for an arm.

She kept walking.

A long time later she fell down. Her knees had abruptly given out. She tried to get to her feet. Her arms and legs would not respond. The pain was much worse. It was as if her body had simply surrendered to it. She lay on her belly, helpless. She would lie there until she died. The thought was strangely comforting. She almost closed her eyes. . .

Then, drawn by some sixth sense which she had not known she possessed, she raised her head to stare at the dusty horizon. And she saw it.

Hovering at the edge of the earth was a spread of darkness, shimmering like black velvet, extending to envelop desert and sky. To wrap her in its lightless folds. To draw her in and suffocate her.

Is it death? she wondered dimly. She was not sure. But she knew it was something evil, something that hated life and fed on it, something seeking her life as a leech seeks blood.

"You won't get me," she whispered. "Not without a fight."

She struggled to her feet. She walked on, hobbling like a cripple. She kept her head down till she got her strength back. Then she looked defiantly at the horizon. The thing was gone. For now.

She needed water. Her canteen had been hooked to the horse's saddle. She tried to moisten her mouth with spit. There was none. Her mouth was as dry as the desert air.

The world was silent, save for the low, ragged sounds of her footsteps and her labored breath. That was the trouble. Too much silence. The thing she had glimpsed, *it* liked silence, the brooding silence of a graveyard. Maybe she could keep it away with sound. With music. The way the cowboys would build a fire to keep out the wild things lurking in the night.

She was too weak to sing. She hummed a tune. It was "San Antone Rose," the old Patsy Cline number. She liked Patsy Cline. She wished Patsy Cline hadn't died in that plane crash. She wished nobody ever had to die. Least of all when they were ten years old and all alone in the desert.

The song gave her strength. She kept going, though every step was agony. She hummed louder. When she grew tired of that song, she tried "Together Again," then "For the Good Times," and then "Life Is Like a Mountain Railway." She ran through all her favorites. She pretended she was lying on the sofa listening to the radio. The *Grand Ole Opry Hour* was on. Yes. Who was up next?

Nobody was up next. She could not hum anymore. She had no breath. She was so tired. Hot poker tips stabbed her back, her ribs, her belly. She fought to force air down her windpipe. She wheezed. Black spots shimmered before her eyes, then coalesced into the lightless, wavering shape of the thing she had seen. It was closing in again. This time there was no escape. She collapsed in the dirt. She tried to get up. She couldn't move. She couldn't fight this pain any longer. Her last awareness, before she lost consciousness, was of the thing gliding over her like a shadow, blotting her out.

She awoke in a hospital bed. From some great distance she heard her parents explain that the arrival of the riderless horse had prompted a desperate search, and that the antivenin had been administered just in time, and that the doctor had said their little girl was going to be all right.

She barely heard them. She was thinking about the thing she had cheated—was it death?—and about music, the music which, more than the antivenin, had saved her life.

"Mommy," she whispered. "I'm going to make music someday. I'm going to be on the radio."

Eight years later. The dressing room of the White Horse Saloon in Taos.

She pulled on her boots and laced them tight. She

slung her guitar around her neck. She stood up and studied her reflection in the tarnished full-length mirror.

I look like I'm thirteen years old, she thought miserably.

She had dropped out of high school in the eleventh grade and run off on a Greyhound bus, leaving a note for her parents. She had expected to make it big in six months or so, maybe a year. Everybody had told her she was good. Whenever she played at school dances, she got the kids clapping their hands and singing along. Only, it turned out that the people who hired nightclub acts were harder to please than her high-school friends. So she wandered from town to town, crisscrossing New Mexico, breathing the dry, dusty air mixed with diesel fumes, trying to figure out what the hell to do.

And now here she was, with her first big chance after playing small-town bars and used-car lots. And she was psyched. Pumped. Hell, yes. She was rarin' to go.

She smiled at herself, then turned and vomited into a wastebasket. She paused, mildly astonished, then did it again. Again. She could not stop. Fear twisted her gut like a knife. She heaved up every meal she'd ever eaten, then went on dry-retching, gasping for air, till her head swam and the floor was suddenly far away.

She came to with the manager shaking her arm and asking if she was all right.

"Yeah," she muttered, fighting to speak past the cotton in her tongue. "I can go on."

"Forget it, kid," said the man. "You just ain't ready. Why don't you go home?"

She did not go home. She wanted to. Pride stopped her. Pride, and the desperate sense that her life was at stake, just as surely as it had been on that desert trail with poison pumping through her veins. To go home meant to finish school, take a job, get a beau, marry and bear children, and grow old and die. It meant giving up on everything she wanted. It meant surren-

der. Surrender to that thing always hovering on the
horizon, just out of sight. A thing which was vast and
evil and empty. Not even a thing, really. A nothingness. She could not define it. But she felt its presence
inside her, on the nights when the bus jounced over
the rutted roads and sleep would not come. It felt like
death. Like insanity. She would not let it win.

Six years later. Holed up in a motel room in Bag-
dad, Arizona, with the guys. Bobby Joe sat on the bed
picking idly at his Washburn guitar, the way he did
when he was nervous. K.C. was in the bathroom clip-
ping his toenails. Gary lay on the floor studying a
Penthouse centerfold. Billie stared out the window at
the dark horizon. Nobody said anything for a long
time.

"Okay," Billie said at last. "Let's cut out the Mar-
cel Marceau routine." She looked at Bobby Joe. "You
guys have something to say?" she asked, knowing that
they did.

He nodded slowly. "We're fed up, boss lady. This
just ain't working out."

"You've got to give it time."

"We've given it time."

"Damn straight," said K.C. from the bathroom.
The steady snip-snip of his clippers went on. "And
where are we? The Twilight Zone." He whistled the
eerie theme song. "Submitted for your approval," he
intoned in a decent Rod Serling. "A band of itinerant
musicians. Lost in a cultural wasteland. Forever struggling toward the distant horizon some call financial
solvency." He dropped the phony voice and looked at
Billie through the doorway. "Sorry, Bills. I want out
too."

"Likewise," said Gary. The Pet of the Month was
draped across his chest, her bare legs spread. "This
is bullshit."

"*You're* bullshit," breathed Billie. "All of you. You
expect to make it overnight?"

Bobby Joe flung the guitar down on the bed. He got up. "It hasn't been overnight. It's been four fucking years. In which time we've done six demos, three albums, and approximately a million one-night stands. And we're still playing happy hours. Background music for drunks. And I'm goddamn sick of it."

"Likewise," said Gary.

"We won't always be playing the happy hours," said Billie.

"No? What's going to change?" Bobby Joe ticked off points on his fingers. "We don't have more than a week's worth of cash in reserve. We don't have a label now that Columbia dropped us. We don't have any management since you got Gordo pissed off—"

"He deserved it," said Billie.

"Because he wants us to play what people want to hear?"

"Because he wants us to play what everybody hears."

Bobby Joe turned away, disgusted. Billie stared at him. They'd had this argument before. It had taken them two years of experimenting before they found the style Billie wanted, a style that was as far from the Nashville, country-pop, urban-cowboy sound as it was possible to get, a sound that returned to country's roots and glorified them. No electric guitar or Moog keyboard, no fancy arrangements, just country music the way their grandparents might have played it, clean and simple and pure. Sometimes they wrote their own songs, sometimes they brushed the dust off forgotten classics, and sometimes they even did the latest top-ten hits on the country charts—but they did the hits their own way and made them sound like nothing on the charts today.

And nobody listened. Nobody cared. Bobby Joe was right about one thing: this was not the sound that people wanted to hear.

They had gone through seven different managers, all of whom had taken on the group with high hopes that gradually gave way to weary discouragement. That was when the suggestions always started. Couldn't Billie do some of Barbara Mandrell's songs? Couldn't they work some more mainstream material into their act? Did they have to sound so goddamn *different?*

"Yes, we do," Billie always said. She wouldn't budge. Not even when the record companies—there had been three so far—began echoing those sentiments. They didn't want traditional country; nobody wanted it; it was dead, buried, and forgotten; so why not just give in? Billie would not give in. And so, one by one, the managers left and the companies terminated their contracts.

She knew they could compromise, sell out, do the same music everybody else was doing, and become another jazzed-up cowboy band wearing rhinestones and sequins, playing Vegas and Atlantic City. They could make a fortune. But, dammit, they wouldn't be themselves. Billie understood that. She had talked long and hard, far into the night, fighting to get her band to understand it too. She had thought they did. But maybe not. Or maybe they just didn't give a damn anymore.

The room was silent for a long moment.

"I've got a friend who backs up Dolly Parton," said K.C. wistfully. "He's making a fortune. I call him up every once in a while, when I want to get depressed."

"Come off it." Bobby Joe sighed. "When did it ever take a phone call to get you depressed?"

Billie wasn't listening. She paced in front of the window, then flopped down in a creaking chair near the TV, which was busted. She gripped the armrests. Her fingernails were squeezed white.

"I just can't figure you guys," she said quietly, cutting off their conversation. "We're trying to do something here, don't you get it? We're not just going through the motions. We're creating a whole new sound, a new direction. We're trying to reshape what country music is about, take it back to where it began,

wake people up. We're going for it all.'' Her voice
was shaky. She fought to control herself. ''Don't you
get it? We're not playing it safe. We're grabbing for
the goddamn brass ring. Sure, we haven't caught it
yet. That's why we've got to keep on trying. If we give
up now, we'll never get it.''

''We'll never get it anyway,'' said K.C. philosoph-
ically.

''I sure as hell haven't gotten any,'' said Gary, gazing thoughtfully at the centerfold, and added in a
warbling falsetto, ''for a long, lo-ong tahmmm.''

Bobby Joe picked up his guitar and strummed a few
bars. Then he put down the guitar gently. He shrugged.

''Sorry, boss lady. I'm cutting out.''

''Likewise,'' said Gary.

'Yeah,'' said K.C., emerging from the bathroom.
''We've been talking this over for a while, see? We
decided last week. Only, we didn't want to tell you till
we finished this gig.''

Billie blinked back tears. ''Where the hell will you
go?''

K.C. looked away, not to see her face. ''I'm heading
to Atlanta. I know a guy who needs somebody for
session work.''

''L.A.,'' said Gary. ''Maybe there I can get laid.''

Billie looked at Bobby Joe. ''You?''

He spread his hands. ''Someplace.''

She got up. She pressed her palms to the window.
She lowered her head till the cool glass kissed her
forehead. She closed her eyes. And in the sudden inner
darkness, she saw it, sensed it, her old enemy, that
black hole, that yawning emptiness, opening up before
her like a chasm. And with a flash of insight she knew
that it was not death. It was something much more,
and much less. She could not identify it. But she knew
that it was all around her and within her. She knew,
and she was afraid.

Once, a few years ago, K.C. had lent her one of the
fatalistic philosophy books he was always reading to

sabotage the band's collective morale. This one was by Nietzsche. *And when you look long into an abyss,* said the book, *the abyss also looks into you.* Billie had caught her breath, reading those words. They had struck a chord in her, a low, ominous C-minor chord. She remembered it now. She pressed her hands tighter to the glass, suddenly afraid she would lose her balance and plunge headfirst into that abyss looming before her closed eyelids.

And then she was angry. Because it was not fair, not right. They had a band here. They made music. They took chances. They were alive. They were *something*. And here was this nothingness, this void, this deaf-dumb-and-blind nonentity, seeking to swallow them up and wipe them out, as it had sought to swallow her in the desert.

She had fought it then. She had won. She would not surrender now. No. No.

"*No,*" she said. She whirled on them. Her face was a white mask, her mouth contorted. "Goddammit, no!"

They stared at her. They had expected her to cry, to beg, anything but this.

"Now, you listen to me, you gutless sons of bitches." She spoke low, in a rapid-fire monotone. "We've got something here. We're good. I know it. If you don't, that's your problem. You don't have to have any confidence in us. You don't even have to have any courage. I've got enough of both for all of us. All you've got to do is haul your asses into the car tomorrow and ease on down the road with me to our next stop. Don't ask questions. Don't think about it. Let me do the thinking. And give me six months. That's all I want. Six more months. If we don't make it by then, you're free, white, and twenty-one. Adios, amigos. But give me that much. You've stuck it out for four years. Another six months won't kill you. It might make the difference. It *will* make the difference. It's *got* to. Because I know we're good. I know it. I *know* it. And sooner or later somebody else is going to know it too.''

She paused for breath. "Six months," she said again.

Gary and K.C. looked at Bobby Joe.

"Okay, boss lady," he said slowly. "You got it. Six months. And that's it."

A year later they were still broke and hungry, but she had held them together somehow, fighting off that abyss which still stared her down on sleepless nights. They were playing at a cowboy bar in Bakersfield. She gazed past the lights at the pale ovals of empty faces. Was that the abyss she saw in their eyes, their black-resin eyes? Was it all around her again? Dammit, was it closing in?

They finished their set. She was putting her guitar back in its case when a man approached her out of the darkness.

"Howdy," he said.

Billie looked him over. He was a short, middle-aged guy with nervous hands. He wore an expensive shirt with a wilted collar. He smiled. He seemed like the sort who always smiled.

"I'll come right to the point," he said amiably. "I think you're good."

He was trying to hit on her, she figured. For once she wasn't in the mood.

"Sorry." She turned away. "Not tonight, Josephine."

"You don't understand. I'm a talent agent."

"Right. I'm Snow White. These guys backing me up are Sneezy, Doc, and Grumpy."

K.C. snickered.

The man was unperturbed. He took out his wallet and removed a business card. He handed it to her.

"The name's Harve Medlow."

She stared at him, then at the card. And, yes, there it was. Right there in black and white.

The boys paused in packing their equipment. K.C. was not snickering anymore.

"You've heard of me," said Harve Medlow. It was not a question.

Billie nodded.

Everybody had heard of Harve Medlow. Everybody in the business, anyway. He had an office in New York, another one in Nashville, and a third on Sunset Strip. He handled some very big names. She would have recognized him right off, except what the hell would Harve goddamned *Medlow* be doing in a pissant hole like this?

"I'm just passing through," he said, as if in answer. "I don't do much business in Bakersfield. This town's not too hot anymore. Used to be, though." He sighed. "They used to call it Nashville West. Did you know that? A lot of great names came out of here. Buck Owens. Don Rich. Merle Haggard." He shrugged sadly. "Times change. Anyway, tonight I wasn't looking for talent. I was just looking for a beer."

He met her eyes. "I found talent, though. Real talent."

Billie swallowed. "Mr. Medlow—"

"Harve."

"Harve . . . I think I'd better warn you, right off, that we've gone through a pile of managers. They all want us to go electric and play top-forty stuff. And we won't do that. We've got our own sound here, and we like it. Even if nobody else does."

She could hear Gary and K.C. groan softly. She ignored them.

Harve Medlow smiled. "Well, shit, honey, I like it too. You know, most of the country acts I handle now sound more like the Beach Boys than the Oaks. I mean, the original Oaks. But I'll tell you something. I think people are ready for a change. Whether they know it or not. I think they're looking for something new. Like you, maybe."

His smile broadened. "You thought I wanted to

make you. Well, I do. I want to make you a star. And if you let me . . . I will.''

Four years had passed since then. Sights and sounds from those years whirled in her mind like a spray of autumn leaves in a breeze. The moment when she heard herself on the radio for the first time, singing ''Waltz Across Texas''—the moment when she led her boys onto the stage at the Dallas Reunion Arena as the Statler Brothers' opening act—the moment when she accepted the CMA award for best new performer of the year—when she won the Grammy for *Lovers' Leap*—when she received a royalty check for $250,000 and sat staring at it, stunned by the line of zeros—when she put down a cool million, in cash, as the down payment on the beachhouse in Malibu—when she was invited to perform at the Opry and stood backstage, white-knuckled as a beginner, flanked by Willie Nelson, Johnny Cash, Emmylou Harris, and the other heroes she had worshiped, kneeling at the altar of her radio, the heroes who now accepted her as one of their own, dear Lord, as their equal.

And still—in dark corners, in starless skies, on sleepless nights—it haunted her, mocking her success, telling her to enjoy her happiness while she could, reminding her of its ageless presence and of a rendezvous it meant to keep with her.

The abyss.

She had cheated it, fought it, beaten it back, but never destroyed it, and somehow she felt a wordless certainty that all those earlier battles had been mere skirmishes, a prelude to the war to come. She did not know why it had chosen her or why she was alone to see it, sense it. She did not know even what the battle was being fought for, what the stakes might be, except that they were life-and-death. She did not know, and in bright sunlight she shrugged off her nighttime fear, but then the dark would fall and it came back. Always, it came back.

* * *

Then she was in the present, twenty-nine years old, and she was flying.

But not in an airplane. No. She was really flying. She glided weightlessly through space. Spiral nebulae pinwheeled around her. A comet flashed past, trailing an opalescent bridal train. She looked around, trying to find the familiar blue-green ball of the earth. It was nowhere in sight. She was far from home, lost somewhere in a riot of wheeling galaxies. She tried to call for help. Her voice was gone. Sound, she remembered, does not travel in space.

But even as she remembered that, she heard a sound penetrating the vast silence. The distant echoes of a song.

She listened. She glided onward. The song grew louder. A haunting song, seven notes endlessly repeated in a minor key. She had never heard a song like this. It sent chills racing through her body, the body that had not shivered even in the icy vacuum of space.

There were no words to the song, only a melody played on an instrument she could not name. A harp, perhaps, or a sitar, or some strange device combining the qualities of both. She had once heard a recording of whale songs. These sounds were similar; they captured the same sense of longing, of mystery, of something utterly alien and very much alone.

Even without words, the song spoke to her. It spoke of death. Of the death of worlds. Of suns. Of galaxies. It knew a secret, whispered the song in its wordless way, and the secret was that at the end of time, as at the far reaches of the universe, there lies darkness. There lies the extinction of light and life. There lies an emptiness so vast that it might swallow all that there is and never be filled. She knew that emptiness. She had seen its looming shapelessness on the horizon. She had shivered under the blankets of her bed, chilled by its touch.

Billie flew on, leaving behind the light of the stars, hurtling into a black tunnel which was the abyss.

The song was loud in her ears. Deafening. She did not wish to hear it. It was all around her, inside her, consuming her. She opened her mouth to scream.

And she awoke, at ten thousand feet over the Great Salt Lake.

She barely remembered the dream. It was fading fast. But the song, out of context and devoid of meaning, still resonated in her mind.

She grabbed a datebook and a pen from her purse. She scribbled down the notes she heard.

"What's up?" asked Bobby Joe from the seat next to hers.

"Dreamed up a song," she said, forcing a smile.

She showed it to him. He studied it critically.

"Pretty strange," he said at last. "Might work with a little keyboard, maybe a Dobro on this part here . . ."

"No." She was startled by the firmness of her voice. "It's got to be done solo. Just my guitar."

"You think?"

"I know."

Bobby Joe shrugged. "Boss lady knows best." He handed back the datebook. "You know, I've heard Johnny Cash got the idea for that trumpet arrangement of 'Ring of Fire' in a dream."

She barely heard him. She was staring at the notes she had marked down, hearing the song in her mind, and wondering why she felt cold all over when the plane was warm.

3

Kenneth Blane sat frozen in his seat as the song went on. He had never heard it before, but he knew it at once, with no flicker of doubt. All his training, his initiation rites, his services and sacrifices had brought him to the point where he could not fail to recognize it.

Slowly he unbuttoned the sleeve on his left arm and pulled it back, revealing the bracelet he had worn since his induction into the Brotherhood. It would provide the final confirmation.

He looked at the bracelet. It was a circle of gold links, holding a single stone in an oval frame. The stone was blue. Had been blue. Now it was . . . changing. Changing even as he watched. Pinpoints of red appeared, like fireworks in a summer sky. They ran together, forming bright streaks of color, swirling and spiraling. Kenneth thought of cream in a coffee cup. He watched, fascinated, till the stone was red all over.

Bloodstone, he thought, remembering the prophecy.

There was no doubt, then. No doubt at all.

He knew what he must do. He did not want to do it. He had no choice. The song had been sung. The Door had been opened. But it could close. That must be prevented. The responsibility, the awesome burden of destiny, had fallen on his shoulders.

Something held him until the modern lyrics fell away, replaced by the ancient words, the right words. Then he knew he was free to act.

He rose from his seat. Beside him, Sharon mouthed a question: You okay?

He did not reply. His wife did not matter anymore. She belonged to some other world, a world of mortgage payments, union dues, and orthodontist bills. She would have to be discarded now, along with his job, their three children, the house in West L.A., and the rest of that dead past. It was all right. A better future awaited him.

He made his way to the aisle, slowly, casually, as if he were simply heeding the call of nature. He smiled, because in a sense he was. Only, this was not nature as men understood it with their chains of syllogisms, their theorems and theories, their feeble rationality. This was a dark nature, a nature which had lain in wait for the world, invisible as a panther coiled in an inkspot shadow, poised to strike. And tonight—let loose to pounce and feed.

He reached the aisle. The orchestra pit, covered with a temporary floor to prevent unwary patrons from falling in, was six feet away. Just beyond it was a partition four feet high. He could vault the partition without difficulty. His leap would carry him onto the bank of lights at the edge of the stage. Another step would put him on the stage itself. No doubt there were security guards and cops stationed in the wings, who would be on top of him a moment later. That was all right. One moment would be enough.

He slid his hand into his jacket pocket. His fist closed over the switchblade.

He tensed. The song was ending.

He had never taken a human life, though he had slit the bellies of the alley cats whose blood, mixed with herbal brew, made steaming clouds of incense in the midnight ceremonies. He did not wish to kill Billie Lee Kidd. But he would. He must.

The song came to a close, the last of the ancient lyrics rising like smoke to dissipate among the stars. From the audience at his back came bewildered murmurs and polite applause.

Kenneth Blane took a breath and prepared to rush the stage.

"Sir?"

He turned. An usher was there. Just a kid, probably working his way through college, donning the red jacket at night for some spending money. His flashlight wavered in the darkness like a will-o'-the-wisp.

"Can I help you?" whispered the kid.

Kenneth tightened his grip on the knife.

"Yeah," he breathed. "I'm not feeling too good."

"Come this way." The kid turned. Kenneth whipped out the knife. The blade popped up with a click. He hesitated for only a split second. Then he plunged the knife into the kid's back. It sank into the soft flesh between the shoulder blades, vanishing up to the hilt. The kid gasped. His hands jerked, groping for the knife. Kenneth jerked the knife free. The kid teetered, then fell in the aisle in a spastic heap.

From a nearby seat came a woman's gasp. Kenneth ignored it. They would all be screaming in a second, and then the cops would be onstage and the game would be up. He had to strike now. Now.

He raced across the orchestra pit, grabbed hold of the partition, and hoisted himself onto the bank of footlights. A light bulb exploded like a gunshot. He flung himself on the stage and sprang erect, less than two yards from Billie Lee Kidd.

She was looking back, over her shoulder, at her band. She didn't even see him.

He had been wrong to worry. Taking a human life was easy. As easy as killing alley cats in ritual sacrifices.

Now he would kill again.

The song ended about five seconds before the man appeared out of the footlights. Billie's head swam back into focus. She looked up, blinking. The stars were still in place. The world had not shattered like a crystal ball. Her vision had been some kind of crazy dream, that was all. Like the song itself, only a dream.

She heard a light patter of applause. Automatically she said, "Thank you," though she knew they were responding out of politeness only. The song had been too weird for them. Shit, a little too weird for her too. Was it her imagination or had she switched to some other lyrics in the middle? No. That was crazy. Just another hallucination or something.

Anyway, it didn't matter. She figured she would follow up with a good hard-rocking tune like "Guitar Town" to get the folks back on her side. She turned to signal Bobby Joe, and that was when the audience screamed.

She spun. A man was on the stage with her, less than two yards away. He had a knife. It gleamed, catching the spotlight. It dripped blood.

He took another step, closing the distance between them. She had time to see his face, a perfectly ordinary face, the face of a guy in his thirties who tightened bolts on an assembly line, maybe, or repaired refrigerators or hawked cars, but not the face of a killer who was going to waste her in full view of six thousand people.

He said one word.

"Deathsong."

He smiled.

His fist shot forward, the knife arrowed at her throat.

Kenneth's body was electric with adrenaline. The seconds crawled by in soundless slow motion. He had time to gauge his thrust perfectly and to visualize its result. The knife blade skewering Billie's neck, slitting the tender flesh like a paper bag. The geyser of blood, sparkling in the spotlight, a tinted fountain. Her body collapsing on the stage in a tangle of jerking limbs. Her tongue swelling up, bluish-purple, as she gasped for breath and gargled blood like mouthwash. Her green eyes flickering madly like the lights on a pinball machine, then fading out. Oh, yes. He could see it so clearly.

Sorry, Billie, he thought. Looks like the show's over for you.

Billie had only a split second to react. Instinctively she jerked the guitar in front of her face. The knife drove into the body of the instrument with a dull thud and a splinter of wood. It lodged there harmlessly.

The man snarled. He wrenched the knife free and prepared for a second try.

In that instant she saw his eyes. They were the black-resin eyes of the sidewinder, the zombie eyes of the crowds she had played for in her poverty days. They were as dark and as bottomless as an abyss. And they wanted to kill her. To snuff her out.

Hello again—she thought, almost incoherently—I've been waiting for you.

She lashed out with a kick. The pointed tip of her boot slammed into the killer's groin. He doubled over, groaning, then glared up at her with those empty eyes.

He raised the knife again.

Time had ceased altogether. He had an eternity in which to strike. Nothing could stop him. Not even the stinging agony in his crotch. He knew how to fight pain. That was only one of the many things which they had taught him. He hummed a little tune, three dancing notes audible only to himself, and shut off sensation below the waist.

He felt fine. Just fine.

He smiled at Billie. Her face was flushed. Her freckles stood out sharply on her cheeks. Strands of reddish-brown hair swung over her eyes. She looked so young—younger even than her years—and so very vulnerable. Like a teenage girl. Only her eyes spoiled the effect. They blazed, darkly green. Tiger eyes.

He would plant the knife in her forehead, directly

between those eyes, and then they would gaze sightlessly, harmlessly, forever.

He lunged for her, bringing the knife down in a
glittering arc.

The man was fast. He had straightened up immediately, then had gone for her face again. Billie barely
had time to leap sideways, dodging the blow. She heard
a whistle of air as the blade slashed empty space inches
from her ear.

She ripped her guitar free of its strap and closed her
fists over the fretted neck, wielding the instrument like
a baseball bat. She swung at him and missed. The
knife flashed, catching the front of her T-shirt, ripping
it open with a long zipper sound. She glanced down
at her chest, half-expecting to see a flood of entrails
spill out. She was unhurt. But already the knife was
sweeping back for another blow, a killing blow.

Fury electrified her body. She swung out with savage force, gambling her life on one swing of her arms.
She connected. The guitar slammed into his forehead
and cracked in half. He staggered backward, blood
streaming into his eyes.

Got you, she thought with almost bestial satisfaction.

But it was not the killer she was seeing. It was the
rattler. The shadow on the horizon. The abyss.

He couldn't see. A red curtain had dropped, blinding him. He clawed at his face with his free hand,
trying to stem the torrent of blood. It was no use. He
was dizzy. He dropped the knife. It clattered on the
stage. He had failed. Goddammit, he had failed.

They'll kill me for this, he thought in sudden terror.

It was true. Oh, Christ, he couldn't give up now.
He had to get the bitch or he was dead. Dead.

He struck out blindly, hoping to wrap his bare hands
around her neck and snap it with one twist of his

wrists, and then two men were on him, wrestling him savagely to the floor, and he was screaming.

Billie watched as Bobby Joe and K.C. tackled her attacker and brought him down. K.C. pinned his hands behind his back. Bobby Joe had him in a headlock. A pool of blood spread in widening ripples across the floor.

Half a dozen cops and security guards reached center stage an instant later. Billie wondered why the hell it had taken them so damn long, an hour at least, till she realized that the whole incident had lasted less than five seconds.

Kenneth Blane put up no resistance as the cops handcuffed him, then jerked him to his feet and frisked him roughly. In the darkness encircling the stage, the audience stirred, mixing anxious murmurs with cries of panic, the sort of sounds that crowds of movie extras always try unsuccessfully to recreate. Other cops had reached the usher, seeking in vain for any sign of life from his body.

Kenneth was barely aware of what was happening. He was so weak, so tired. Anyway, it didn't matter. He was a dead man. But—he thought coldly—Billie was dead too. Yes. He would see to that. It would take only one phone call. And the police always allowed you one phone call, didn't they?

He smiled.

You're dead, Billie. You are one dead bitch.

"What's so funny?" hissed a cop.

Kenneth just smiled at him. A voice interrupted his thoughts. Sharon's voice raised in a quavering falsetto.

"Ken . . . ?"

He glanced down at the foot of the stage, where she stood, her face a clown mask of bleeding mascara.

"What happened? Why did you . . . ? Why . . . ?"

"For a better world," said Kenneth softly.

Sharon bit her trembling lip and turned away.

* * *

Billie fought to catch her breath.

"You all right?" K.C. asked, slipping an arm around her shoulder.

She nodded, not trusting her voice, and buried her face in K.C.'s chest.

"No."

The word came from a few yards away. Billie raised her head. The killer glared at her. "She's not all right," he said quietly, his mouth frozen in a humorless grin.

"Get him out of here," said Bobby Joe.

The cops hauled the man toward the wings. He twisted his head to look back over his shoulder. His eyes locked on Billie's. And as she gazed into their dark depths, she saw that door again, opening wider, spewing forth insanity.

"She's *not* all right," he said again, louder. His voice boomed like cannon fire, echoing from the far corners of the amphitheater. "She's *dead*. You hear me? *She's dead!*"

4

Frank Lancett sat in the overstuffed armchair of his private screening room, watching swirls of marijuana smoke dance in the flickering projector beam. On the screen swam grainy images of shackles snapping shut, leg irons clamped in place, torture racks laid out in a neat row. Three naked women—girls, really, not one of them older than sixteen—were tied down to three hard wooden slabs in a shadowed room. Nearby stood a man, rummaging through a briefcase filled with shiny household objects which, when used properly, could inflict great pain. He selected a pair of hedge clippers. Lancett leaned forward expectantly.

He liked this flick. He had threaded up the 16mm Bell & Howell projector himself and left it running unattended while he settled back to watch the first reel. It always got him up. The best part was when the blond bitch got it with the corkscrew and died, gargling bloody froth and screaming to the Blessed Virgin in her peasant Spanish. Oh, yes. That was nice. And what made it even better was that it was real. No makeup and special effects, no phony simulation. Uh-uh. This stuff was the genuine article, and when these three bimbos got snuffed, they were getting it for keeps.

Just the way his bimbos always got it—thought Frank Lancett dreamily, as the clippers began to snip, snip, snip and the screaming started—ever since that night up in Frisco, seven years ago.

He had been wandering in the streets of Chinatown, restless, looking for something he couldn't quite define. He had thought it might have been sex. So he found himself a chink whore, a pretty little doll-faced thing with long black-stockinged legs tapering to six-inch heels. But he was wrong. He didn't want sex. He couldn't even get it up. He lay with the whore in his hotel-room bed, grunting in frustration, kneading her small firm breasts and trying to get hard. He was nearly ready to call it a night when suddenly a thought occurred to him, an intriguing possibility.

She had gone along with the idea. She had not known the full extent of what he had in mind. Maybe he hadn't quite known either, not at first. Anyway, she didn't protest as he tied her hands with his belt. She seemed to enjoy it, in fact. She giggled and asked if he wanted her to beg for mercy.

He didn't smile. His heart was racing. He had an erection. He knew this had been the right idea.

The girl had cost him a hundred bucks. He found

his wallet and pulled out a thick wad of bills. He waved them in front of her face.

"You want more money, baby?" he whispered. "You want more?"

"Sure," she said. She giggled again. "I like money."

"Then eat it," said Frank Lancett. He peeled off a crisp twenty and stuffed it in her mouth. She smiled, thinking this was some kind of kinky game, a profitable game. He peeled off another bill, then another and another. She accepted them greedily. His fingers were smeared with lipstick. The money crackled like lettuce between her parted lips. Her mouth was very full now, too full. Instinctively she tried to spit some of it out. He would not let her. He shoved the rest of the wad at her face. He crammed it into her mouth. She twisted her head violently back and forth. Spit flew from her lips. Suddenly she was afraid. Suddenly it was not a game. And in that moment, Lancett knew it never had been.

"You know who you've got in your mouth?" he whispered feverishly. "You've got Andrew Jackson and Alexander Hamilton and old Honest Abe. Good men. You like to eat good men, don't you? Don't you, you slant-eyed bitch?"

Green paper jutted out at crazy angles from her mouth. Her eyes were wide, staring. She squirmed, fighting to free her hands. But he had looped the belt tight around her wrists and fastened it securely. She could not break free. She kicked. He straddled her, laughing. He raised the pillow and brought it down on her face. He pressed down hard. Her body jackknifed wildly under him. It was like riding a bucking bronco. He held on to the pillow, hearing her faint, muffled cries. His erection was huge now. He watched the muscles of his bare arms bulge with the strain of holding the pillow in place. A trickle of sweat ran down his forehead and dripped off the tip of his nose.

In the moment when she gave a final shudder, he

had an orgasm. She died under his hands as he pumped semen into the bedsheets.

And it had been good. Oh, yes. So damn good.

For months afterward, he lived in fear of being found out. Then, one day he was.

He was dining by himself in a restaurant on Gateway, chewing refried beans and listening to the blare of mariachi music on the radio, when he saw a man watching him from across the room. Their eyes met. The man rose, approached Lancett's table, and introduced himself, giving—as Lancett later learned—a prudently false name. Lancett had not known what to make of the encounter; it had, he thought, definite homosexual overtones, which, for reasons he preferred not to explore too deeply, he did not find entirely without appeal. The man joined him. They talked far into the night, about this and that, one thing and another, casual conversation of no consequence, except that Lancett was sure that it was not casual, that the man was feeling him out, that there was a hidden purpose to the seemingly random drift of their discussion.

A purpose which became clear when the man observed that Lancett was dining alone far too often, five nights in a row this week, and that was a shame, for surely in a city of three million there was no shortage of nubile young things for him to wine, dine, rape, and kill.

Lancett did not answer at once. He could not guess how the man had learned his secret or followed his trail, but there was no need to panic, not yet. Blackmail could be paid, if the sum was not too large. Or there were other possibilities. He had murdered once. He could do it again.

Blackmail, however, was not the issue. Instead Lancett was informed—as he sat in stony silence, neither confirming nor denying anything—that an organization existed which did not frown on such pastimes as his, an organization which, in fact, encouraged recreational activities of all kinds, promoted them, subsidized them, and would supply Lancett with a limitless quantity of the playthings he desired, in exchange for certain considerations.

By the end of the night, Frank Lancett was on board. It was hardly even necessary to ask him if he wished to join. He had no choice. But more than that, he wanted to.

In the years since, Lancett had proved his value to his employers, and they, in turn, had proved their value to him. He rose swiftly through the ranks. He never learned the precise reasons for his selection—whether it was his vulnerability, his inherited wealth, or the media contacts he had made as a producer of low-budget films, mainly slasher flicks and porno reels, with an occasional secret foray into the snuff pictures which were his real passion—but he supposed it didn't matter.

His main function was to procure new recruits. He sought them out in bars and massage parlors, in shopping malls and movie theaters. He became adept at spotting potential converts, men whose eyes betrayed them, eyes which belonged in a mug shot. He did research, hired spies, learned his marks' weaknesses, then struck. Of the fourteen men he approached, only two turned down his eventual offer. Those two were killed—standard procedure—his employers could not permit the existence of outsiders who had glimpsed their secrets. It was not standard procedure for Lancett to do the killings personally, but what the hell, membership had its privileges.

His recruits had a variety of jobs, income levels, interests, beliefs, and aspirations, but they were united by frustration, by unfulfilled longings and unrealized dreams, like bricks cemented by a gray paste of mortar. Frustration made them candidates for recruitment to any movement that promised a better life and a larger purpose. Like the angry, aimless young men who had drifted into the ranks of Hitler's brownshirts, they needed something beyond themselves, an escape from self, from impotence, futility, and despair. Lancett had provided them with that. It was a public service, really.

Thinking back on his life now, his mind soaring on cannabis clouds, Frank Lancett had to smile. It was ironic, wasn't it? He had always been a loner, and yet his most profound contentment had been found in the arms of a movement older than history, cloaked in secrecy, operating underground, unknown and unsuspected. An organization to which he had given, quite literally, his life. He had no regrets.

He loved the Brotherhood.

The phone rang, interrupting his thoughts.

Who the hell could be calling here? he wondered, irritated. And at—he glanced at his watch, digital readout glowing greenly—1:15 in the morning, for Christ's sake.

The ringing continued. He thought about letting the machine answer. But, no. At this hour it might be important. It had better be.

He got up and crossed in front of the screen. A riot of blood and blond hair was printed briefly on his back. He picked up the phone.

"Yes?"

"Greetings," whispered a nervous voice, "my brother."

"May you hear the song," Lancett replied automatically. "Who is this?"

"Blane."

Lancett frowned. His operatives were forbidden to call him here. Except in case of an emergency. And every man in his department knew what that meant.

"What's up?" he asked, keeping his voice level.

"I'm at a police station in Irvine. I'm under arrest. This is my one phone call. You've got to help me."

Lancett sighed. So that was it. The jerk had gotten himself in trouble, drunk driving or something, and he was calling good old Frank to bail him out. Jesus.

The nerve of some of these bastards. Here he was, breaking company rules, calling in the middle of the night, and ruining the best part of the movie, to boot. And now he expected help.

"Fuck off," growled Lancett. "Call a fucking lawyer. There's enough kikes in this town."

He nearly hung up. The voice from the receiver, as distant and shrill as the buzzing of a fly, stopped him.

"I heard it."

Lancett pulled the receiver up close to his ear again. He drew a breath and exhaled it slowly. "Say again."

"The Deathsong." Blane's voice was a whisper. "It's been sung. Tonight. Maybe an hour ago. I was there."

"Okay, hold on. Take it easy. You sure?"

"Of course I'm sure."

"Where?"

"At the amphitheater."

"Come off it."

"I went to see a show with my wife."

"What show?"

"Billie Lee Kidd."

"You wasted or something? You fucking with me?"

"Mr. Lancett, I swear to Christ. Check it out for yourself."

Lancett cradled the phone between his neck and shoulder, then shrugged off his jacket and let it fall to the floor. He stared at the bracelet on his left wrist. It glowed, bright red, as red as blood.

"Jesus," he hissed.

He rubbed his forehead. Suddenly he had a headache. He wished he hadn't smoked tonight. He wished he could think straight. On the screen behind him, the blond was begging for mercy as the worm of the corkscrew began to spin, rotating like a drill head, closing in.

He pressed the phone's mouthpiece to his lips again.

"Did you run the program?"

"I tried. But . . ."

"There was a glitch."

"Please, Mr. Lancett . . ."

"Don't beg, Blane. It's bad for our corporate image. Almost as bad as failure. Almost as bad as fucking up royally, like you did tonight." He took a breath. "Now, listen to me. Listen real close. Because I'm going to give you some new instructions, and this time you'd better not screw up. You listening?"

"Yes."

Frank Lancett hummed a little tune, a cheerful, unmelodic fragment musty with age. It was not a powerful song. It could not bring on deathly paralysis or bring up a vomitous flood, as—it was rumored—some songs had the power to do. It was more of a lullaby, really. Just a gentle song to rock Kenneth Blane to sleep. To sleep . . .

He finished humming. "You hear that, Blane?"

Blane's voice was slow, torpid. "I hear it."

"Then you know what you have to do."

Lancett cradled the receiver, then stood for a moment trying to sort out the emotions washing over him in dizzying waves. He was scared, yes, because the song had been sung, and he knew damn well what that meant. But he was excited too. Excited at the prospect of what lay ahead, in the new world about to begin. And excited, as well, at the knowledge that he had just taken a man's life, taken it without even so much as laying a hand on him. He had a sudden urge to masturbate. He resisted it. There was work to do.

He punched in a number he had committed to memory long ago. His hand shook a little, the way it always did when he called this particular number, as the phone rang at the other end. Five rings. Six.

"Yes."

The voice he heard was cold and somehow dark. Lancett had never thought a sound could be dark, pitch dark, so dark that hearing it was like drowning in black waves . . . until he first spoke with the Director, five years ago.

Lancett had never met the Director. Nor did he want to. He knew of only one human being who had ever met the Director, and that man, his predecessor in this office, had never been seen again.

"Greetings, my brother," said Lancett, swallowing his fear.

"May you hear the song," came the ritualistic response. "What is it, Lancett?"

"Director. The Bloodstone has turned."

"I have eyes," rasped the shadow voice. In the background was the murmur of the traffic. Lancett had spent long, fruitless hours replaying in his mind his rare phone conversations with the Director, trying to guess where the man's office might be. It faced a busy street—that much was certain—and, of course, it was in the part of town covered by the 213 area code. Beyond that, he could not say. The number could have been traced easily enough, but as far as he knew, no one had ever dared to try.

"The Deathsong was sung," said Lancett.

"I told you, I've seen the stone."

"It was sung here."

There was silence. On the other end of the line, a distant car blasted its horn, a brief caterwauling sound.

"Here?" croaked the voice. For once, it registered an emotion. It registered shock. And something more. Something very much like glee.

Lancett smiled, pleased that he had been privileged to deliver the news.

"One of my operatives just called in." Rapidly Lancett summarized the situation. "I terminated him," he concluded.

The Director grunted. "Where does the songbird live?"

"Malibu, I think." He was fortunate to have seen a *People*-magazine spread on Billie Lee Kidd only a couple of weeks ago. He had not bothered to read it— his musical tastes ran more to heavy metal of the particularly vicious kind, music with teeth, as he thought of it—but dimly he remembered a photo of Billie lounging barefoot on the hammock of a modernistic beachhouse.

"It's Reynolds' department, then," said the voice.

For a moment, Lancett was disappointed. He would have liked to handle the job himself. Maybe even do it personally. Then the Director's voice dissolved into what might have been static, but was in fact a mirthless chuckle, and Lancett was suddenly glad he didn't have the job.

"Make sure he doesn't blow it," said the voice, still chuckling dryly. "Make sure our Mr. Reynolds understands the gravity of the situation. Make sure he knows that if our songbird is still chirping at sunrise, he won't be alive to hear her."

The line went dead.

5

Officer Jack Pierce of the Irvine Police Department watched as Kenneth Blane cradled the phone. Blane's face had gone oddly slack, expressionless. It reminded Pierce of the kids in the drug clinics, fifteen- and sixteen-year-old kids who'd shot up so much smack that their brains had just given out like dead batteries. They had faces like that. But Blane hadn't worn that kind of face a minute ago. He must have heard some real bad news from his lawyer, Pierce figured. What a shame.

"Okay, asshole," he said. "You've exercised your rights. Now make like a monkey and get in your goddamn cage."

Blane stood motionless, blinking. He surveyed the landscape of empty desks, his eyes moving slowly, as if hypnotized, along the rows of desks cluttered with coffee cups, photocopies, newspaper clippings, family snapshots in gilded frames, paper clips, and pens. Ball-point pens.

He took a step toward the nearest desk, where Pierce stood, waiting.

"Come on," he snapped. "Move it."

Blane took another step, then flung himself at the desk. His hand closed over a ball-point pen like a weapon. For an instant it hung quivering in the air, catching the glare of the fluorescent ceiling panels. He brought it down, gouging Jack Pierce's cheek like a letter opener slicing an envelope. Pierce leapt back, his face hot with a spurt of blood and agony. He fumbled at his holster.

"You fucker," he breathed.

Kenneth Blane ignored him. Calmly, deliberately, he twisted the pen so that the pointed tip was aimed at his own face, then thrust it into his right eye.

Pierce stared at the man. He forgot his gun. For a moment he was too stunned to react. Then he lunged, trying to snatch the pen away. Blane braced himself against the desk and pistoned out both legs to deliver a stinging kick to Pierce's knees. Bone cracked. Pierce staggered backward, then collapsed on the floor. He shouted for help. Footsteps pounded through the station house.

Blane's face was a grotesque carnival mask. His lips were stretched taut, teeth bared to the gumlines. He gripped the pen with both hands. He drove it deeper into his eye. A milky stream, dripping like egg yolk, bubbled down his cheek. The pen sank into his eye socket in fits and jerks. It struck an artery. Blood spurted out in a pink rainbow. He gasped. Pain contorted his body. He slid off the desk, as boneless as a rag doll, and lay in a knot of trembling muscles on the tiled floor. He did not stop. He jammed the pen all the way into his skull, rupturing the bony wall at the back of his eye socket, puncturing his brain. Then there was no further resistance. The pen sank easily into the spongy gray matter, sliding in like a pin in a pincushion.

A dozen cops reached him in the moment when he dropped his hands, smiled, and died.

"Motherfuck," whispered Jack Pierce, still curled on the floor, clutching at his fractured knees. "Did you see that?"

They had seen it.

6

Billie guided the Lamborghini Countach off the Pacific Coast Highway onto the side road that led to the gates of the Malibu Colony. In the passenger seat, the pretty blond boy was tense and silent. She was not certain if he was nervous about going home with her or simply about entering the Colony, that exclusive fenced-in, mysterious compound of the super-rich. Maybe both.

Through the glass wall of the gatehouse, a guard was visible, his face illuminated by the bluish flicker of a TV. Billie knew him—his name was Chet, though she had never learned his last name—and she knew his nightly routine. He always brought a VCR with him and hooked it up to the TV, then played a movie he had rented from a place up the highway. It was a way to pass the time.

She pulled up alongside the gatehouse and lowered the driver's-side window. Chet leaned out. He was a trim-looking man in his fifties, wearing the standard uniform for security personnel at the Colony—navy pants, light blue shirt with red patches on the shoulders, and a cap. He tipped his cap politely, as always.

" 'Evening, Miss Kidd."

"More like the morning, Chet," she said. "What's playing at the Bijou tonight?"

He gestured toward the TV. "John Wayne double feature. *Fort Apache* and *She Wore a Yellow Ribbon.*"

"Around her neck," Billie sang, "she wore a yeller ribbon . . ." The gate swung up and she drove through.

The Countach glided down the main road, then hooked left. Rows of houses, jammed preposterously close together on minuscule plots of land, passed by in the darkness. Halfway down the street, she turned into the carport of a house facing the beach.

"We're here," she announced.

The boy smiled. Still nervous. Well, that was okay. They were usually nervous at first. Maybe they figured she was going to whip out a tape measure and grade their cocks. Or maybe they were simply afraid of her. It didn't matter. She knew how to put a man at ease.

She studied him in the light of the analog gauges studding the dash. He was about twenty-five, she figured. Tall and lanky, his long frame sunk deep in the hammocklike seat. His straight hair fell neatly to his shoulders. He wore a tweed jacket over a Raiders T-shirt, stone-washed jeans with a hole strategically cut in the knee, and battered Nike running shoes. His features were sharp, clean-shaven, and regular enough to be considered handsome. She did not know why she had picked him out of the crowd. She never knew.

"Could I ask you a question?" he said over the low idling of the engine.

"Ask away."

"How much did this car cost?"

"Well"—she smiled—"it retails for a hundred and thirty-five, but I knocked a few bucks off the sticker price. And they threw in the floormats, no charge."

"A hundred and thirty-five grand?"

"Sickening, ain't it?"

He gazed, awestruck, at the cream leather seat cush-

ions and ergonomic dash. The four-cam V12 engine,
455 horses, purred sensuously.

"Shit, no. It's great." He laughed. "Fucking
great."

"I'm not usually so extravagant, but, see, I used to
travel by bus a lot." She looked at him. "And I didn't
like it."

She killed the engine and released the door latch.
The door swiveled vertically on its gas strut, coming
to rest at a ninety-degree angle to the car. She got out
and lowered the door. On the passenger side, the boy
did the same. He stared at the machine, its low-slung
blue-black form faintly ominous in the semidarkness,
like some alien spacecraft temporarily grounded on
planet Earth. Then wordlessly he followed her through
the carport to the front door.

She was almost surprised to find herself going
through with this, considering what had happened
barely two hours ago. But what the hell. She was alive,
wasn't she? And tonight—even more than usual—she
felt the need to be reminded of that fact.

She found her key. She led him inside. The living
room was lit by a single lamp on a corner table, throwing orange sunrays across her framed Degas. The rest
of the house was dark. Somewhere waves beat against
a shore.

He stopped in the middle of the room, looking
around.

"It's . . . nice," he said softly.

"Thank you. 'Course, around here, the view's the
thing. Take a peek."

She opened the door to the sundeck and led him
outside, to the ladder that descended to the beach.
Spotlights shone on the sand. It glittered, a white carpet, wondrously litter-free. The air was cool here,
laced with moisture and fragrant with salt, a blessed
relief from the desert dryness inland.

She walked hand in hand with the boy. They stopped
a few yards from the house, at the edge of the surf.

They looked back at the line of houses in semisilhouette against the stars.

"Looks like Disneyland, doesn't it?" said Billie.

The boy looked at her. "Huh?"

"This place. These funny little houses in a neat row. All so spanking clean. And all different colors, too, though you can't really tell at night. That one there is pink, and the one next door is green, and mine is bright blue. . . . Well, I'll tell you. The first time I saw this place, I thought it looked just like Main Street in Disneyland."

"Except in Disneyland," said the boy, grinning, "it only costs twenty bucks to get in."

"Well, hell," said Billie, "you got in here for nothing."

She let her hand stray to his pants.

"You might have to give me something before I let you leave, though," she added quietly.

She squeezed his buttocks. They were small and firm. Gently she pulled him toward her, without preliminaries, and kissed him deeply, probing his mouth with her tongue. His thin body trembled, electric with tension.

Finally she pulled away. "Maybe we'd better continue this inside," she whispered.

He nodded.

She led him back inside the house, upstairs to the bedroom. It was a large room with an adjoining bath, the two rooms together taking up the entire second story of the house. The seaward wall was a semicircular sheet of glass framing the spotlighted beach and glittering surf. This morning she had opened the smaller window in the side wall to air out the room. Lace curtains rustled, ghostlike, in the breeze. Moonbeams slanted through the net of lace, washing the walls and the unmade bed. Billie sank down on the bed and gently pulled the boy on top of her. They lay together in a tangle of silken bedsheets.

In the darkness, he chuckled.

"What?" she asked.

He looked away, embarrassed. "Nothing."

"Come on. Give."

"I was just thinking . . . I shouldn't say this."

"Tell me or I'll fry you in oil."

"Well . . . it's just that . . . I can't wait to tell my friends about this."

She smiled. "They won't believe you."

"I know," he said. He laughed again. She joined him, giggling. Playfully she rolled him over onto his back and straddled his hips. They kissed. Then his hands were fumbling with her shirt. She shrugged it off and tossed it aside. He kneaded her breasts. She dug her thighs into his pelvis.

The telephone rang.

Billie moaned. Damn. She had to answer it. Only a handful of people knew her home number. And nobody would call her at this hour without a good reason. Unless it was a wrong number. Oh, God, let it be a wrong number.

Reluctantly she pulled herself free.

"I'm sorry," she whispered.

"It's okay." He patted her rear. "You're worth waiting for."

She smiled at him, slid to the edge of the bed, and lifted the receiver.

"Hello?"

A man's voice—a stranger's voice—reached her ear. "Billie?"

"Yes. Who's this?"

He did not reply. Instead, very softly, he began to hum.

She listened, fascinated. The tune was oddly hypnotic, not unlike the song she had heard in her dream. It made her feel . . . sad. More than sad. Suddenly it was as if all her friends had died. As if she were alone in the world. And such a rotten world. A friendless, heartless world. Who would want to go on living in a world like this? Why even try, when it was so easy to be free? So very easy . . .

The humming went on, low and mournful. She barely heard it. She was thinking of the full-length mirror mounted on her bathroom door.

"Do you understand?" whispered the phantom voice.

"Yes," said Billie slowly.

The line went dead. She hung up. She got out of bed, moving in weightless slow motion.

"Hey." The boy rolled over to look at her as she glided past. "Billie? What's wrong?"

She said nothing. She went into the bathroom, shut the door, and locked it. She turned on the light. The overhead fan came to life with a whir. Very calmly she wrapped her fist in a towel. She turned to the mirror. She lashed out. The silvered glass erupted in a spider-web of cracks. She hit it again. The mirror crumbled. Glass sprayed the floor.

The doorknob rattled. The door shook under a hammering of fists. The boy was shouting her name.

She stooped. She picked up a large triangular shard. She raised it slowly, then held it, quivering, poised to open her neck in a sluice of blood. She hesitated.

The glass caught a reflection. A face. A familiar face. One she was sure she had seen before. A face composed of dark green eyes, a serious mouth, a wisp of auburn hair curling over a sun-freckled forehead. The face that had gazed back at her from the mirror of the dressing room of the White Horse Saloon. The face printed on the cover of six million copies of *Lovers' Leap*, the album that had won her a Grammy, the album she had struggled for ten years to make. Her face.

That's me, she thought, blinking. That's me.

My God, what am I doing?

Her hand shook. Her features wavered blurrily. She dropped the glass shard. She stared down at the floor. Scattered pieces of her face gazed up at her from the fragments of the ruined mirror. Like a jigsaw puzzle, she thought. Only, who scrambled me all up like that? Was it the phone call? Was it—

The door burst open.

"Are you okay?" gasped the boy. He stood in the doorway, his pants sagging comically around his thighs. The door slanted on smashed hinges. "What the hell happened?"

"I don't know," said Billie. She shook her head slowly. "I don't know."

From the bedroom, the phone rang.

He turned automatically. She grabbed his arm. "No!"

For some reason she could not define, she did not want him answering that phone. It was dangerous. There was death on the line, death in the form of . . . of what?

She could not remember.

The phone kept ringing. Shakily she stepped out of the bathroom and picked it up.

"Hello?"

There was a pause, then a click. The connection was broken.

Billie stared at the receiver, hearing the dial tone. It hummed tunelessly, meaninglessly. Harmlessly.

For a moment she almost remembered what she had heard on the phone. Then, in the next moment, the memory was gone, leaving only ripples of gooseflesh spreading over her arms.

"Billie?" said the boy from the doorway.

She looked at him.

"No questions," she whispered. "Just hold me. Please."

7

What followed was good, very good, but strangely unmemorable, because it was not special. That, Billie knew, was the penalty for having had so many lovers. After a while they blended together and became indistinguishable. She supposed it was wrong—dangerous, even—to live like this, picking up strange men, men who might beat her up or kill her or infect her with a deadly disease. But she did it anyway. She didn't seem to be able to stop.

She sometimes wondered if she were some kind of a nympho or simply the liberated female of today, the one in the cigarette ads. She didn't know. Maybe it was just one consequence of the life she led. Maybe a person couldn't put it all on the line, night after night, exposing herself in public before thousands of strangers' eyes, without some sort of outlet. Maybe.

Or maybe there was something more. She thought about it now, as she lay in the bed, in the dark, with the boy asleep beside her. She had started picking up men on a fairly regular basis around the time when she was getting her first jobs. She earned ten bucks a night, strumming Merle Haggard tunes in smoke-filled honky-tonks, playing for an audience of empty barstools and rare, empty faces. The men in those bars were lonely. They went there in order to forget their dusty apartments, their telephones which never rang, their mailboxes stuffed only with bills and advertising circulars. They went because they needed at least the illusion of human contact. And they tried to talk to her. Not because she was beautiful or because they admired her talent or because she had moved something in their souls. Just because she was a woman and they sensed that she was lonely too.

When she was onstage she was alive. Those moments kept her going and made it worthwhile. But afterward . . .

Afterward, she needed company. She needed a friend. Or even a stranger. Because lying alone in the dark was too much like death. Too much like being swallowed in that darkness she hated and feared.

The darkness that had nearly swallowed her tonight. Twice.

She shivered. The sea breeze was cool. Naked, she got out of bed and shut the window. She found her shirt, slipped it on, then spread a blanket over the boy. He murmured but did not awaken. She kissed his cheek.

She left the bedroom and went downstairs. The clock in the living room said 4:15. She paused before her Degas. It had cost a fortune. But she had wanted it, because it was a street scene of Paris, rendered in bright colors, alive with people and dappled sunlight. She needed things like that in her home, for the same reason she needed a man in her bed.

She went into the den, where she kept her stereo console, a modest little system which had cost as much as two of the luxury options on her Lamborghini. She put on headphones so as not to disturb her guest, then found a CD and loaded it. The tray vanished with a whir of gears. Over the hiss of the analog transfer rose the voices of Willie and Waylon, singing a ballad about two other outlaws. She lay down on the sofa, stretching her legs across the pillows, and listened.

It was nearly 6:30 when she shut off the stereo and climbed the stairs to her bedroom again.

The boy lay as she had left him. She slipped under the blanket. The sheets were damp with sweat.

She snuggled close to him. She put her hand on his leg. It was wet. With semen, she guessed, or with sweat. She let her hand slide slowly up his thigh. Funny. He was wet all over. His skin had the tacky quality of fresh paint. She found his groin. She groped blindly for his penis. Suddenly she needed to be reassured that it was still there. Which was crazy. Of course it was still there. Only it wasn't. Her fingers sank into a spongy ooze. A long time ago, when she was a little girl, she had stuck her hand into a thick, stagnant pond, reaching deep down into the muck. It had felt like this.

Slowly she pulled her hand free. It was gloved in red.

"Oh," she said.

She flexed her fingers stupidly. They dripped.

Suddenly she was shaking. With fear. Simple, animal fear. She had to get away from him. She had to get out of bed. She could not move. Her muscles would not respond. Her teeth chattered crazily.

In the darkness, she heard a sound, a low, desperate, apelike grunting. It grew louder, closer. It became a series of hiccuping gasps. It was all around her now. It was her. She was doing it. She was making the sound.

Get hold of yourself. Calm down. Calm down, dammit.

With effort she rolled over on her stomach and gripped the edge of the bed. Her bloody hand left a red palm-print on the sheet. She stared at the sheet, her eyes moving from that stain to another one, then to another, and more, still more. They were everywhere. She had thought the sheets were damp. Damp with sweat. It was not sweat. She looked at her body. Her skin was streaked in red, like war paint. Candy-cane stripes banded her arms. Her shirt clung to her nipples in dripping patches. Even her hair was wet. Cherry-colored teardrops rolled down her cheeks. She blinked flecks of blood out of her eyes.

She pulled herself forward, across the sheet that was suddenly limitless, stretching before her like a red sea.

She reached the edge of the bed. Her head hung over the floor. Her hair bobbed across her face. She grabbed hold of the carpet, her fists knotted around clumps of the thick pile. She hauled herself out of bed, sliding down onto the floor like something poured out of a can. She lay in a quivering heap.

Then she crawled on hands and knees to the foot of the bed. She gripped a bedpost for support. She pulled herself to her feet. She stared down at the huddled outline of the body under the blanket. Just a shape in the darkness. An anonymous shape.

The breeze stirred her hair. The breeze through the open window.

Oh, Jesus.

She turned. She stared outside, half-expecting to see a killer's face staring back. There was nothing. Nothing but a spread of moonlit sand and surf. They were gone. Whoever they were, they had come while she was downstairs, cocooned in her music. They had scaled the outside wall somehow, forced the window, then killed the sleeping figure in her bedroom, thinking it was her. Probably they had used silencers. Then they had left, losing themselves in the night, as invisible as the wind.

She turned back to the bed. She took hold of the blanket. She drew it back, an inch at a time, uncovering the boy. As she did, she noticed for the first time that the blanket was peppered with small round holes. So many holes.

He had been shot at least two dozen times. His legs, arms, and chest were tattooed in red. His genitals were bloody pulp. His face was unrecognizable. His left cheek, the cheek she had kissed before leaving, was a nest of splintered bone. A gray mush of brains was seeping out onto his pillow through a hole in the back of his skull.

Billie stood trembling, staring down at the bed.

He would not get to tell his friends about it, after all.

She hitched in a breath. "Jesus," she managed to say at last. "Jesus. Jesus. Jesus."

She moved away from him, circling the bed. She picked up her pants and tugged them on. Barefoot, she stumbled out of the room and down the stairs, leaving a trail of bloody footprints. She ran out the door and fell sprawling on the concrete floor of the carport, skinning her palms. She got to her feet, gasping. Her hands bled freely. Her own blood was mixed with his. It was all over her. She was drowning in blood, in death. She reached the car and stabbed the driver's-side door release. The door hinged up with a hiss of air. She flung herself behind the wheel.

Then she was gunning the engine, still saying, "Jesus, Jesus, Jesus," over and over again, the word devoid of meaning now, as the seat cushion darkened with a spreading burgundy stain.

The Countach shot out of the carport and ripped forward, accelerating to a hundred miles an hour in three seconds flat. Billie swung the wheel sharply to the right. The car rounded the curve with a squeal of Pirelli P7's. The gatehouse expanded in the windshield. Both gates were up. But that was impossible. Chet never left the gates up. Unless . . .

She hit the brake and shifted down. The car screamed to a stop outside the gatehouse.

"Chet!" she shrieked. *"Chet!"*

White static hissed on the screen of the portable TV. Chet sat in his chair, watching.

Billie's voice dropped to a whisper. "Chet?"

He did not seem to hear her. He just sat there, motionless, staring blankly, his lower jaw hanging down. For an instant she thought he was dead. But no. She could see the slow rising and falling of his chest with each breath.

His eyes blinked once. She looked closer and saw that they were not focused on the TV. They were not focused on anything.

Then, over the hiss of the TV, she heard a low, insistent sound, a strangely familiar sound.

Slowly Billie lowered her eyes to Chet's lap.

A telephone receiver, off the hook and screeching angrily, lay in his open palm.

8

Frank Lancett paced the balcony. Ten stories below his feet, the palm trees lining Ocean Avenue rustled languidly. On the horizon, where the sea met the sky, the lights of a jetliner circling into L.A. International Airport flashed like a distant beacon. The topmost points of the seaside cliffs to the north were already brightening with the promise of dawn.

The glass door slid open. Mack Reynolds joined him on the deck.

"Hell of a view you've got here," said Lancett, though in truth he had barely noticed it.

"You said it, Frankie."

Reynolds leaned on the railing and sipped his seltzer water, the only thing he ever drank. He was a fitness nut, addicted to wheat germ and low-impact aerobics. Pushing fifty, ten years older than Lancett himself, he still sported the trim waist and lithe muscles of a college boy. Still played the field like a college boy too, damn him to hell. Lancett often found himself sucking in his gut in Reynolds' presence. He knew he'd consumed too much booze and too many pills to be considered college material anymore.

"Santa Monica is the place, all right," Reynolds went on, smiling, his tanned face awash in the faint pink light of sunrise. "No smog. No hassles. Just blue skies and the sea breeze. It's the life, Frankie."

Lancett frowned. He hated being called Frankie.

"If life's so good," he said quietly, "what are you doing in the Brotherhood?"

Reynolds shrugged. "Always room for improvement."

"Think it will be? An improvement, I mean."

"Sure. That's what they told us. A better world." Reynolds looked at him. "Cold feet, Frankie?"

"Maybe I never expected it to really happen. After four thousand years . . ."

Lancett looked at his bracelet, still glinting redly. Reynolds pulled back his own shirtsleeve and did the same.

"I expected it," said Reynolds. "I'm an optimist. And I believe it's for the best. I really do."

"What time is it?" asked Lancett, though he had a watch.

"Six-forty-five."

"She ought to be dead by now."

"She is," said Reynolds confidently. He glanced at Lancett. "Ever hear one of her albums?"

"I hate that hayseed shit."

"She's good, though. *Was* good."

"You were a fan?"

Reynolds made an indifferent gesture.

"Must've been tough for you," said Lancett, intrigued.

"What the hell. Nobody lives forever."

"Except maybe us, huh?"

They laughed together.

"That's right," said Reynolds, pleased with the thought. "Maybe us. Just think. We'll never grow old. Never die. Never have to wheeze our guts out in some fucking hospital bed."

"And never have to take any shit from anybody."

"You think Caesar ever had it so good? Sure, he had his games and his slaves and concubines. But we'll have all that too."

"Better believe it," said Lancett softly. He gripped the railing tighter.

"And even Caesar had to die," said Reynolds. "That's the trouble with getting what you want. You can't keep it. The house always wins in the end. But not this time. We're going to beat the house. We're getting it all and we're never giving it up. Caesar was a fucking piker, compared to us."

"And old Nero too."

Reynolds chuckled. "And Borgia. And Bonaparte."

"And Hitler."

They were silent for a moment.

"It's not like that," said Mack Reynolds finally. The enthusiasm had gone out of his voice. "I told you, Frankie. It . . . it'll be a better world."

They said nothing more for several minutes. A few cars sped by on the street below, their headlights sweeping along the blacktop like shooting stars. A man and woman, very drunk, wandered down the sidewalk singing a medley of Simon and Garfunkel. A cat screeched briefly somewhere. Lancett stared out to sea, squinting to make out the curve of multicolored lights which was the shoreline of Palos Verdes, fifteen miles south of here. And fifteen miles north, he knew, was Malibu. And death.

He could have handled the job himself, but that would have been breaking the rules. And the Brotherhood had very strict rules. He and Reynolds were both Department Heads, of equal rank within the organization; but they controlled different territories. Lancett handled the nebulous area known as the Westside, stretching inland from the eastern border of Santa Monica to the outskirts of Hollywood. It included some prime real estate—Brentwood, Beverly Hills, and Mulholland Drive—as well as Inglewood, which he thought of as Niggertown, and Culver City, home of the MGM lion and more spics than Tijuana. Reynolds was in charge of the coastal strip, the winding, vertical ribbon of land from Long Beach to Oxnard. Included in that territory was Malibu. So the job was his.

He and Reynolds controlled roughly the same number of operatives—staff members, they called them—scattered throughout their respective territories. The staff members were men like Kenneth Blane, who lived—*had* lived—in West L.A. and therefore reported to Lancett. They had been selected in part for their loyalty but in greater part for their strategic value. Many were in the police department and the various city governments. Others worked for the phone companies, insurance firms, and banks. The sorts of places where information and, if necessary, large quantities of money could be obtained.

Not that money was a problem for the Brotherhood. All of its members held down regular jobs. All of the Department heads, including Reynolds and Lancett himself, were in the highest tax bracket. And none took a deduction for the ten percent of his income secretly devoted to charity—one particular charity, not listed in any IRS file.

Most of the staff members, though by no means all, held far less glamorous positions. Kenneth Blane had worked for a computer firm. He had been only a low-level technician, of no importance to the company or, for that matter, to the world; but he'd had keys to everything. He could have been useful. Lancett sighed. Oh, well.

It was by pooling the resources of the membership, from the nickel-and-dime contributions of the boys at the bottom to the million-dollar tithings at the top, that the organization maintained its operations. There were rumors of other, less savory resources which were also tapped—Lancett knew that the prostitutes and runaways delivered to his house for fun and games came from somewhere—but it was not prudent to inquire too closely into such matters.

Each Department Head also had access to men who

were not staff members, men thought of as free-lance
help. Most of them took the form of experienced criminals, streetwise and dangerous, capable of murder. It
was two men like that whom Reynolds had phoned
three hours ago to arrange the job tonight.

At first, neither Reynolds nor Lancett had considered that step to be necessary. It was necessary only
to obtain Billie's phone number, then call her house.
Reynolds had hummed the lullaby which Lancett had
used to rock Blane to eternal sleep. They assumed it
would have the same effect this time. But when Reynolds called back a few minutes later, the bitch herself
had answered.

Her will was strong, then. Stronger than poor Kenneth Blane's willpower had ever been. Strong enough
to resist the feeble magic of that spell. There were
more powerful songs, but Department Heads did not
learn them. Still, there were other, more conventional
ways to achieve the same purpose.

Billie might be immune to magic. But not bullets.

Now they were waiting only for confirmation that
things had gone as planned. No glitches this time.
Then Reynolds would call the faceless Director, who
would contact his still-more-mysterious superior, a
man known only by whispered rumors, believed to
live on another continent, directing by remote control
an enterprise which spanned a hundred cities and perhaps a hundred thousand men.

And only men. No women were used. Orders were
explicit on that score. And those orders, it was understood, came from the very top.

Inside the apartment, the telephone rang.

Reynolds smiled. "Sounds like it might be time to
notify the next of kin."

Lancett said nothing. He waited. He heard the door
slide open. The ringing of the phone was abruptly cut
off as Reynolds lifted the receiver.

"Yes."

Lancett listened tensely.

"Drake? What the hell?"

He stiffened. Something had gone wrong.

Drake was not one of the free-lancers hired to do this job. He was the desk sergeant on the night shift in the Malibu P.D., a member of Reynolds' staff. Reynolds had called him earlier this evening to obtain details of the Malibu Colony's security. The man had informed him that there was a patrol car on duty at all times, but it was not likely to stop any car that got through the front gate without raising an alarm. That was the key.

Well, it had been easy enough to arrange. Reynolds merely phoned the Colony's security office and hummed a little lullaby to the man who picked up the phone—a song calculated, not to kill him, but merely to put him to sleep for a couple of hours. And everything was fine. Everything was smooth.

Except that now Drake was calling, when he had no reason to. No reason, except one.

"All right," said Reynolds. "I understand." He hung up.

Lancett entered the apartment and stood mute, waiting, with the breeze at his back. He did not like to admit it, but he was enjoying the look of cold terror on Mack Reynolds' face.

"They fucked up," said Reynolds slowly. His lower lip trembled. A bead of sweat glistened on the bridge of his nose like a third eye. "Kidd is alive. She's at the goddamn police station right now."

"What happened?" asked Lancett quietly.

"How the hell should I know?" Reynolds was already dialing a new number with a shaking hand. "Goddammit. Goddammit to hell. Why is this woman so fucking hard to kill?"

9

Billie had driven to the police station at bullet speed. She arrived, a blood-streaked, hysterical mess. An inner voice had told her to explain things calmly and logically, but she couldn't, just couldn't. It was all too much. The concert . . . the phone call . . . the boy in her bed . . . Chet, staring like a zombie . . .

Two sympathetic young officers, whose names were Ramirez and Edwards, led her to a chair, got her a drink of water, and bandaged her hands, still bleeding from the fall she had taken. A fortyish, vaguely hungover man emerged from his office with bags under his eyes and a steaming cup of coffee in his hand. She was able to grasp that he was a lieutenant and that his name was Pratt. He sat by her, holding her hand for a good long time. In the back of the room, the desk sergeant, whose name she hadn't quite caught, watched her expressionlessly.

Gradually she regained the ability to speak in declarative sentences. She told her story, one word at a time, omitting the phone call and the suicide attempt, because those things still made no sense at all. She ended with the gatehouse and the phone off the hook. "He was just staring," she said, fresh tears welling in her eyes. "Just staring into space . . ."

"It's okay, Miss Kidd," said Pratt softly. "It's okay."

The day was brightening, already heating up with the promise of another mid-August scorcher, the kind of day when the dust-dry Santa Ana winds blew in off the desert, robbing the air of moisture and threatening the parched hills with brushfires, a day when even the most hardened L.A. natives went scurrying for the nearest air conditioner. Shafts of sun broke through a tremulous curtain of mist. Sea gulls wheeled in the dawn sky, cawing. Their shrill cries seemed sad and lonely, like cries of mourning for the dead.

Billie sat in the passenger seat of the unmarked car, with Pratt at the wheel, speeding down the Pacific Coast Highway. The two patrolmen, Ramirez and Edwards, followed in a black-and-white.

The first thing she saw as the cars pulled onto the side road and approached the Colony was that the gates were no longer raised. Then Pratt pulled to a halt alongside the gatehouse and Chet leaned out, smiling.

"Good morning, Lieutenant. You're up early today."

He was conscious again. He was himself. Billie closed her eyes, experiencing a blessed wave of relief.

Pratt stared at him, then threw Billie a questioning glance.

"Uh . . . good morning," he said quietly. "I think you know Miss Kidd."

Chet tipped his cap. "Sure do. Glad to see you're okay."

She blinked. "What?"

"Well, I hate to say so, but you were acting kind of peculiar when you left."

"Me? You're the one who was doing the potted-plant impersonation."

"Miss Kidd seems to think," said Pratt slowly, "that you might have been drugged. She says she drove out of here about forty-five minutes ago, and at that time you didn't respond when she shouted your name."

Chet shrugged. "Well, I certainly don't like to disagree with any of our people. But I recollect things differently. Miss Kidd did leave here, all right. I logged her out. She was in a real hurry. She looked all . . . out of sorts. Kind of frazzled, you could say. I asked her if there was anything wrong, but she just yelled at me to let her through.''

Billie whirled in her seat to face Pratt. "That's a bunch of bullshit!" she hissed. "He didn't ask me any damn questions. He was about as talkative as a scarecrow—"

"Okay, Miss Kidd." Pratt put a hand on her shoulder. "Just relax."

She brushed his hand away. "Hell if I will! There is something very weird going on here!"

"We'll get it all straightened out," said Pratt soothingly. "A look inside your house should settle everything." He turned back to Chet. "Mind if we go through?"

"Sure thing."

The gate swung up a second later.

As the car pulled forward, Billie leaned out the rear window with a sudden thought.

"Hey, Chet. How'd that movie turn out, anyway?"

For a moment—just one moment—a flicker of doubt registered on the man's face. Then it was gone and his features smoothed out into a smiling mask.

"Just fine," he said. "You should see it sometime."

"So should you," she muttered, turning away.

She said nothing more as the two cars rolled down the street and parked outside her house. The three cops entered the carport. She trailed them, a nervous shadow. The door to the living room was open. She had not thought to close it when she fled. The four of them stepped inside. Bloody footprints stained the carpet. Wordlessly they followed the trail of blood up the stairs.

The bedroom was just ahead. The door had swung half-shut, blown by the breeze. It swayed, creaking on its hinges, a shivery horror-movie sound. Pratt pushed the door open, then stepped inside with the two cops. Billie took a breath and followed. Her heart thudded in her ears. Her hands were knotted into fists. Suddenly she wished she had not insisted on coming along. The memories in this room were too vivid. The stink of blood, of death, was all around her. She fought back the impulse to turn and run.

She stared down at the carpet, spotted with red stains. She was afraid to look up, to see it again—the boy's pockmarked chest leaking blood, his eyes staring sightlessly out of a ruined face. With an effort she raised her eyes to the bed.

It was empty.

Billie stared. The sheets were still bloody and tangled, a hideous pinkish shade in the early light. But the body was gone.

"Well, Miss Kidd?" asked Pratt softly.

She shook her head. "I don't get it."

Ramirez and Edwards were already checking out the rest of the room. Edwards found the bathroom and switched on the light. The ceiling fan whirred.

"Hey, Lieutenant. Take a look."

Pratt stepped into the bathroom. His eyes moved from the litter of glass to Billie.

"How did this happen?" he asked.

She swallowed. "That was something else. It had nothing to do with . . ."

"Did you do it?"

"It was an accident."

The cops looked at one another, then at her. Their expressions were no longer as friendly as they had been in the police station.

"I'll tell you what I think, Miss Kidd," said Pratt slowly. "I think you broke the mirror. I think you cut up your hands pretty good in the process. They were bleeding like crazy when you got to the station. You might have opened an artery, even."

"No. I told you, I fell down—"

"Then I think," he continued relentlessly, "you got this idea in your head that somebody had been killed in here. Maybe you saw all the blood and freaked out.

Some people can get pretty upset at the sight of blood. Particularly their own blood. And particularly if they're kind of juiced, say.''

"What's that supposed to mean?''

"Have you ever taken any illegal substances, Miss Kidd?''

"No.''

"Not even a little something to calm your nerves after what happened at your show?''

"I said no, dammit.''

The three men stared at her, disbelief printed on their faces.

"Please,'' she whispered. "You've got to believe me. A man was murdered in my bed. It was supposed to be me. There's something going on. Something big, involving a lot of people, I think. The man at the concert . . . and whoever came here . . . they're all after me. They're . . . they're trying to kill me.''

She hated herself for saying it, for the paranoid way it sounded: They're all out to get me. It's a conspiracy. Little green men in flying saucers.

Pratt watched her coldly.

"You're sticking to your story?''

"It's not a story,'' she moaned. "It's what happened.''

"Then maybe you'd care to give us some information about the deceased. Something for us to go on, if we file a missing-persons report.''

"What kind of information?''

"How about his name?''

"His . . .''

She stopped. Slowly she raised her hand to her face.

She had picked him out of the crowd, driven home with him, whispered to him in the darkness, made love with him in her bed . . . but she had never asked his name. She had never thought to ask.

"His name, please?''

She stared forlornly at the bed.

"I don't know it. I don't know his name. I don't know anything about him."

10

Two miles away, a rusted 1976 Pontiac Firebird pulled off the coast highway onto a dusty turnout. It sat there, engine idling fitfully, exhaust clouds spurting from its rear and nearly obscuring the faded bumper sticker that read EASY DOES IT.

Johnny drummed his fingers on the steering wheel. In the seat next to his, Roadrunner fiddled with the radio, turning up the volume till rap music throbbed like a pulsing migraine in the confines of the car. Johnny reached over and snapped the radio off.

"What's the matter with you?" said Roadrunner petulantly.

"We fucked up," said Johnny in disgust. "That's what's the frigging matter."

"Little mistake, that's all." Roadrunner giggled. "Tell you, Johnny-O, I'm kind of bummed. I mean, I really wanted to do it. Yeah. Really wanted to tell people I wasted Billy the Kid. Like in the O.K. Corral or something."

"Her name's Billie Lee Kidd, ass-wipe. And you better hope sorry is all you are. 'Cause I've got a feeling the guys we're working for aren't real tolerant when it comes to screwing up."

"Fuck 'em." Roadrunner hefted the Llama 9mm automatic. The deep blue finish glinted coldly. "They hand us any shit, I'll give 'em an extra eye to see with. Right in the middle of their face."

Johnny considered making a reply. He didn't bother. There was no point. Roadrunner, he knew, was a certifiable moron. But he was damn good with a gun. And always willing. Christ, yes. He'd blow the head off a six-year-old kid if you told him to. Or maybe even if you didn't. And he never lost his nerve. That was important in this line of work. Johnny figured maybe Roadrunner was too dumb to ever get scared enough to lose his nerve.

Johnny wasn't dumb, though. He knew they had been playing for high stakes this time. They'd done some odd jobs for these people before, but never anything like this. Never a murder.

Not that he was exactly a virgin in that department. He'd been broken in a long time ago, at the tender age of fifteen, running with the Skitters gang in South-Central. He had started as a cop-spotter and worked his way up to gang-banging full time, toting an AK-47, blowing away the rival Second Street punks in drive-by shootings that left twisted corpses littering half a city block. He had neither enjoyed nor hated the work. He had felt no pride or shame afterward. Some people would say he was immoral for doing shit like that, but the way he had things figured, this world was only fit for tough bastards, and if you wanted to survive, you had to be the toughest bastard there was. And he was a survivor. Oh, yeah. When the dust cleared, he would always be standing. Count on it.

A couple of years ago, around the time he turned eighteen and was no longer a kid in the eyes of the law, the heat came down hard on the Skitters. To save his ass from a term in prison, Johnny went solo. Now he made a damn good living as a hired gun, drug dealer, arms smuggler, jack-of-all-trades. He had a reputation for doing whatever he was told, quickly and well, and not mouthing off about it afterward. He figured that was how Reynolds had heard of him, and why he had been hired to do this job. And now, goddammit, he had fucked up.

"So what do we do now?" asked Roadrunner, breaking in on his thoughts. The question was a perennial favorite. Left on his own, Roadrunner did not have the smarts to figure out which movie he wanted to see.

Johnny sighed. "Got to call in. Talk to the man."

"Don't let him rattle you, Johnny-O." Roadrunner giggled stupidly. His gapped teeth made a leering crescent. He looked like that cartoon character on the cover of *Mad* magazine. "We can handle him. We can handle anything."

"Right," said Johnny, who was not at all certain this was true. Not when it came to the people they were dealing with today. People who could contract the execution of a top-of-the-charts country queen without a second thought. People who had drugged that security guard, or done something weird to his head anyway, so the Firebird could ease through the front gate without a hitch. Yeah. People like that.

Then he shook his head, dismissing all doubts. He was a survivor. He always made it. Nobody could knock him down for the count. Not Reynolds or his people or anybody else. He could take them all on and win. Count on it.

He climbed out of the car. A telephone booth stood a few yards away. He walked to it, taking deep breaths, filling his lungs with ocean air. He stepped inside and dialed a number.

"Johnny," he said when his employer's voice answered.

"Did you take care of it?"

"Yeah."

"Trouble?"

"None. In and out. Like a cheap date on the Strip." He tried to sound cool, but he was uncomfortably aware that he sounded merely stupid. "Pretty major carpet-cleaning job, though. No way we could fit that into our schedule."

"Uh-huh."

"Then we disposed of the goods. Where nobody'll go looking for 'em."

There was some kind of wildlife preserve next to the Colony. The body, weighted down with tire chains, had vanished into the lagoon with a splash. A flock of ducks had been bobbing half-asleep nearby. The noise scared them into the sky. Roadrunner had laughed at that. Roadrunner laughed at everything.

Johnny waited for an acknowledgment from Reynolds. He heard nothing.

"Anything else you need?" he asked finally.

"No. Nothing." A pause. "Except this."

Then Reynolds did a strange thing, a thing which Johnny could not quite comprehend. He began to sing. A high, reedy, mournful sort of song. Johnny blinked, listening. The song went on for a few bars, then stopped.

"Got it?" breathed Reynolds.

Johnny nodded. "Count on it," he said softly.

Johnny climbed behind the wheel and smiled at Roadrunner and listened to the song in his mind. Catchy tune, he thought distantly. Like a TV jingle. Hard to forget.

"No problem," he said calmly.

"Told you." Roadrunner shrugged. "So what do we do now? Lie low for a while?"

Johnny shifted into drive and pulled out onto the highway. "Yeah," he said, cracking a smile. "We lie low. Real low."

He walked the Firebird up to fifty-five, a little fast for this winding road, but not too fast for him, not now, not with that song still bopping in his brain.

"Hey, Johnny-O," said Roadrunner. "You think they're going get that bitch?"

"They can get anybody."

Johnny accelerated to sixty. Sixty-five. Seventy. The wind, laced with salt, whipped through the open windows.

Roadrunner stuck his arm out the window to feel the breeze.

"All *right,*" he said, grinning that Alfred E. Newman grin.

Roadrunner was into speed. That was how he had gotten his name—he was always streaking along like that cartoon bird with a dizzy smile on his face. Last year, on his birthday, he had insisted on going out to Magic Mountain just to ride the Ninja. Johnny had practically barfed. Roadrunner had loved it.

Well, today wasn't his birthday. But he was getting a little present anyhow.

The Firebird hit eighty miles an hour. Johnny swerved into the opposing lane and shot past a station wagon creeping along at fifty, then veered back across the double yellow. The driver blasted his horn. Roadrunner gave him the finger.

"This is great, Johnny-O." He was giggling. "This is fucking great."

"It gets better," said Johnny, still smiling, as the song played on.

The needle of the speedometer edged ninety. The highway twisted and looped and coiled, a roller-coaster ride, better than the Ninja, better than anything. Johnny skidded into the northbound lane to pass three more cars, and a little VW Rabbit rounded a corner, heading north, coming right at him. The driver, a woman, screamed. He could see her eyes bulging fishlike out of her head, her lipstick-smeared lips parted in a doughnut hole. At the last second she swung onto the shoulder. The Firebird whipped past, grazing the Rabbit with a hiss of metal, then careened back into the southbound lane.

"Man!" Roadrunner was in heaven. "You are really doing it!"

"You ain't seen nothing yet, my friend."

Johnny put his foot on the floor. The speedometer passed the century mark. The tires shrieked on every curve. The car leaned on two wheels. The road was a blur. The wind cut through the open windows like a knife.

Roadrunner jumped up and down in his seat like a kid, like a puppy, like the fucking mental defective he was. He was laughing hysterically. Ropes of spit flew from his mouth, spraying the dashboard.

"Faster," he said. "Come on, Johnny-O. Let's do it. Let's take it to the fucking limit!"

"To the limit," said Johnny very quietly, his words all but stolen by the wind. "That's right. So right."

That high, sweet, sad song still played in his mind.

Up ahead, a truck rumbled into view, heading north. Not a big truck. A little Ryder job. Some asshole, thought Johnny calmly, hauling his shit from one apartment to another. Some asshole who wasn't going to be moving in on time.

Johnny's hands tensed on the steering wheel. He was doing a hundred and ten. Hundred and fifteen. Hundred and twenty.

"I tell you, Johnny-O," said Roadrunner, "I'm loving this."

Johnny spun the wheel to the left. The Firebird careened into the northbound lane, directly in the path of the oncoming truck, leaving no time and no room for either vehicle to maneuver.

Roadrunner had time to open his mouth and utter one word, which would be his epitaph.

"Shit."

Then came impact.

The Firebird folded up. The tires exploded. The front seats flew off.

Roadrunner sailed headfirst through the windshield and landed on the pavement on a rag-doll heap, his head lolling on a broken neck, his lips still stretched wide in a gap-toothed smile.

Johnny slammed into the steering wheel. His ribs splintered like toothpicks. A shaft of bone punctured his heart. He vomited blood. Somewhere a horn was blaring.

And the song was gone.

Jesus, he thought as his mind cleared and he gazed

down in helpless horror at the river of blood drenching his shirt. What did I do to myself? What the fuck did I do?

He died without hearing an answer.

11

Reynolds put down the phone slowly.

"They got rid of the body," he said. "And I got rid of them."

Lancett, sprawled on the sofa of Reynolds' living room, grunted indifferently.

"I called that security guard again." Reynolds' voice quavered slightly. "An easy subject. No willpower at all." He gave a short, hysterical laugh. "By now, he's probably told the cops exactly what we want them to hear."

Lancett shrugged. "She's still alive," he said quietly. "All this other stuff is bullshit."

"It helps cover our ass."

"Your ass, you mean."

Reynolds swallowed. His tanned face was ghostly pale. His nostrils contracted and dilated rhythmically, but with no sound of breath. He cracked his knuckles. Scared. Oh, yes. So goddamn scared.

Well, Reynolds had never been much of a Department Head anyway. And maybe—thought Lancett with the hint of a smile—once Joe College here was out of the game, the Director would figure out that there was no time to promote a new man to the position. Not now, with the song already sung and the clock ticking. So maybe he would just consolidate the coastal strip into the existing territories. In which case, by simple geography, guess who would get the biggest slice. Just guess.

Reynolds got up slowly. He went into the kitchen. Lancett watched him through the doorway as he removed a plastic container of unflavored yogurt from the refrigerator. He dumped the contents into the blender, then added some milk, a dollop of molasses, and a sliced banana. He switched on the blender and reduced the mixture to a foaming milkshake. His hands shook as he poured it into a tall glass and came back into the living room, sipping the drink slowly.

"These are great," he said, his mouth flecked with white, his voice quavering worse than before. "Healthiest thing you can drink. I have one every morning. Usually sit out on the deck and look at the sunrise."

"Before or after you go do your six miles?" asked Lancett in what he hoped was a tone of sarcasm.

"After. Not good to exercise on a full stomach. Plays hell with your digestion."

"I'll remember that."

Reynolds finished the last of the drink and put down the glass. He sighed. "I just wanted one more," he said, his voice low and thoughtful. "One more for the road."

He looked down at his hands. Slowly he pulled back the sleeve of his jacket to reveal a glittering bracelet with a blood-red stone. He fingered the chain.

All at once, Lancett knew what Mack Reynolds was going to do.

"Hey," breathed Lancett. "Wait a minute."

"What for?" Reynolds chuckled. "I'm a dead man anyway. You know it as well as I do."

"Yeah, but . . ." Lancett swung his legs around to a sitting position. He dug his fingers into the sofa. "Not here." He swallowed. "Not right in front of me."

Reynolds was laughing now, a low, hysterical sound.

"So long, Frankie," he said with insane cheerfulness. "See you in hell."

He tightened his grip on the chain. Then with one jerk of his arm he snapped the bracelet off. It dangled in his fist. He spread his fingers. The bracelet dropped to the floor, sinking into the carpet's thick pile.

Lancett opened his mouth to say something, he did not know what. He said nothing. He stared.

He had been warned of the consequences, should he ever remove the bracelet which bound him to the Brotherhood. All the members had been warned. He had never seen a man do it. He had heard stories but, well, everyone knew how stories were. Things were never as bad as they were rumored to be. Almost never.

He watched, horrified and fascinated at once. He did not want to look. He wanted to close his eyes, turn away. He could not do it.

Mack Reynolds opened his mouth to scream. No sound came. His lips worked frantically. His tongue clicked in his throat.

He was . . . changing.

Black fur sprouted on his forehead, his chin, his knuckles. It rippled up his arms. The thin cotton of his shirt crawled. Lancett thought crazily of those old Lon Chaney Jr. pictures, the ones with the withered Gypsy woman always warning of the nights when the moon is full. But this was not quite the same. What he was seeing now was not those smooth, graceful Hollywood dissolves from man to makeup creation. This was something crude, shocking. Ugly bristles of hair burst out of Reynolds' pores like porcupine needles. His skin fell away in bleeding patches, ripping free of his body like the sudden tatters of his shirt and pants. His face was contorted with pain.

He fell on his knees, gibbering. He groped for the bracelet, seeking to snatch it back. He had changed his mind. This was worse than he had expected. Worse than anything *they* could do to him. Worse than anything he thought possible. His hands almost closed over the bracelet, and then they were not hands any longer, they were thick, fumbling animal paws. They scrabbled uselessly at the chain, buried in the thick pile carpet. They could not pluck it loose.

His body was racked with spasms. His legs and arms jerked wildly. He could not control his muscles anymore. He gave up on the bracelet. He curled up in a tight fetal ball. His skin went on shedding like a snake's hide. His bones shifted, expanding and contracting like Silly Putty in the hands of a restless child. His skull flattened. His forehead sloped. His eyes crawled farther apart as the bridge of his nose caved in. His nostrils flared, horselike. His jaw jutted out. Yellow teeth shot up like dandelion stalks, distorting his swollen lips. His back hunched. His rib cage expanded. His arms lengthened, unspooling like film reels. He rolled over on his belly, grunting, and raised himself to a crouch. He stood on his knuckles. A ribbon of spittle ran down his chin.

Not a wolf, thought Lancett past numbing shockwaves of horror. An ape. Some kind of ape.

Reynolds groaned, a low, tortured, hopeless sound. His hands moved over his body in a desperate quest for the familiar form that had once been there. His eyes rolled in their sockets. Tears streaked his cheeks. He crawled on hands and knees toward the bracelet. He stopped, halfway there, frozen by the sight of his reflection in the polished brass frame of the fireplace screen. He stared at himself. He lashed out with one fist and smashed the screen to twisted wreckage.

Then all at once he lifted his head, feeling something, something which Lancett saw as an earthquake shuddering through his body. Cracks shot through his flesh like the crisscrossing veins in a crumbling statue. The ape skin shattered into a webwork of jagged lines. Then, as Reynolds howled and beat his chest in animal rage, his skin fell away in a cloud of hair, exposing a new body underneath, a stunted midget body crawling with silvery fur. His buttocks swelled up and split open with a sickening tear of flesh. A long serrated tail sprang out like a jack-in-the-box. His hands curled into white-tufted claws. Talons sprang up like switchbades. A pink tongue flicked in his mouth. His nose twitched and wrinkled, gray whiskers quivering. His face was wall-eyed, fuzzy, pointy-eared. A rat face.

He hunched down on all fours. Only his shirt and, grotesquely, his Jockey shorts still clung to his body. He squeaked frantically in a high-pitched rodent voice that was somehow still human. He was a rodent-thing, some sort of hybrid of rat and monkey, about the size of a German shepherd. He dragged himself across the floor, still seeking the bracelet with monomaniacal desperation. He prodded it with his snout, making damp, snuffling noises. He turned the bracelet over and over, pushing it along the floor, unable to hook the chain around his nose.

Lancett understood what was happening, of course. It was evolution. The whole course of evolution, just like old Mr. Brindell had taught it in tenth grade. Only in reverse. From man to missing link to giant shrew to . . . what?

Reynolds was mutating again. He shed his rodent fur in a shower of loose hairs. What was left of him was only a pale, embryonic, torsolike thing, slimy and boneless, perhaps two and a half feet long. It had no arms or legs. It had flippers. Fins. A mosaic of scales was printed on its skin. Its eyes, round and unblinking, bulged out of a fish head. It flapped wetly on the floor, wriggling free of the last of Reynolds' clothes.

The fish-thing jackknifed wildly on the carpet, spraying the walls with droplets of moisture. Its skin peeled away in long strips like fleshy zippers. Out of its bleeding chest cavity scurried a lobsterlike creature with twitching eyestalks and snapping claws. A trilobite, thought Lancett, remembering some sort of slideshow in Mr. Brindell's class. A thing extinct for better than two hundred million years. Its only legacy, fossil imprints in Paleozoic rock. He thought about a guy he had known once, a guy who was obsessed with tracing his family tree. Finding his roots, he called it. Well, shit, Reynolds had that guy beat by a country mile. He had found his goddamn roots, all right; and like the people who learn that their great-great-granddaddy was a horse thief or a slaveholder, he clearly was not relishing his discovery.

The trilobite scuttled weakly across the floor, leaving a trail of slime. Lancett saw in mingled amazement and disgust that it was creeping toward the bracelet. Seeking to hook the chain in its claw, perhaps. Still trying to undo what it had done. If that was even possible.

It made no difference. The bracelet was still a yard away, and already the creature was losing its shape, the brittle exoskeleton cracking apart like an eggshell, the abdomen sagging on ruptured legs, the eyestalks drooping like smashed flower stems. A milky amoeboid puddle oozed out of its remains, foaming like a pool of dishwashing liquid. Shapeless pseudopods extended from the thing and slithered feebly toward the bracelet. They could not reach it.

The thing that had been Mack Reynolds bubbled down into the thick pile carpet, shrinking as it went, until finally, mercifully, it was gone.

What remained was only the clothes, the bracelet, and—like a confirmation of what had taken place—a bloody snowdrift of tattered skin flaps and animal hair.

12

Despite everything, Billie had to smile at the expression on K.C.'s face.

"Guess what?" she said cheerfully as his eyes ran over her blood-matted clothes and rat's-nest tangle of hair. "You boys have got company."

"Bills." He blinked as if just remembering how. "What the hell happened to you? What are you doing here?"

"It's a long story, pal of mine." She sighed. "So am I just supposed to stand here, or could a lady come in and rest her weary toes?"

"Huh? Oh. Sure. Come on in."

She stepped inside the spacious sun-streaked living room, looking around slowly. She rarely visited K.C., Gary, and Bobby Joe in the penthouse apartment they shared, living the bohemian bachelor life. She wouldn't have been here now if she'd had anyplace else to go.

After the discovery of the shattered mirror, there had been little point in further conversation with the representatives of the law. Billie had found her wristwatch and snapped it on, then pulled on her boots, grabbed her wallet, and stuffed it with extra cash from a desk drawer. She figured she might need money for a hotel or something, because she sure as shit wasn't coming back here.

Wordlessly she rode with the cops to the police station, where her Lamborghini was waiting. She picked up her car keys from the desk sergeant, a man named Drake who was studying her with intense gray-blue eyes. A fan, she figured.

"Anyplace we can reach you if something turns up?" he asked casually.

She thought for a moment, then gave him the number of her band's apartment on the Sunset Strip.

The Countach's interior was mottled in red, sickeningly bright in the morning sun. She drove slowly down the coast highway to Sunset, then along the winding road, past the manicured lawns of Brentwood and Beverly Hills, into West Hollywood. The streets were uncharacteristically empty, as they always were on Sunday mornings. Along the Strip, billboards shouted news of movies, records, and Vegas shows. Barry Manilow was playing the Tropicana. His stylized likeness, forty feet high, sparkled with sheet-metal sequins, shimmering in the slow waves of heat like a mirage in the desert.

Billie turned down Doheny, then swung left onto a side street. She parked before a luxury high-rise featuring rooftop tennis courts, an indoor swimming pool, and penthouse apartments with spectacular views. Some very famous names could be found inside, names as prominent in the entertainment business as those on the billboards lining Sunset. They included a record promoter, a brat-packer movie star, an author of historical novels, and a former sports figure turned talk-show host. Most of them were gay. West Hollywood was a largely gay neighborhood. Boys' Town, the locals called it.

Her band members, however, were not gay. Hell, thought Billie wryly, after they find out I'm staying with them, they won't even be cheerful.

The bad joke made her smile, just a little, for the first time in hours.

She rode the elevator to the top floor, rang the doorbell, and now here she was.

She flopped down on a futon butted up against a wall plastered with stolen street signs. That was Gary's hobby. He liked collecting signs from cities where they played. He had at least a hundred of the things.

"Were you in a goddamn car crash or something?" asked K.C., interrupting her thoughts.

"I should be so lucky." She looked up at the ceiling. Dust bunnies inhabited the corners. "Let's just say the past few hours haven't been my best. Where are the other guys, anyway?"

As if on cue, Bobby Joe and Gary shuffled into the living room in their underwear. They were trailed by two sleepy-eyed suntanned blonds who were not twins but could have been.

"Yo, boss lady," said Bobby Joe.

"Hey," said Billie with all the enthusiasm she could summon, which was none.

"What brings you here?" asked Bobby Joe.

"Must have been my charm," said Gary. "Knew it would work eventually."

"Hey, you're saving your charm for me, remember?" said one of the girls. She glanced at Billie. "Who is she, anyway?"

"You kidding?" said her clone. "That's her. You know. *Her.*"

"Oh," said the first one. "She's a lot shorter than I thought."

Billie closed her eyes. Suddenly she had a massive headache. A warm hand closed over her own. She opened her eyes. Bobby Joe was standing over her.

"You feeling okay?"

She forced a smile. "Never better."

"That nut at the show didn't throw you too bad, did he?"

"The show?" She had almost forgotten. "No. Not too bad."

"How'd it work out with the guy last night?"

For a moment she felt a rush of faintness. She saw it again. The bed, dripping. The naked body scored with bullet holes like a silhouette target in a shooting gallery. The gray ooze of brains on the pillow.

"Not so hot," she said weakly.

"Tell you the truth," said Gary, "he looked like a dead fuck to me."

She shuddered. Two sightless eyes, glassy in the moonlight, stared up at her. She said nothing.

"So, give," said K.C. "What's up?"

"Look." Billie sighed. "I'd rather not talk about it right now. Okay?"

"Sure, sure." K.C. shrugged. "Be mysterious. See if we care."

"I'd just like to stay with you guys for a bit. Hang out here. Only for a few days. If that's okay."

"Hey, wait a minute," said one of the blonds. Billie honestly could not tell them apart. "Vicki and me, we're not going for any, you know, menagerie de trois."

The telephone rang, sparing Billie the necessity of a reply. Bobby Joe swore, muttering who-the-fuck-could-that-be, and picked it up.

"Yeah? . . . Oh. Yeah, how you doing? . . . What? . . . She's here. Right here. Hold on." He cupped a hand over the mouthpiece and looked at Billie. "It's Harve."

She sat up. Bobby Joe carried the phone to her. "Hello?"

"Billie, is that you?"

"Sure is. Aren't you still in New York?"

"Got in this morning. Didn't even see a goddamn newspaper till I got home. They were piled up on the front step. Today's edition on top. I practically choked. You're front page news, you know. The *Times* has got a picture of you squaring off against a knife with your guitar."

"Talk about dueling banjos."

"Don't make jokes." His voice was hard. "Damn, that was a close one. I should've been there. I swear to Christ, I'll never miss one of your shows again."

"If you went to see all your clients perform, you'd never get any work done. But thanks for the offer. And for calling too. How'd you know I was here, anyway?"

"I didn't. I called your place. No answer. So I figured maybe you'd be with the guys."

"You must've been Sherlock Holmes in a previous life." She debated telling Harve about the incident last night, but it would have required letting Bobby Joe and Gary and K.C. in on it too, not to mention the Bobbsey Twins, and she didn't want to do that, not now, not yet. Besides, enough people thought she was crazy as it was.

"You sure you're still in one piece?"

"Don't worry, Harve. My head bone is still connected to my neck bone, and my neck bone is et cetera, et cetera."

"I might come by later. Just to . . . you know . . ."

"Pay your last respects?"

"Dammit, I said don't joke about it!"

Jeez, he must be really shaken up. She had never heard him so wired before. She remembered suddenly that his first and only wife had died ten years ago, long before Billie had become his client. She wondered if he was relating that loss to what had nearly happened to her last night. Or if, in some subtle way she had never quite perceived, he thought of her as the wife he had lost or the daughter he would never have.

"Sorry, Harve," she said quietly. "I didn't mean to get you upset."

He sighed heavily. "It's just . . . I've always cared for you, Billie. You're more than a client to me. You're my friend . . ." His voice trailed off. She realized with a wave of shock that Harve Medlow—the biggest talent agent in the music business, the man known by the affectionate nickname of the Shark, who drove the hardest bargains and cut the sharpest deals in town—Harve Medlow, *that* Harve Medlow, was on the verge of tears.

"It's all right, Harve," she said anxiously. "Everything's all right."

Except it wasn't. She knew that. Because there were people out there, hidden in the shadows of the city, lurking in dark corners, people who wanted to kill her for some reason she couldn't guess. They had tried twice. They had failed. But she knew with sick certainty that they would not give up.

She went on talking with Harve, trying her best to sound cool and calm and unafraid, while ribbons of gooseflesh rippled up her arms.

13

Sergeant Martin Drake put down the phone slowly. A busy signal. Again.

This was the third time in the last two minutes that he had called the number given to him by Billie Lee Kidd. He had to get through.

He looked around with unseeing eyes at the clutter of his one-bedroom cabin on Old Topanga Canyon Road, where he had just returned after completing the night shift. Ramirez and Edwards and the other guys at the station house ribbed him a lot about still leading the wild life of a bachelor at thirty-two, partying up here in these hills known for marijuana gardens and all-night bashes; but their jokes rang hollow and they knew it. His life was not wild; it was empty, as empty as the bare shelves of his refrigerator and the blank pages of that photo album he had always meant to start someday. He slept most of the day, worked most of the night; even on weekends he could not break out of his sleep cycle; he was like a vampire, shunning daylight and humanity.

He had no friends, no family, no joys. He existed for one purpose only. To serve his gods.

Eight years had passed since the night when he joined the Brotherhood, eight years of torchlit gatherings and mystic rites. There was danger in this life, and loneliness, a sense of isolation from the rest of the world, the nagging knowledge of a secret never to be shared. And there were other hardships. His initiation had been difficult. He did not like to kill living things, not even stray cats squirming and screeching in burlap sacks. He had done it. He had slit their bellies and watched their blood pour out like sparkling wine. He had obeyed, so that he might serve the cause which called him. The cause which had led him to last night. And to his destiny.

He had heard, on the radio, about the incident at the concert, but he had never thought to connect it with the Brotherhood or to look at the bracelet hidden under the sleeve of his uniform. A short time later, he got the phone call from Mack Reynolds, requesting information about security at the Malibu Colony. He answered Reynolds' questions, speaking softly so as not to be overheard. Then the line went dead and, very slowly, he pulled down his sleeve and looked at the bracelet on his left wrist. It was red. Blood-red.

When, three hours later, Billie Lee Kidd stumbled into the police station looking like somebody's blood-drenched nightmare, he knew that the prophecy had come true at last, that the Deathsong had been sung, and that he was looking at its singer.

And she was still alive. Still capable of undoing all that had been done. Still able to close the Door she had unknowingly opened, and put an end to the new world dreamed of by the Brotherhood before it had even begun.

He had known what he must do.

Now, alone in his house on a Sunday morning, he picked up the phone and dialed again, and this time, at last, he got through.

14

Billie hooked K.C.'s Mustang left onto Hilgard and barreled down the winding street, past UCLA, into Westwood Village. She had been afraid to take the Countach. The car was too recognizable, and they would be looking for her by now. She was sure of that. And Drake had sounded pretty certain of it too, when he called half an hour ago and arranged this little get-together because, he said, he had something important to tell her, something to do with last night.

She had taken the call, then left without explanation, pausing only long enough to change her clothes. Her T-shirt and jeans, sticky with dried blood, were gratefully discarded. From Bobby Joe she borrowed a pair of black corduroy pants, a leather belt with a brass buckle, and a button-down denim shirt which, as it turned out, had originally been hers. She rolled up her shirt sleeves in deference to the steaming weather outside. Her white cowboy boots were clean, which was lucky, since none of the guys' shoes would have been her size anyhow.

She glanced at herself in the mirror of Bobby Joe's bathroom before leaving and saw a scared little girl in the dressing room of the White Horse Saloon, a girl on the verge of puking her guts into a wastebasket. Only, the enemy she was facing now was not a hostile audience but a gang of killers. But maybe there was no difference. Maybe it was all the same, somehow, the same evil, the same . . . She had no time to think about it. She had an appointment to keep.

Now, as she turned onto Weyburn, the thought occurred to her that this whole thing could be a trap.

Maybe the caller had only claimed to be Drake. But
no. That was crazy. Nobody else would have known
enough to reach her at that number. Anyway, she recognized his voice.

And besides, dammit, she had to trust somebody.
She had to take a few chances or they would get her
anyway.

They. She kept using that word as if it had some
meaning. It didn't. It was just an empty sound, a word
that stood for nothing, for a blank, for—she winced—
for an abyss.

According to the digital readout flashing on her
wrist, it was only eleven A.M., but already Westwood
Village was crowded. A month from now UCLA would
be in session and the streets would be swarming with
college students. For the time being, they were filled
mainly with shoppers, marching resolutely down sidewalks that were streams of white fire, their sunglass-
visored eyes squinting against the glare.

On-street parking was impossible. Billie pulled into
a parking garage and took a ticket. She got out of the
Mustang and glanced around the building's cavernous
interior to see if anyone was watching her. She saw
nobody. Which meant nothing, since how the hell
would she know if she were being watched, anyway?

At least she had not been followed. She was reasonably certain of that. She had checked the rearview mirror at every traffic light. She had even pulled off Sunset
at one point, leading any potential pursuer on an aimless detour through Beverly Hills. She had seen no one
behind her. But maybe they didn't need to follow her.
Maybe they were already here. Maybe it really was a
trap.

"Christ," she said out loud. "What a goddamn cry-
baby."

She shook her head, mildly disgusted with herself,
but still looked self-consciously around as she left the
garage and crossed the street. She was supposed to

meet him on the terrace of the restaurant above Crown Books. She looked up at the people at the tables overhead, but the terrace was screened by a glass canopy bright with hanging plants, and she could not make out their faces. The place seemed crowded enough, and for a moment she told herself that there were too many witnesses for anybody to try anything. Then she remembered a killer on a lighted stage in full view of six thousand pairs of eyes, and she figured there was not a whole hell of a lot of safety in crowds. She shrugged. Damn the torpedoes, full speed ahead.

A wide red-brick stairway rose to the terrace. She started up the stairs, trying not to think about who might be waiting for her at the top, and a hand closed over her arm.

She had time to think that she had been right, it was a trap, goddammit, how could she have been so stupid—and then she spun to face a teenage girl gazing up at her from the sidewalk.

"Billie? Billie Lee Kidd?"

Billie caught her breath. "Yes. That's me."

"Oh, my God, this is so great, I can't believe it's you. You're my favorite singer in the whole world, I mean, except for Reba McEntire. Could I have your autograph?"

Billie exhaled slowly. She never had the heart to refuse a request like this. Even now.

"You have a pen?" she asked resignedly.

The girl pawed through her purse and produced a felt-tip marker, then plucked a paperback from her shopping bag.

"I wish I had one of your records with me. Maybe you could write on this instead. If that's okay."

Billie managed a smile. She took the paperback, a gothic romance, and scribbled on the title page: "I didn't write this book but I'm signing it anyhow, which gives you some idea of the sort of person I am." Her signature slanted across the bottom of the page in large, angular, slashing letters. She handed back the book. The girl clutched it tight.

"I'll treasure this. I mean, I know that sounds so bullshit, but I will. Really."

"Take care now, darling."

Billie turned and headed up the stairs before the girl could snare her in further conversation. Her heart was still beating like a son of a bitch. She had been sure it was them. Them. Whoever the hell they were.

She reached the top of the stairs, scanned the terrace, and saw Drake, in a sport shirt and faded jeans, seated at a table overlooking the street. She expelled a long-held breath.

See? she told herself triumphantly. It really is him. It's not a trap, after all.

"I almost didn't come," she said without preamble as she slipped into the chair facing him. "I thought maybe this might be dangerous. And I've had enough excitement for a while."

Drake smiled at her, a strange smile full of hidden meanings.

"I'm sorry to hear that, Miss Kidd. Because I'm afraid you're in for a little more excitement."

"Why? What's going on?"

He was about to answer, then fell silent as a waiter stopped at their table. Billie almost said she wasn't hungry, then realized she was. Starving, in fact. She ordered two eggs over easy, a side order of bacon, and tomato juice. A meal fit for a condemned man, she thought randomly. Or woman.

Drake ordered coffee. The waiter left. Billie forced a smile.

"Am I nuts to be pigging out, under the circumstances?"

His eyes were not on her. He was studying the other tables, the passing traffic, the pedestrians. He didn't answer.

"Yo, Sarge," she said. "We're supposed to be having a conversation here."

He turned to her. "Sorry. Just . . . thinking." He smiled. It looked wrong somehow. False. Forced. "You don't have to call me Sarge. The name is Martin. Martin Drake."

"I'm Billie. We don't stand on ceremony in my line of work."

He said nothing for another long moment. She studied him. His face was a geometry lesson, all sharp angles and plane surfaces. His jaw was a ruler-straight line. His nose was narrow, a shade too long, oddly hawklike. His eyes were bright crumbs of steel, glinting gray-blue in the sun. They made a sharp contrast to the paleness of his skin and the jet-black luster of his hair, close-cropped, slicked back, accenting his high, unlined forehead.

A hard face, she told herself. Almost a cruel face.

She did not know why she was suddenly afraid.

"Billie," said Martin Drake softly, "there is an organization, a secret organization, which is out to assassinate you. The man who tried to kill you at your show last night belonged to this organization. And the people who murdered your friend—the one whose body disappeared—they were under orders from the same authorities. This . . . group is still after you. They must kill you. It's their highest priority. They will not stop until you're dead."

She swallowed. She had assumed as much, but it was not exactly reassuring to hear it confirmed.

"How do you know all this?"

Slowly he smiled.

"Because I'm one of them."

Billie stared at him. She drew back in her chair. She was aware, with unnatural clarity, of the pressure of her fingertips gripping the edge of the table, her nails squeezed white.

Oh, Jesus. A trap. It's a trap. It really is.

She had walked right into it. And there was no way

out. Not this time. They had set her up. They had her right where they wanted her.

Twice before, she had nearly bought it. Three strikes—said a mocking voice in her mind—and you're out.

She sat rigid, frozen, like a rabbit huddled in the path of an onrushing train. The worst of it was not knowing where he was. The man with the gun. Because it wasn't Drake. She knew that. He could hardly conceal a gun under the thin cotton of that shirt. There must be someone else, maybe at the table behind her, or on the roof of the building across the street, or somewhere, anywhere. Someone with a bead on her. Someone who could kill her with one shot.

"Okay." She swallowed. "So come on. Do it. Get it over with."

She closed her eyes. She waited, knowing that in a moment she would be gone, just gone, forever.

"I'm not going to hurt you, Billie."

She looked at him, not quite daring to believe it.

"Say again?"

"Listen to me." The steel-blue eyes locked on hers. "I'm part of the Brotherhood. But I'm a traitor. A traitor to their cause, but not my own. I'm here to help you. You have to believe that."

She stared at him. Her thoughts whirled. She didn't know what the hell to think. Part of her warned that this might be only another kind of cruelty. A way to lift her hopes before finishing her off. Like promising freedom to a hostage, then leading him to the firing squad.

He seemed to read her thoughts. "Look," he said calmly. "I knew you were coming. I have a clear view of the street from this position. If somebody were going to put a bullet in you, don't you think they would have done it already?"

She relaxed a little. That made sense. She guessed.

"Maybe," she said cautiously.

"You're safe. At least, as safe as you can be."

She forced a smile. She could not quite manage it. "Which is not very."

He nodded.

"So what's the story?" she asked, hating the tremor in her voice, the aftershocks rippling through her body. "What kind of organization is this? And why in God's name do they give two shits about a poor little country girl like me?"

He shushed her with a wave of his hand. Breakfast arrived. Billie waited, gazing out over the balcony, letting her body regain some semblance of control as she marveled at the simple fact of being alive.

On the street below, a line was forming for the noon showing of the new Spielberg flick. A woman emerged from a frozen-yogurt parlor licking a vanilla cone. A teenage couple jaywalked across Westwood Boulevard, dodging traffic. They all looked so happy. The sun was out, the day was warm, they were alive and so was she and everything was okay. For the moment, at least, everything was fine.

Then Drake was speaking again, and she realized that the waiter was gone.

"This organization is called the Brotherhood. It's a religion. A cult, you would call it, though naturally they don't use that term." He glanced at her plate. He smiled. "Go on, eat."

Reluctantly she stabbed at her eggs with a fork. She had lost her appetite a moment ago. She chewed without noticing the taste.

"The Brotherhood is the oldest continuing religious movement on earth. It dates back before Babylonia, to the time of ancient Sumer. Its point of origin was a city-state called Antarok, which existed somewhere in the Middle East, in the desert east of Mesopotamia. Antarok was a dictatorship ruled by a succession of high priests who worshiped dark, evil gods. The priesthood had absolute power over the population. They built temples to their gods and made human sacrifices—children and virgin girls. Just like many other primitive cultures. Except . . .'' He took a breath. ''Except the gods of Antarok are real.''

Billie stopped eating. She stared at him.

''I know you don't believe me,'' he went on implacably. ''Not yet, anyway. But it's true. I know. I've seen their powers at work.''

''Why haven't I ever heard of this religion of yours?''

''Because it's been kept secret ever since the fall of Antarok. The city was destroyed in a single night— utterly annihilated. Not a trace remains above ground, although some subterranean tombs do survive. A few of the tombs have even been excavated secretly by the faithful. But no mainstream archeologist or historian knows anything about that—or about Antarok itself. You won't find a mention of it in any reference book. I know. I've looked. The Brotherhood likes it that way. They don't want publicity. They keep themselves hidden. They gather in secret meeting places. They talk in code.''

''And nobody blabs?''

''The penalty is death.''

''You're willing to risk that?''

''Yes.''

''Why?''

''Because I've sworn to fight them. I joined the Brotherhood for that single purpose.''

''You just lost me, pal.''

''Within the Brotherhood, there are a handful of people like me. People who have infiltrated the cult in order to learn its secrets and undermine its efforts from the inside. And above all, to frustrate its ultimate goal. The goal which is now within its reach.''

''You belong to a rival faction. Is that it?''

''I serve different gods.''

''Oh, Jesus.'' She rubbed her forehead.

''I know it's hard to believe. But at least give me a hearing. You don't have to call them gods. That was the way our ancestors saw them thousands of years ago, in a more primitive age. Think of them instead as . . . as spiritual forces . . . energies located in a plane of existence parallel to our own. Nonmaterial, intangible, but real. As real as your own mind and spirit. And locked in a deadly struggle. A struggle which has reached its climax.''

Billie took a long, slow breath and tried to think clearly.

"Okay," she said softly. "Suppose, just for the sake of argument, that I wanted to take all this stuff seriously. So what? I mean, two different sets of deities are at each other's throats. What do I care which side wins?''

"You've got to care. Because you're part of it now. Your own life is at stake. And because this is more than a skirmish on a street corner. This is a battle—the ultimate battle—between good and evil. And that makes it a matter of life and death for all of us.''

"So you're on the side of the angels. Is that it?''

He shook his head. "They aren't angels. I don't know just what they are. I don't think they want me to know. But I do know what they're fighting against. I was indoctrinated into the Brotherhood, remember. I've seen it from the inside. And I've learned first-hand what it stands for—and what it wants.

"Throughout history the Brotherhood has been at work behind the scenes, unknown and unsuspected, shaping and directing events. They have been a force for evil—for slavery, dictatorship, and war. Members of the cult have sat at the right hand of many of humanity's worst tyrants. Helping them, by means of magic, to crush their opposition and gain total power, then goading them on to wage war and smash whole continents.

"And they're still at work today. One man runs the cult. Nobody but his immediate subordinates knows his identity or his whereabouts. He lives somewhere abroad, a recluse, directing the whole worldwide operation without ever revealing himself. He's the only one who knows exactly who on the world stage is under the Brotherhood's control.

"But there are rumors. Names that surface in conversation a little too often. Names like Qaddafi, Castro, Pol Pot. And Usu Ndamos. He's the crucial one right now. Have you been following the papers?''

Reluctantly Billie nodded. She rarely kept up with the news while on tour. But vaguely she was aware that the African dictator's troops had recently invaded two neighboring countries in a twin-pronged attack that had plunged the southern half of the continent into war.

"That was the final prophecy,'' said Drake. "It was foretold that war would come at the decree of a tyrant who had risen to power by first spilling the blood of a child. Usu Ndamos murdered an eight-year-old prince to pull off his military coup.''

Billie looked away, not wanting to hear any more. "People have been murdering princes and starting wars for centuries.''

"But the prophecies follow a definite chronology,'' said Drake insistently. "And this was the last. The last link in the chain. For thousands of years the Brotherhood has been working to bring about this series of events, in this sequence. Finally they've succeeded. They've reached their goal.''

"Look.'' She sighed. "I don't buy conspiracy theories. I still think Oswald acted alone. So let's just flunk me out of Paranoia 101 and move on, shall we? What's the point of all this?''

Drake watched her through the plume of steam rising from his coffee.

"You're the point, Billie. As it turns out.''

"Why?''

"Because you sang the Deathsong.''

Slowly Billie put down her fork. She remembered the last time she had heard that word.

"What the hell does that mean?'' she whispered.

"When Antarok fell, only one man among the population escaped alive. The last of the high priests. His name, according to legend, was Kuruk. He is said to have wandered for years and to have wound up in the ancient Sumerian city of Ur. This was in the middle of the Third Dynasty, probably during the reign of Gimil-Sin, one of the last Sumerian kings. In other words, roughly two thousand thirty B.C. And during Kuruk's stay in Ur—so the legend goes—a song was foretold to him. A song which the Brotherhood has been awaiting ever since. A song that can be sung only once the last of the prophecies has been fulfilled." He shrugged. "The song you performed at your concert last night."

"You mean 'Dark Waters'?"

"Is that what you call it? It's appropriate."

"There's nothing ancient or sacred about that song. I wrote it myself."

"Did you?" The hint of a smile flashed on his face like heat lightning. "Or do you only believe you wrote it?"

"I . . ." She stopped. "I don't know," she said finally. A new thought occurred to her. "Last night wasn't the first time I sang that song, anyhow. I'd rehearsed it in sound checks and motel rooms and all over. Played it probably a hundred times, trying to get it down."

"Only for yourself."

"There were people around."

"But no members of the Brotherhood. One of them must be within reach of your voice. Last night, one was. He heard the song, and he knew instinctively what it was. And his understanding, his recognition, would have been like the closing of a circuit, uniting song and listener, giving the Deathsong its power. Its terrible power."

"So this guy tried to kill me just because he had a gut feeling about a song? What if his gut was wrong?

What if he had nachos for dinner and they were acting up on him?''

"He wasn't wrong."

"How do you know?"

"The Bloodstone doesn't lie."

"I assume you're going to translate that last remark into English."

Drake put down his coffee cup. He hesitated, glancing around, then slowly rolled up his shirt sleeve. Billie saw a bracelet with a fine metallic chain and a crimson stone glittering on his left wrist. It looked oddly familiar to her, as if she had seen it someplace before. Or a bracelet very much like it. She wasn't sure.

"The Bloodstone," said Drake softly. "We all wear one. The bracelet is given to each new member at the start of the initiation rites. It's fused with us, not physically, but spiritually. Fused with our very being. It can never be removed. To take it off would mean instant death."

He gazed down at the bracelet, his eyes veiled and faraway.

"The stone was blue until last night. Then it turned. That was the confirmation. All around the world, at that precise moment, the Bloodstones turned."

Slowly he buttoned his sleeve.

"So that man knew he had to kill you. He failed. His superiors tried again. One of them even contacted me for help. And I did help. I told him how the security system was laid out at the Colony. And later, when you showed up at the station, I called to tell him that you were still alive."

He met her eyes; his face was pained with the memory of what he'd done and with a silent plea for understanding. "I had to. They would have learned all of it anyway, with or without me. And if I had done anything less, I would have aroused their suspicions. And we would not be having this meeting."

He dropped his gaze. "Fortunately, they haven't

succeeded in killing you. Yet. But they'll keep trying. They won't give up. They must kill you. It's their only purpose now."

"Why?"

"Because you sang the song. Which means you fulfilled the prophecy. And for that reason, you can stop it. Reverse it. Undo what you've done."

Billie shook her head in helpless anger. "I can't reverse a goddamn thing. I didn't start anything. I didn't *do* anything."

"Not intentionally. Not knowingly."

"So what was this terrible thing I did?"

"You opened the Door."

She was about to ask a question, something like *What in the name of all that's wholly owned and operated are you talking about?* when she froze. All at once the memories came flooding back, images of a doorway opening in space, spewing forth a Pandora's box of chaos and insanity, and suddenly she was not seated at a table on a terrace in the sunlight, no, she was hanging weightless in space above the asteroidal remnants of the earth, watching galaxies shatter like crystal chandeliers, and somewhere far away she heard a voice, her own voice, singing.

She blinked, and reality was back.

"Billie? Are you all right?"

"Huh?"

"You went all pale."

"Oh. Oh, yes." Her palms were slick with sweat. "I'm fine. Just fine and dandy."

His eyes narrowed. "You remembered. Didn't you?"

"Remembered what?"

He looked at her. She looked away. She could not meet his gaze.

"Go on with what you were saying," she said finally. Her voice was shaky. "But . . . but don't expect me to believe a damn word."

"I was saying that you opened the Door. The mystic

aperture through which the dark gods of Antarok can return to our universe after their long exile.''

''I suppose this isn't any ordinary door?''

''It isn't really a door at all. It's a point of intersection between their world and our own. There is an infinite number of such points, scattered throughout the universe, like wormholes in space, like time warps. But only one Door will be open to them. The one nearest to the site where the Deathsong was heard. Somewhere in this general area, probably within a radius of a hundred miles. Already that Door is opening a crack or so. The pressure on the other side is building. The dark gods are gathering there. Straining to force it wide, to break through. And they will. Unless that Door is closed again, sealed for good.

''You can do it, Billie. You only need to find the Door, track it down. I'll help you. Then you must stand before it, face it, and sing the Deathsong, note for note—backward. And you'll reverse the spell.''

She stared at him, held by the intensity of his own belief and by those memories she could not quite deny. Her voice was a whisper: ''What will happen if I don't?''

''Then, at midnight tonight, precisely twenty-four hours after you sang the Deathsong, the Door will open wide. The dark gods will be set free. And they will usher in a new world, ruled by the Brotherhood. A new Antarok, risen from the dead. An empire, spanning the universe. An evil kingdom built in the image of evil gods. Of Ragnaaroth, the Spider King. Toth, the Wind That Hungers. Bethshul, the Screaming Woman. Narantos, the Hidden One. Garnarlit, the Stealer of Light. Dasharoom, He Who Eats Souls. And others, all the others, so many others. Their number is legion. For four thousand years they have been cut off from mankind. Sealed behind the Door. Trapped and helpless. Soon they will be set free. Free to rule. To kill. All-powerful, all-consuming, everlasting. You can stop them, Billie. You—and only you. You have the power. You have a greater power than any you have ever conceived.

"You can save the world."

Billie stared at him. Her heart thudded in her ears.

"You're crazy," she whispered.

His hand shot across the table. He seized her arm. His fingers dug into her skin. She could feel red welts forming.

"You remembered," he breathed. "Goddammit, I saw you remember. I can see it now. In your eyes. You know. You just won't admit it. Because you're scared."

She tore free of his grip. She got up. Her legs were unsteady. The floor rippled. She took a step away from the table.

"Where are you going?"

"Thanks for the chow. We'll have to do this again sometime."

"You can't leave."

"Watch me."

She crossed the terrace. He caught up with her at the top of the stairs. He spun her around. She pulled away.

"Get away from me or I'll start screaming," she said, white-lipped.

He reached out, pleading. "Billie—"

"Get away!"

She turned and raced down the stairs, pursued by his voice.

"You'll change your mind. You'll come around. You've got to. When you do, call me. My number is 555-3742. You hear me?—555-3742. I'll be waiting—"

"*Go to hell!*"

She reached the street. She ran, blindly.

Three blocks away, she stopped, out of breath, huddled in an alley behind a video store. She looked out at the street, afraid to see him chasing her. He was nowhere in sight.

She retreated to the rear of the alley and doubled over, clutching her stomach, fighting for air.

Oh, Christ, Billie Lee, what have you gotten yourself mixed up in?

She waited in the alley, staring sightlessly at cans of spilled garbage, till finally she could breathe again and she had a plan.

She would drive back to the guys' apartment and pick up her stuff and some more money, then hit the freeway, speeding out of town, in the general direction of Phoenix, maybe, or Vegas or Frisco. She would put five hundred miles between herself and L.A. She would hole up in a motel. She would stay there for two weeks or longer. Long enough for these wackos to see that the world was going to pull through no matter what song she happened to sing. Long enough for them to forget the whole thing. And while she waited, she would just lie in her motel bed with her head under the covers and sleep without dreams. That was important. No dreams.

Because in her dreams she would see that Door opening, galaxies spiraling like pinwheels on the Fourth of July, sputtering and dying, and the universe fading out like the last reel of a movie, going, going . . . gone.

It was crazy, what he'd told her. It had to be. Otherwise, she would have to stay and face it. And she couldn't do that. She just couldn't.

Because Martin Drake had been right about one thing.

She was scared. Oh, yes.

So goddamn scared.

15

By the time Billie returned to the apartment, she was almost in control again.

Drake had been nowhere in sight. He had not followed her as she had feared. Maybe he was afraid that their little altercation in the restaurant had drawn attention. Or maybe he had just given her up as a lost cause. She hoped so.

Gary, K.C., and Bobby Joe were hanging out in the living room. The girls were gone. They hadn't seemed like the type to stick around for quiet conversation. The Nashville Network was blaring Alabama's latest video. The glass doors to the balcony framed a panorama of the city from the airport to the skyscrapers downtown, everything washed brown in a smoggy haze.

"Yo, gang," she said, shutting the door wearily.

"So where'd you run off to?" asked K.C., sprawled on the sofa.

She sighed. "The funny farm, I think."

"We all knew it was inevitable." That was Gary. He got up off the floor, where a pile of fan mail was scattered like a drift of autumn leaves. He showed her a letter, handwritten in pencil. "Guy in Tennessee wants to marry you. Says his horoscope told him you'd accept."

"Tell him I went to Sweden and got balls."

"What? An extra set?"

She gave him a look. "Cute."

Bobby Joe glanced up from the battered rosewood-body dreadnought resting in his lap. He was always messing around with the thing, patching up the soundboard, trying to make it play as good as new. Right now he was at work replacing a busted string. "You really aren't gonna clue us in on what you've been up to?"

"Christ." She stopped in the middle of the room, looking around at them. "What is it with the Torquemada routine? I told you before, I'd rather not talk about it. Okay?"

"Hey, come on, Bills. Chill out." K.C. swung his legs off the sofa, got up, and crossed the room. He put a hand on her arm. "We're worried, is all."

Something about the touch of his hand disturbed her. K.C. was not the touchy-feelie type. Hell, he wasn't even the understanding type. Tell him you had a problem and he'd tell you that man is born to suffer as the sparks fly upward, or something equally reassuring. She pulled away.

Another hand found her waist. Gary.

"Yeah," he said, leaning close. Too close. "You're acting awful funny. Like you're in some kind of trouble."

"I'm not in any trouble. Give the lady a little air, will you."

Suddenly Bobby Joe was behind her. His hands rested lightly on her shoulders. She looked up into his face. She wondered if she had ever really noticed how tall he was. How he towered over her.

"We're your friends, boss lady," he said. "We want to help."

There was nothing wrong with the words, not even with the way he said them, but dammit, there sure as shit was something wrong here somewhere. They were crowding her. It wasn't normal. K.C. on her left, Gary on her right, Bobby Joe at her back. She tried to take a step forward. Gary circled his arm around her waist.

"Let go," she said softly.

"Hey, come on." Bobby Joe massaged her shoulders. "Why so unfriendly?"

"You know our Billie," said Gary in a low, mocking, vaguely threatening voice. "She's never too friendly. Not with us. She'll pick up any guy in the audience with a Jimmy Dean in his pants and take him home for fun and games, but do we ever get any? Hell, no."

"We're just the hired help," said K.C. "A lower caste. The untouchables. We get the crumbs from the table, that's all."

"You know I don't think of you guys that way," she said, fighting the sudden terror constricting her throat.

"You don't think of us at all," said Gary bitterly.

"That's right," said Bobby Joe. "She's too busy being a bigshot." His breath was hot on her neck. The caress of his hands was unpleasantly rough. They were powerful hands. "Ordering us around. Having the spotlight to herself. Yeah. Boss lady's having herself some fun, all right."

There was a new video on the tube. Emmylou Harris singing about that old mystery train, thirteen coaches long.

"What's going on here?" whispered Billie. "Why are you acting this way?"

"What way?" K.C. took her hand. His grip was clammy. She tried to pull free. She could not. "We're just having a friendly little chat."

"Well, let's have it later, okay?"

"Uh-uh, sweetheart." Gary smiled. "We've been putting this off long enough."

She looked at him, then at K.C. Their eyes were empty. Dead. The eyes of the killer on the stage.

"What have you been putting off?" she breathed, knowing the answer.

"This," said Bobby Joe.

What happened next took less than a second. The three guys acted at once, in perfect synch. K.C. yanked Billie's arm backward, pinning it painfully behind her shoulder blade. Gary seized her other arm with his free hand. She opened her mouth to scream and something closed over her neck from behind, digging into the tender skin of her throat, searing her like a red-hot wire, and it took her another split second to understand that it was a length of guitar string, a yard of roundwound stainless steel gripped taut in Bobby Joe's strong hands.

Gary and K.C. hung on as she fought to tear herself free. She shook her head in helpless protest, spraying the room with streamers of spit. Her legs jackknifed wildly. The steel loop gouged her neck, garroting her. She could not breathe. Her mouth was open wide, her tongue bulging out from between parted lips, but no air came. Her lungs shrieked for oxygen. Her hands and feet were going numb, all pins and needles. Blood pounded in her head. White specks shimmered across her field of vision. The world was one of those little plastic paperweights with glitter inside, and somebody had just given it a good hard shake to watch the pretty snowfall.

This is it, she told herself from someplace far away. I'm going to die.

The snowflakes turned darker. Black specks instead of white. They whirled and danced. They ran together into black pools. She remembered lying in the desert and watching the abyss take shape before her eyes. Here it was again. It had been waiting. Waiting patiently, all these years. Now, at last, the wait was over. It had won.

Fury rose in hot waves. She would not let it win. She had beaten it before. She would beat it now.

She swung both legs off the floor, parallel to the ground, and pistoned them out with her full strength. Her boots slammed into the wall. The force of the kick thrust her backward. The three guys were knocked off-balance. They loosened their grips for one instant. She tore free.

She ripped the garrote from her neck and flung it aside. She wanted to run but she had no strength. She fought for air. Her knees were weak. She was seeing

double. The room flashed from light to dark. The floor
was tilted and she couldn't find her balance.

K.C. grabbed for her. She thrust her hand into her
pants pocket. Her car keys came out, wedged between
her middle fingers. She lunged at K.C.'s face. He
dodged. He backed off, retreating into the kitchen a
few yards away. She had a momentary exhilarating
sense of triumph. Then Gary seized a clump of her
hair from behind. She whirled on him, acting on pure
animal instinct, with no time for thought. She drove
the keys into his right eye. Egg yolk bubbled out. He
let go of her and sank to the floor, his face cupped in
his hands. He was screaming.

She spun toward the door, still clutching the bloodied keys. Get out, her mind was screaming. Get out.
Get out. Get out.

She could not get out. Bobby Joe had already retreated to block the door. He stared back at her, ropes
of hair swinging over his forehead.

"Shouldn't have done that, boss lady," he breathed.
Spit lathered his mouth. "It would have been quick,
our way. Now look what you've done to poor old
Gary." Involuntarily her eyes moved to Gary, sunfish-
ing wildly on the floor. "You've got to pay for that,
bitch. We're going to do it slow now. Nice and slow."

She looked back over her shoulder. K.C. was moving forward, closing in. He flexed his fingers rhythmically, clenching and unclenching his fists.

She ran. Across the room was the hallway leading
to the rear of the apartment. She arrowed toward it.
That was a bad tactic, suicidally bad. There was no
rear exit. She would be trapped. They could hunt her
down and kill her at their leisure. She knew it. She
had no choice.

Halfway down the hall, she looked back. They were
not following her. Not yet.

She stopped to get her bearings. Three bedrooms
and a bath opened onto the hall. She chose the farthest
door. It swung open on an unmade bed, a checker-

board pattern of street signs plastering the walls, heaps of discarded clothes and dirty magazines. Gary's room.

She stepped inside, shutting the door quietly. She wanted to lock it but, goddammit, the lock was busted. There was a phone near the bed. She moved for it, thinking that she could call 911, knowing it was hopeless, because response time in this neighborhood was eleven minutes on a good day, and in eleven minutes she would be dead.

Footsteps drummed ominously on the hardwood hall floor outside. She listened, her heart hammering in answer.

They were coming. She had no time even to make a call. Unless it was Dial-a-Prayer.

She looked helplessly around the room. There was nowhere to hide except the obvious spots. Under the bed. In the closet. The first places they would look. Then she saw it.

Their tour had ended last night. Gary had not had time to unpack. Not that he ever unpacked anyway. A large jet-black trunk sat in one corner of the room, drooling shirts and underwear out of its half-open lid.

The footsteps detoured off the hallway, into the first room. They must be checking each bedroom in turn.

She crossed the room, wishing the heels of her boots wouldn't clump so loudly, grateful at least for the deep pile carpeting which muffled the sound. She crouched by the trunk and raised the lid. She winced at the squeak of hinges. The trunk was filled with clothes of all kinds in a disorganized mess. She flung handfuls of socks and Jockey shorts and sweatshirts into the closet. They wouldn't notice that. Gary never picked up a damn thing off his floor. He had pants and shirts scattered around here that hadn't been worn since the Nixon administration.

She made a well for herself in the trunk, then climbed in. The thing was suffocatingly small. She squatted down inside, doubled over, and groped blindly for the lid. She lowered it. She was in darkness. She stiffened with a rush of fear. She hated the dark. The nameless thing which she thought of as the abyss, *it* dwelled in the dark. Was it in here with her? Had she climbed into its yawning mouth? Had it swallowed her whole? Was she dead already?

She shuddered. She tried to force the crazy thoughts out of her mind. She concentrated on her surroundings, on reality.

The trunk was maybe three feet tall, two feet wide. Hunched inside, squeezed into a tight fetal ball, she was nearly immobile. Her arms were wrapped around her knees. She might be able to pry them free if necessary for self-defense. The walls were claustrophobically close. Her shoulders butted up against them. She had the feeling she could stick out her tongue and lick the wall before her face without difficulty. She did not test her theory.

The smell of old laundry surrounded her. She loosened one arm enough to grope among the clothes at her feet. She found what felt like an old shirt. She hauled it up and draped it over her head and shoulders. Camouflage. Even if they opened the trunk, they might not see her if they gave the interior only a quick glance.

Then she waited.

After an endless span of time she heard the door open. Footsteps entering. Heavy breathing. The guys were tired. They must have been searching the other rooms like wild men. Now they had reached the end of the line. The last place she could be hiding. They knew she was in here someplace. Which meant they would not leave until they found her.

"Okay, boss lady," said a voice, Bobby Joe's voice. "Come on out. Playtime's over."

"Ollee ollee ox-en-free," said K.C. mockingly.

She did not hear a third voice. She had put Gary out of commission, anyway. It helped even the odds. A little.

She hugged her knees. Already her muscles were

stiffening up. She tried not to breathe. The trunk trembled slightly with circling footfalls. She heard the creak of mattress springs, then a thud. They had lifted the bed to look underneath, then dropped it, finding nothing. There was a groaning sound, the protest of a large, heavy piece of furniture being moved. She guessed that they were looking behind the chest of drawers. That was stupid. There was no room to hide back there. They must be getting desperate.

"Where the fuck is she?" hissed K.C., confirming her thought.

"Shut up. She's in here. I can smell her."

One set of footsteps approached. She waited, rigid with fear. The footsteps traveled past the trunk, to the closet. She heard a clatter of metal. Wire coat hangers being flung to the floor.

"Nada," said K.C. in disgust.

The footsteps approached again. K.C. stopped directly beside the trunk.

Then the lid of the trunk creaked in a sullen complaint as a weight settled on it. She took a second to grasp that K.C. was sitting on the trunk. Sitting right on top of her. Oh, Jesus. It was almost funny. She bit her lip to keep from laughing out loud.

"Man, she's gone," said K.C. His fingers drummed on the side of the trunk. The sound was amplified inside. It was like listening to one of Gary's percussion tracks on headphones in the mixing session.

"She fucking can't be," said Bobby Joe, from several yards away. "You covered the hall the whole time, right?"

"Yeah."

"She couldn't get by you."

"No way."

"So she's around. She's somewhere."

A second set of footsteps approached. They died out a yard away. Bobby Joe must be standing before K.C., looking right at him, which meant that he was looking right at the trunk.

"Get up," said Bobby Joe softly.

Billie's heart stopped. Waves of cold rippled over her.

He knew. She had heard it in his voice.

She wished she had a weapon, some way to fight back, to make a last stand. She had nothing. She was helpless. She could not even move in this confined space. She could not even lift her head more than half-way.

The lid creaked again, as if in relief, as K.C. stood up.

"What is it, big guy?" asked K.C.

A beat of silence. Billie waited, huddled in pitch darkness, her body electric with adrenaline and terror.

"She outmaneuvered us," said Bobby Joe quietly. "She got away. I guess that bitch was smarter than we thought."

Billie took a breath, the first one she had permitted herself in what seemed like days.

She had made it. She had beaten them. All she had to do now was stay put till they left the room, then call for help or sneak out of the apartment or—

She was still sorting out her options when she heard a loud double click. The twin latches on the trunk, snapping shut.

Then . . . laughter.

"Nice try, boss lady," said Bobby Joe. His voice was louder, closer than before. "But no cigar."

She remained silent. Frozen.

"We were just kind of playing with your head," said K.C. easily. "We know you're in there." The trunk resonated with a slap on the lid. "Any last words?"

She would not answer. Didn't dare.

"Come on, boss lady. When did you ever pass up an opportunity to exercise that award-winning mouth of yours?"

Maybe they weren't absolutely sure. Maybe if she

kept quiet, she could bluff them into opening the lid. Then she might spring up, take them by surprise, maybe have some kind of chance.

"Well, have it your way," said Bobby Joe. He chuckled. "This is it, boss lady. Say good-bye to Hollywood."

A knife exploded through the side wall of the trunk. She jerked sideways. A scream rang out like the echoing clang of a bell. Her own scream.

The blade hung in the darkness, inches from her face, then withdrew, leaving a razor-thin slit glowing with the light from outside.

"We got you, Bills. Oh, yeah. Got you now!"

It was K.C., laughing. He pounded his hands wildly on the sides of the trunk, a manic drumroll. Another knife burst through the opposite wall. It caught her arm. Her shirt sleeve shredded with a long ripping sound. The knife point sank into her skin. She felt a lance of pain. She pulled free, gasping.

That knife vanished, leaving another vertical slit.

Billie was thinking of those magic acts where the magician would place his female assistant in a trunk, a trunk just like this one, and then he would stick swords through it, one by one, skewering the woman like a pincushion, except of course those acts were all fake and this was real.

"Please," she said helplessly, knowing it was no use. "Please don't do this."

A knife was thrust down through the lid of the crate. It grazed the side of her head. The blade tangled in her hair. A second knife followed. It ripped empty space, inches from her nose. She stared at the knife, faintly visible in the light from outside. A long stainless-steel carving knife with a serrated blade. From the kitchen. That was why they had been delayed in following her. They had armed themselves. Then hunted her down.

Both knives were pulled out with a hissing sound.

"We're having some fun now, huh, Bills?'' That was K.C.

"No,'' she said, her words distorted by the sudden frantic trembling of her lower lip. "No, it's not fun, let me out, please, let me out, do whatever you want, just let me out.''

"That's it, boss lady. Keep begging for mercy. We're loving every word.''

"Let me out!'' she shrieked. "Let me out, God, don't do this!''

She was crying. Tears burned her eyes. She rocked crazily from side to side, banging her head on the walls. Clothes spilled everywhere, ensnaring her like rumpled ghosts. She twisted her arms free of her knees. She hammered at the trunk with her fists.

She was so scared. She didn't want to die. Especially not this way. Not in the dark.

She moaned incoherently as the knives struck again, penetrating the trunk from the front and rear. One blade got her left hand, slicing through the web of skin between thumb and forefinger. The pain was blinding. Her head reeled. She jammed her bleeding hand into her mouth. Blood bubbled down her chin.

Presto, the knives were gone. *Voilà*, they were back, attacking from new directions. Her right thigh erupted in agony as a blade punched through her corduroy pants, the pants she had borrowed from Bobby Joe, and sank into her flesh. She shrieked in pain and terror. She hurled herself against the side of the trunk, seeking mindlessly to break through the wall. The trunk teetered like a drunken thing. Paper-thin shafts of light from the multiple cracks in the walls played over the interior like miniature searchlights.

The knives pulled free, then slammed through the lid, barely missing her head. She kept on screaming. She was unable to speak, to think. She was some kind of animal in a cage. This was a nightmare and if she screamed loud enough, she would wake up. She had to wake up.

Runners of mucus swung from her nose. She snuffled noisily, inhaling snot and tears. Goddammit, Billie, complained a voice in her mind, at least go out with some fucking dignity. She didn't listen. She couldn't help it. She was afraid.

"Guess this hasn't exactly been one of your better days, boss lady," said Bobby Joe as the knives hissed out.

She caught her breath. She gripped the walls, seeking to hold on to something in reality, something firm and tangible.

"You guys were my friends," she croaked. "What happened? What the hell happened to you?"

"It was the man," said K.C. "He showed us."

"Yeah," said Bobby Joe. "It was the man."

She didn't know what in Christ's name any of that meant. She had no time to ask. The knives came again, bursting out of the lid and the side wall, at right angles to each other. One blade shaved her cheek. The other missed her eye by a half-inch. They vanished magically.

How soon before one of them found her throat, her heart? How soon before she felt that final, total pain that signaled death?

She heard a low, desperate, pitiful whimpering and wished to God she could shut up. Her shoulders jerked with sobs. Her breath was ragged. Blood leaked down her arm and leg, collecting in a brackish pool in the laundry on the floor of the trunk. It occurred to her that she was going to die kneeling in her own blood and Gary's come-stained underpants. She laughed. She couldn't stop laughing. It was funny, all of it. It was a riot.

"Okay, boss lady," said Bobby Joe. His voice was suddenly cold sober with murderous intent. It cut off her laughter like the flick of a switch killing a light. "I think we've been playing this cat-and-mouse number long enough. The next one stops your heart."

"You know it," said K.C.

She drew back, expecting a dual assault from the front. She pressed her palms to the sides of the trunk. She tasted copper. The taste of death. A bitter taste.

Then from some great distance came a sound.

The phone, ringing.

"Shit," said K.C. "Think it's . . . him?"

"Better find out," said Bobby Joe. "Boss lady can wait a minute." He chuckled, a dry-cough sound. "She ain't going anywhere."

She lowered her head and tried to remember exactly how to breathe.

From outside, footsteps. Bobby Joe was crossing the room to pick up the phone.

Billie hugged herself, blinking to hold back fresh tears.

16

The bitch had to be dead by now.

Frank Lancett was sure of it. And if she was dead, those stupid hick friends of hers should have called in with their report, the way he'd arranged it. But they hadn't, and he was getting increasingly uncomfortable as he paced the living room of his house in Bel Air. He had not forgotten the penalty for failure. His hand strayed occasionally to the bracelet on his wrist.

So finally he decided to place a call of his own and find out what the hell was going down.

He had no doubt that his plan had worked. It was foolproof, perfect, despite its somewhat improvisational quality. Its only flaw was that he had not been there to do the honors himself.

He had arrived at the West Hollywood high-rise at eleven o'clock. As he rode the elevator to the top floor, he mentally reviewed his arsenal. Strapped to his right forearm, a seven-inch hunting knife with a serrated blade. Concealed under his jacket, holstered to his vest, a Beretta Model 20 semiautomatic. In his briefcase, a Walther MPK collapsible machine pistol, folded neatly in half.

He smiled. Loaded for bear, he thought coolly.

He was ready to take out Billie Lee Kidd and anybody else who might be hanging out with her. He expected a crowd. His informer had told him that the three members of Billie's backup band stayed there. Still, there was a chance Billie might be alone—and on that chance, he had brought along two other little toys, a pair of handcuffs and a roll of electrician's tape. He would cuff her hands and tape her mouth, and then he would do things to her, unpleasant things, and finally, when her eyes were dull and staring and glazed over and he knew she wasn't feeling the pain anymore, he would wind tape over her nostrils and watch her sunfish crazily, fighting for air, till her face turned purplish-blue and her eyes were eggshells and she was dead.

He hoped it would be that way. But he doubted he'd have that kind of luck.

He got out of the elevator and strolled down the hallway, swinging the briefcase in one hand. He found the door to the apartment. He leaned his fist on the doorbell. The door opened. A young man with longish hair and the shadow of a beard looked at him past the security chain.

"Yes?"

"Is Billie in?" said Lancett, smiling.

"Who?"

"Billie Lee Kidd."

The young man's eyes narrowed. "What makes you think she'd be here?"

"She told me. I'm Detective Lancett, with the Irvine P.D. I have a few more questions about the incident last night."

"I was there last night. I remember a cop asking questions. Nobody mentioned your name. And Billie never said she'd be here. Tell your magazine, no dice."

He started to shut the door. A tough customer, Lancett figured. Well, that was okay. He could deal with tough customers.

He whistled a tune, a string of six notes, high and haunting and mellifluous.

The young man paused.

"Let me in," said Lancett quietly.

The man unhooked the chain. The door swung open under Lancett's hand.

"Now tell Billie to make herself visible. She's got company."

"Billie's not here," said the man matter-of-factly.

Lancett took a breath. Damn. The bastard could not be lying. Not now.

He was about to ask where the hell she was when the other two band members appeared from out of the hallway.

"Hey," said one of them. "What's going on here? Who is this guy—"

Lancett sang.

The men froze, their faces slack and blank.

He interrogated them briskly. About an hour ago, Billie had gotten a call. They didn't know from whom. All they knew was that she left immediately, without explanation, pausing only to borrow the keys to K.C.'s Mustang. Which was weird, because what was wrong with the Lamborghini? Anyway, she had been gone since then. None of them had a clue as to where.

Lancett considered the problem. Billie might have taken off for good. He doubted it. She would have told her friends where to reach her. Unless she knew that the Brotherhood had tracked her here. But how could she? No, most likely she had just gone out to meet somebody for some reason or other. Which meant that, sooner or later, she would be coming back. Coming back . . .

He leaned close to the three men, one at a time, his mouth inches from each man's ear.

"Do you like Billie?" he asked.

"Yes. Sure." A note of uncertainty, of doubt. Lancett seized on it.

"What don't you like about her?"

"I like her fine." The voice was querulous, defensive.

"Come on. You can tell me. You can say anything. Reveal what you feel deep down. No one will ever know."

And then it came. From each of them, a confession.

"She orders us around," said the first one sullenly. "Boss lady always knows best. Makes me want to smack her good. Break her goddamn jaw."

"She'll fuck anything in Jockey shorts," said the second. "But when I come onto her, she treats it like a joke. Too good for me, I guess. I hate her guts sometimes."

"She thinks she's going to live forever," said the third. "If she's ever been afraid of any damn thing, she hasn't let on. Just once I'd like to see her scared. Really for Christ's sake scared. Scared shitless. Just once."

Lancett smiled. They were petty, conventional hatreds, born of envy, lust, and neurotic fear, but they would serve.

He gave them instructions and left, certain that if Billie Lee Kidd returned to this apartment, she would not be leaving, except in a plastic bag. Or maybe several bags.

Now he waited impatiently as the phone rang in the apartment. Once. Twice. Three times.

"Hello?" said a voice.

"This is your friend," said Lancett quietly. "What's the status there?"

"Hey," said the voice to somebody not on the line, "it's the man."

"Give me a fucking answer, Jethro," said Lancett. "And give it fast."

"Yes, sir. We got her."

Lancett expelled a sigh of relief.

"I mean to say," the voice added, "we've got her under restraint."

Lancett frowned. "She's still alive?"

"Not for long."

"Cut the crap, asshole. Do you have the situation under control or not?"

"Yes, sir. Under control. We got her locked up. We were just about to finish her when you—"

"Right. I understand." Lancett thought about it. A slow smile crept over his face. "She can't get away? You're sure?"

"No way."

"Keep her like that. I'll be over." The smile broadened. "I'd like to handle this personally."

"You said we—"

"I changed my fucking mind. Got a problem with that?"

An audible swallow. "No, sir."

Lancett cradled the receiver. He stared into space, thinking of a certain Chinese girl in a hotel bed, and of another young lady who would be providing him with similar entertainment very soon.

17

She wished to hell Bobby Joe had not tied the knots so damn tight. She had been working to free her hands for the last ten minutes without success. At least she had finally stopped bleeding. Her left arm and right thigh ached with knife cuts. Her shirt and pants were sticky with blood.

She sat in a chair in a corner of Gary's room, near the open trunk from which, minutes ago, she had been unceremoniously removed. Bobby Joe had bound her hands behind her back with one end of a torn strip of bedding, then knotted the other end to an armrest. She had to sit at an angle, her body twisted awkwardly. That wasn't too comfortable either.

She supposed she shouldn't be complaining. The way things looked, she would be feeling no pain mighty soon.

From the living room came the low murmur of K.C.'s voice, comforting Gary. From what Billie understood, the eye was lost. Copious quantities of alcohol were being applied to Gary's innards in an effort to keep him quiet.

Bobby Joe sat on the bed, watching her, his face blank.

"So what's this guy going to do to me when he gets here?" Billie asked softly.

"Three guesses."

"Is he the one that put you up to this?"

"Shut up, okay?"

"Well, excuse me for living." She cleared her throat. "So to speak."

Somewhere a clock ticked. Each second was a beat of time she would never get back. A moment of life, irreplaceable and precious. That had always been true, but she had never felt the truth of it quite so keenly before.

She was going to die. It was that simple. There was no way out. Even if she could free her wrists, she would have to overpower Bobby Joe, not to mention K.C. down the hall. Which was impossible. Both were armed with knives. Both were taller and stronger than she was. And anyway, she couldn't get her goddamn wrists free in the first place.

Dead meat, she thought with a ripple of gooseflesh up her arms. That's what you are, Billie Lee.

Her only hope was to establish communication. Bobby Joe had been her friend once. Only a couple of hours ago, in fact. Then something had happened. Something had changed him. Had changed all three of them. She couldn't fathom what it was. Drugs, maybe. Hypnosis. Neither answer seemed right. But whatever it was, it had been done, and maybe, just maybe, it could be undone.

She swallowed dryly. "Did you always hate me like this?"

"I don't want to talk about it."

"If I did something to hurt you—"

He stared at her from under heavy, hooded eyelids. "You open that fat mouth of yours one more time and I'm going to cut you. Not real bad. Just bad enough to hurt."

"I'm already leaking like a sieve."

He raised the knife. "You can leak worse."

She shut up.

He smiled and settled back on the bed on his elbows. He crossed his legs, looking up at the ceiling.

She kept on tugging uselessly at the cotton strip binding her wrists. Communication seemed hopeless. Everything seemed hopeless.

She remembered her meeting with Drake. His story about mystical prophecies, supernatural powers. She had almost believed him. Except she hadn't wanted to believe. But maybe there was no other explanation. Her whole world had gone crazy in the past twelve hours.

If there was such a thing as the Deathsong and she had sung it, then maybe the rest of what he'd told her was true as well. Maybe there really was a Door somewhere, threatening to swing wide and expel a vomitous stream of destruction and death. And maybe, just maybe, she was the key to it all, the one hope of reversing the spell before midnight tonight, when it would be too late.

She shook her head. It was too much. There was a man on his way over here, a man who had warped her best friends' minds, turned them into psychotic killers, and who was now planning to polish her off personally. That was enough to deal with, thank you very much. More than enough.

So deal with it, she told herself sternly. Do something. Anything.

Softly she began to hum.

She recognized the tune. "City of New Orleans." The old Woody Guthrie song. She had heard it on the radio, on the *Grand Ole Opry Hour,* when she was growing up.

It seemed natural to be singing. She remembered wandering down a desert trail with an infected arm and a fever-spinning brain. She had sung then too, till she was too weak to go on. The singing had kept death from her door. And last night, when she was afraid, she had gone downstairs and listened to music to keep the panic down. That particular decision had saved her life, at least temporarily. Music, she thought vaguely, had always been her salvation. Maybe it would save her again.

She hummed louder.

Bobby Joe looked at her. "What the hell are you trying to prove?"

"Nervous habit. Sue me."

"I don't like it."

She went on humming.

"Stop it."

She didn't listen.

Bobby Joe studied her a moment longer, then shrugged. She hummed the refrain. She rocked to the rhythm. The chair creaked. She whispered the lyrics in a breathless undertone.

Bobby Joe got up.

"At least do something decent. I hate that one."

She stopped, surprised. "It's a classic."

"Do something from our repertoire."

She took a moment to answer. She had caught the word "our." And something else. Some quality in his voice that had not been there before.

"Sure, Bobby Joe," she said carefully. "Anything in particular?"

"I've always been partial to 'Blue Moon Blues.' "

"You ought to be. You wrote it."

"Damn fine tune, if I do say so myself."

She did her best to find some moisture in her mouth. She sang the opening bars. She stumbled over the second line. It was hard to concentrate on the lyrics. She was watching Bobby Joe's face. Something was flickering there, some suggestion of humanity.

She reached the chorus. The part where, according to his arrangement, he would join in. She was halfway through the stanza when she heard his low tenor, barely audible, a whisper of breath harmonizing *a cappella* with her own.

She sang louder, daring him to do the same. His own voice rose. It was working. He was getting into it. He was remembering how things had been.

Abruptly he broke off.

"Fuck this." He flung himself down on the bed with a cymbal-crash of mattress springs. "I know what you're up to."

"I was just singing, Bobby Joe," she said helplessly, desperately, sensing her chance slipping away.

"Go to hell."

She shut her eyes. She had been close. So close. Goddammit.

Still, there might be a way.

She let a moment pass before speaking again. "That old song sure does bring back memories, doesn't it?" Every word was a step along a crumbling ledge. "I remember you writing it down in the back of the van.

We were crossing the desert, I guess. Heading for Al-buquerque.''

That was wrong. She knew it. She was hoping he would swallow the bait. An endless second crawled by.

"Tucson," he said from the bed, without looking up.

She took a breath. So far, so good.

"That's right. Tucson. I guess we had just come from Albuquerque."

"Shit, boss lady. You must be getting senile, the way your memory is going. It was Oklahoma City. That's why I put in that line about the rodeo."

"Hell, I nearly forgot about that." She forced a smile. "Ride 'em, cowboy."

He propped himself up on an elbow to look at her. His eyes were dark and faraway. "At least I gave it a try. Old Gary was too busy coming on to that ticket-taker girl."

"And K.C. kept quoting Kierkegaard or Bertrand Russell or somebody, anyway, who you can bet had never been on a bronco."

"Yeah. He was full of excuses. Told me he'd only ride Caligula's horse. Said if he was going to get his neck broke, he wanted it done by a duly elected official."

He almost smiled. Her heart missed a beat, like a bad drummer. She forced herself to sound casual. She had to lead him on. Just a little further.

"How long did you stay on that goddamn thing anyway?" she asked.

He snorted. "Twenty-three seconds. Which was a damn sight longer than some of those local boys."

"You did us proud, pardner."

"We came to play. The way I always had it figured, if you're going make music, why not have yourself some fun?"

"We've had plenty."

"Yeah. Good times." He swept stray hairs off his

forehead with the back of his hand. "I don't regret it, boss lady. I'm glad I stuck it out with you. Even if you are kind of a bitch sometimes, I guess . . . I guess . . ."

His words trailed away. Slowly he turned his head to stare at her. His eyes cleared and seemed to come into focus from some great distance. She watched him, not daring to speak, to move, even to breathe.

"Jesus," he said in a strangled voice, his own voice. "What the hell's going on here? What the hell are we—?"

The door swung open and the moment was lost.

18

Billie's first impression was of his hands. They were delicate, long-fingered hands, like the elongated claws of a movie vampire. Cruel hands.

The rest of him seemed almost disappointingly ordinary. He stood in the doorway, his tall body thrown into semisilhouette by the light from the hall. He was overdressed for the occasion, suited up in a jacket and tie. The jacket bulged ominously in several places. He had stooped shoulders, an angular chin, and a receding hairline. He was perhaps forty years old.

All in all, he looked no different from a hundred thousand other slightly unsavory Hollywood businessmen, the sort who existed on the fringes of the entertainment industry, forever on the make for a quick buck and an easy lay.

Then she looked into his eyes. They were not the eyes of a promoter or a hustler or even a con man. They were the eyes of a killer. Dead, empty eyes. The thought flashed in her mind that a killer's first victim was always himself.

He grinned, skull-like.

"Allow me to introduce myself, Miss Kidd," he said, his voice a velvet whisper. "My name is Frank Lancett."

Slowly, reluctantly, she turned to look at Bobby Joe. He was staring at the man named Frank Lancett. There was nothing in his face now, no remembrance, no humanity. It was not a face at all. It was an expressionless mask.

Billie moaned.

"You've proved yourself most resourceful," said Frank Lancett. "But all resources are exhausted eventually." He took a step forward. His smile floated above the skeleton outlines of his face, a Cheshire-cat smile. "I've never met such a big star before. So talented. And so pretty. Yes. Such a pretty little thing," he breathed. "Sweet. Sweet."

She heard the low, psychotic undertone in his voice. He loosened his necktie, then pulled it off. She watched it slide free of his collar like an eel gliding out of its cave. She had time to think that he was going to strangle her with his tie, and then in the next instant he stuffed one end of the tie in her mouth, gagging her, then wound the rest of it around her face in a double loop and knotted it at the back of her neck. She did not even have time to protest.

Feebly, uselessly, her hands still struggled to work themselves free.

Lancett drew back and studied her like an artist admiring his subject.

He reached into his vest pocket and withdrew a cigarette lighter. He flicked it. A jet of blue flame shot up. Billie let out a muffled whimper. Then from his side pocket he produced a pack of cigarettes. He tapped one out and lit it. He took a long, thoughtful drag. She fought to control her thudding heart.

"You know, Miss Kidd, most people think of in-

struments of torture as arcane devices. Medieval racks
and iron maidens. Or electrodes and nerve gas."

He held the cigarette between thumb and forefinger,
puffing lightly, expelling black clouds.

"But they're wrong. The most effective methods are
always the simplest. You can't imagine the things I can
do with a pair of kitchen shears or a sewing needle or
even an ordinary tablespoon."

He took another step toward her. He placed one hand
on the armrest of her chair. He loomed over her.

"Or a cigarette."

She stared at the glowing tip as if hypnotized. The
rest of the world seemed to fade away into hazy twilight. There was only that burning spot, expanding
like the headlight of an onrushing train as he lowered
it toward her face.

"Your skin is very soft, my dear. Very tender. I am
going to do things to your face that will not be pleasant. Not pleasant at all."

She twisted her head sideways. She shut her eyes.
She could feel the heat of the cigarette on her cheek.
Hotter. Hotter. The thing was less than an inch away
now.

"And once I get through with your face, I am going
to unbutton your shirt and unbuckle your pants and
then I am going to hurt you very badly, very badly
indeed."

Her heart slamdanced wildly in her chest. Her head
pounded in syncopated rhythm. She clenched her
teeth. She squeezed her eyes shut. White stardust
whirled before her eyelids.

She wished she could scream. Oh, Jesus, she needed
to scream.

Then suddenly she heard a scream, long and agonized and impossibly high-pitched, like the whistle of
wind up a chimney.

She opened her eyes. She looked past Lancett to
Bobby Joe. She stared at his face. And . . . oh, my
God, he was back. He was himself again. She had

reached him, after all. Not all at once or right away, but she had done it, she had gotten through, and now he was on her side.

"Get away from her," said Bobby Joe, brandishing the knife.

Lancett seemed to grasp the situation instantly. He tossed the cigarette on the floor, spun around, and shook Bobby Joe roughly by the shoulders.

"You hate the goddamn slut," he whispered, his voice a python hiss. "She's always hogging the spotlight. Pushing you around. Just once, you'd like to crack her skull—"

"No!"

The knife lashed out, slicing through Frank Lancett's cheek.

Billie pulled desperately at the cotton strip binding her wrists. She had to get free. This was her chance. Her last chance.

Lancett retreated, clutching his bloody face. Bobby Joe advanced on him. The knife glittered in his hand.

"You fucker," said Bobby Joe. "You played with my head. You made me crazy."

"No. It was her. The bitch. The boss lady. She made you crazy." Lancett's voice was a hypnotic monotone, low and almost irresistibly persuasive. "Not me. Her. Her."

Bobby Joe blinked as if to clear his head. He kept coming.

"Listen," said Lancett softly. "Listen to me for one second and everything will make sense. Just listen."

Lancett began to hum a tune—six notes arranged in a haunting melody.

Billie wanted to shout a warning, to tell Bobby Joe not to fall for it. Fall for what? She did not know. But there was something about that song that frightened her.

She couldn't warn Bobby Joe. The necktie jammed in her mouth still choked off sound.

It made no difference. Bobby Joe was in no mood
to listen to a musical recital, anyway. He swung out
again with the knife. It swept past Lancett's throat,
missing its target by half an inch.

Lancett gave up on the song and dived for Bobby
Joe. The two men hit the floor, rolling and twisting in
a tangle of limbs. Lancett grabbed Bobby Joe's wrist
and bit down and wrenched the knife out of his grasp.
He raised it in triumph, brought it down in a sweeping
arc, and buried the blade in Bobby Joe's groin.

Billie wanted to close her eyes, to turn away, anything so as not to see the geyser of red spurting like
Old Faithful out of Bobby Joe's pants. She could not
turn away. She watched, transfixed by horror.

Frank Lancett gripped the knife handle in both
hands. Slowly, protestingly, the knife zigzagged north
to Bobby Joe's belt buckle, slitting his belly wide.
Blood foamed up from between tattered skin flaps.
Intestines spilled out, accordioning onto the carpet like
link sausages. The stench of excrement flooded the
room.

Bobby Joe was whimpering like an animal. His
hands fumbled wildly, trying to scoop up his steaming
entrails and stuff them back inside his body. Blood and
feces smeared his fingers. He squeezed a ropelike
length of intestine and it burst, spraying the room with
diarrhea.

The knife advanced north in a series of rapid zig-
zags. It plowed through Bobby Joe's belt, then carved
his belly, popping the buttons of his shirt. A river of
blood splashed out. The carpet was a mudhole and
Bobby Joe was a stuck pig, grunting and squealing and
shitting himself.

Die, thought Billie with desperate pity. Please,
Bobby Joe. Don't fight it anymore. Just get it over
with. Just die.

Bobby Joe did not die. Not right away. He went on
writhing, limbs flapping bonelessly, while blood
streamed out of his chest and mouth and nostrils, and

the knife danced on, moving of its own will, like the planchette of a Ouija board spelling out a message from the dead.

Then with a final thrust the knife sank into Bobby Joe's ribs and found his heart. He stiffened. His eyes rolled up in their sockets, eggshell white. His tongue erupted out of his mouth and hung there, lolling stupidly. He gave one last shudder, then lay still.

Frank Lancett straddled the corpse, gasping. His business suit was soaked in blood and human waste. He tried to pull the knife free. It would not budge. He gave up on it. He got to his feet. He turned and looked at Billie. He smiled.

"You're next."

He wanted to scare her, she figured, but it didn't work that way. Fury surged through her in a white-hot wave.

Fuck you, she said silently, fuck you to hell.

She was not speaking to Frank Lancett. She was speaking to the darkness in the hollows of his eyes. To the bottomless pit looming there. To the abyss.

She tensed her arms, took a breath, then with all her strength tore her hands free.

Instantly she was out of the chair. She flung herself at him. At the last second he tried to jump clear. Too late. She body-slammed him into the wall. His fist swung at her in a circling blow. She took it square in the face. Teeth rattled in her jaw. She coughed, trying to spit up blood, but the gag was still in place, choking her.

Her hand dived into his pants. She felt the short hairs of his groin, then his cock, his balls. She grabbed hold. She made a fist. She squeezed him like a sponge.

Frank Lancett was screaming. An oddly feminine sound, like the midnight shriek of an alley cat. Suddenly he seemed to forget about fighting back. He seemed to forget about everything but pain.

You can dish it out, thought Billie pitilessly, but you can't take it. Right, asshole?

She released her grip and pulled her hand free. It came away bloody. A stain was spreading over Lancett's crotch. She had ruptured him down there. She had done some major damage, all right. It looked like Planned Parenthood could take Mr. Frank Lancett off their mailing list for good.

He sank to his knees, gargling a mouthful of bloody froth.

She turned. She escaped from the bedroom. Halfway down the hall, she tore the necktie out of her mouth. It flapped around her neck like a scarf.

She reached the living room. K.C. was there. He stood blocking the front door, knife in hand.

"You just don't want to go gentle into that good night, do you, Bills?"

"You got it, pal."

She faced him. Behind her came the sound of movement from the bedroom. Lancett must already be recovering, getting back on his feet like some horror-movie monster that just didn't know when to quit.

She seized the first object within reach, a folding chair. She flailed it at K.C. It struck him hard on the shoulder. Wood cracked. The chair's wooden stiles and armrests flew off. He dropped his knife and clutched his shoulder.

"Shit," he hissed. "That hurt."

She backed off, still holding one leg of the chair like a baseball bat.

He came at her with his bare hands. She swung the chair leg. It whacked solidly into his chin. His head snapped sideways with the force of the blow. He staggered back, regained his balance, and sprang at her again. She leapt to one side and caught him in the back of the neck as he flew past. The chair leg split halfway down the middle. He hit the floor, groaning. He rolled over on his side and tried to get to his feet.

She did not want to have to hurt him any more. She

had never wanted to hurt any of them. She had no choice.

He was on hands and knees, halfway up. She raised the chair leg high over her head and brought it down in a vicious arc. It slammed into his skull. Amazingly, there was no blood. K.C. simply dropped to the floor, spread-eagle like a bearskin rug.

She stood over him, fighting for breath, as her stomach heaved dangerously and the shattered remnant of the chair leg, still clutched in her fist, dripped blood like a leaky faucet.

Behind her, the bedroom door burst open.

Lancett stared at her down the length of the hall.

"Oh, you bitch," he whispered. The velvet voice was sandpaper now. "You fucking bitch."

She hurled the chair leg at him. She did not wait to see if it struck home. She was running for the front door. His voice rose behind her.

"You're going to regret ever checking into this life, sweetheart. You're going to be real sorry your dear old mommy didn't have you scraped."

She reached the door. She fumbled blindly with the knob. Her fingers were sticky with blood, his blood. She could not get a grip on the thing. She could not get it to turn.

"I'm going to cut your eyes out and feed 'em to you. Going to stuff 'em down your fucking throat."

She knew, without turning to look, that he was closing in. She could hear his heavy footsteps, his ragged breath. She remembered those bulges in his jacket. If one of them was a gun, he could shoot her now, in the back. She dismissed the thought. He did not want to shoot her. That would be too quick.

The doorknob still would not yield. It was smeared with blood from her hands. The blood made an oily film on the brass. The knob kept slipping through her fingers.

"Going to take your fingernails off one at a time.

Pull the nipples off your tits. Cut your ears off like a matador carving a bull.''

He was right behind her. Maybe two yards away. Or less.

She got a good grip on the knob and this time, hallelujah, it turned.

The door still would not open.

She rattled the knob wildly. Jesus. What the hell was wrong with the goddamn thing?

She remembered the dead bolt.

K.C. had bolted the door, that was it, that was the problem.

She reached for the latch and Lancett's hand closed over her neck.

He hauled her backward, off her feet, and sent her reeling to the floor. She landed on her side. All the wind was knocked out of her. She wheezed. She looked up through a net of hair plastered to her face. Lancett stood over her. His pants clung to his legs in bloody patches. Droplets of red dripped from his trouser legs onto his shoes in a slow, steady rain.

She tried to crawl away. He took a step forward and planted the heel of his shoe on her hand, pinning her down.

''You're not going anywhere, you fucking bitch. You're dead.''

''Oh, man,'' Billie moaned. ''I only wish.''

Lancett laughed out loud, enjoying her fear, savoring it, and she joined him, laughing helplessly, hysterically, and while they were sharing this moment she took the opportunity to raise her free hand in a vertical sweep, arrowing her fist at the open wound between his legs. She connected. Hard.

He tried to scream but no sound came out. He stumbled backward. A fresh torrent of blood splashed down his inseams. He doubled over, clutching his groin.

She got to her feet. She ran past him to the door, unlatched it, and flung it open. She ran for the elevator. She jabbed at the call button. The elevator would not come. She looked back.

Frank Lancett staggered into the hallway, still after her, refusing to give up.

She abandoned the elevator. She ran to a glowing exit sign and pushed open the heavy steel door underneath and then she was racing down the stairwell, taking the steps two at a time, hearing the echoing clatter of her boots on the iron grillwork.

She reached street level and staggered through the lobby to the revolving door at the front of the building. A man was coming in. He stared at her as she flew past, and she had time to think that she must look like a refugee from a bad dream, disheveled and blood-spattered and wild-eyed.

Then she was running across the street to the parking space where her Lamborghini sat waiting for her, just as she had left it four hours and a lifetime ago. She groped desperately in her pants pockets, praying she had not lost the keys when she used them as a weapon. Her fist closed over the key chain, still sticky with blood. She unlocked the car. The driver's-side door swung up. She sank into the bucket seat behind the wheel, gunned the engine, and screamed away from the curb.

She rounded the corner and tore onto Sunset, careening through traffic, blasting her horn, giddy with exhilaration, racing away from Frank Lancett and death.

19

You really couldn't blame Billie Lee Kidd, thought Martin Drake as the Angeles Crest Highway unspooled under the hood of his '62 Fiat. The top was down, the interior open to the cloudless sky and the cool mountain air.

Two hours earlier, he had been standing on the terrace of a restaurant in Westwood, watching Billie run out on him. He had not tried to stop her. He knew that she would come to him when she was ready. And in the meantime, there was work for him to do.

Her voice had opened the Door between this world and another. Unless that Door were closed by midnight, only ten hours from now, the dark gods would stream out like the eruption of evils from Pandora's box. Only the singer of the Deathsong could close the Door; but he, at least, could locate it, track it down so Billie could go there without delay once she changed her mind.

Because he knew she would change her mind sooner or later. His gods would not have chosen her if she were not equal to the challenge. She needed time, that was all.

No, he thought again, you really couldn't blame her for running away, for not wanting to believe. Not very many years ago, he wouldn't have believed it himself. But that was before a night in Rampart, a trip to the hospital, and a revelation.

Rookie cops rarely saw duty in the Rampart district, a concrete hell in the City of Angels, a war zone of drug deals and drive-bys, where young lives were zippered up in body bags at a rate of one per week, two when things were jumping. It was the kind of place where a man could die for wearing a shirt of the wrong color, a place that ate cops alive, especially rookie cops still wet behind the ears, ate them up and spit them out on the sidewalk.

Not a place which Martin Drake—then all of twenty-two, three months on the force, scared green—had ever expected or wanted to be.

But on that night, ten years ago, the LAPD was going full tilt on another gang crackdown, one of the periodic sweeps initiated for the benefit of the TV news crews and the local pols. The idea was to assemble as many surplus cops from as many other districts as possible, pay them all time-and-a-half, and throw them into Rampart on a Saturday night to see how many of the usual suspects they could round up.

Already Drake and his partner, a thirty-year veteran named Garcia, had bagged sixteen suspected gang members and assorted lowlifes, and now, shortly past midnight, they were cruising for more.

They rolled past an alley where a huddle of slouching figures cast a rippling shadow dance on the brick wall.

"Looks like something's going down," said Garcia, smacking his Juicy Fruit and smiling that jackass grin, the way he always did.

"Okay," said Drake, trying not to sound afraid. "Let's do it."

The squad car pulled slowly and silently to a halt, no squeal of tires or screaming siren, no theatrical stuff. Drake and Garcia approached the alley, their boots crunching on the litter-strewn pavement.

"Hey, you guys," said Garcia in his best don't-mess-with-me voice. "You got company."

Slowly the gang came forward into the purple glow of the mercury-vapor streetlamp. Five kids, none older than twenty. They stared at Drake and Garcia with hard, cold, unseeing eyes.

"Yeah, man," said one, the tallest and oldest of the bunch, apparently their leader. He spoke in a tone of perpetual indifference that robbed his words of a question mark.

"What are you bastards up to?" asked Garcia, nice and mean, the way cops in this part of town had to be.

"Hanging, man. Just hanging."

"That's called loitering," said Garcia. "You're breaking the law."

"Fuck off."

Drake grabbed the kid and slammed him up against the alley wall. "Hey, punk," he breathed, doing his best Clint Eastwood number. "You heard the man."

That was when the trouble started.

Later, Drake was able to piece together what had happened from the arrest reports. It seemed that these five had been doing more than just hanging out. This particular garden party had been a highly exclusive affair, and only those dealing in the highest-quality imported goods had made the guest list. A very important deal was going down here. Too important to be fucked up by two uniforms with an attitude.

Which was why, in retrospect, it should hardly have been surprising when the kid nearest to Garcia whipped out a knife and sliced a brand new smile on the cop's face, stretching from ear to ear.

Drake fumbled with his gun. A boot caught him in the groin. A fist slammed into the back of his skull. He went down on both knees, a yard from Garcia, who was writhing crazily, strangling on his own blood, trying to yell for help with severed vocal cords and producing only a series of wheezing gasps.

The kid who had done all the talking stooped down, seized Drake's .38, and yanked it free of its holster. He aimed it point-blank at Drake's forehead. He pulled the trigger.

At the time Drake thought it was luck, just plain dumb luck, although later a different suspicion entered his mind—but for whatever reason, chance or fate, the gun, which had never failed him in a dozen hours of target practice in the shooting gallery, jammed.

"Fuck," breathed the kid. He tossed the gun aside. It clattered on the pavement.

"What do we do with him, man?" asked one of his partners, panting.

If the kid had been thinking clearly he would have remembered Garcia's gun and that would have been the end. But he was too wired on his own product or maybe just too goddamn stupid to engage in analytical reasoning. His mind seemed to work slowly, turning over the problem like a complex equation of higher mathematics, finally reaching a solution.

"Take him in back," he said.

The other four dragged Drake off the street, to the rear of the alley, and then the festivities began.

They took turns kicking the shit out of him, snapping ribs like wishbones, then slammed him against the alley wall till his nose gushed blood, then pummeled him with their fists, laughing like the low-grade morons they were. Finally their leader picked up a length of lead pipe discovered among the heaps of trash spilling out of overturned garbage cans. He advanced, wielding the pipe like a baseball bat. He grinned down at Drake, lying helplessly on his back.

"Okay, asshole," he breathed. "It's bedtime."

The pipe crashed down on Drake's skull and he was gone.

They left him for dead. A half-hour later, two other cops stopped to investigate the parked patrol car and found Drake and Garcia. Garcia died en route to the hospital. But as for Martin Drake, he was fine, just fine, after eight months of physical therapy and, oh, yes, after the coma.

He was comatose when they found him, and he stayed that way for sixteen hours. The doctors told him later—because he asked, specifically and repeatedly— that he had not dreamed. His brain-wave activity was proof of that. They even showed him the EEG's, though the charts of zigzagging lines meant nothing to him.

He believed the doctors. He had not dreamed. But something had taken place in his mind during that long darkness. In his mind, or perhaps somewhere else.

Visitors had come to him, ghostly visitors with healing fingers, soothing to the touch, and spectral voices, mellifluous as woodwinds. They told him of their cause. They made no deal with him, no quid pro quo. They would not blackmail his acquiescence by holding his life hostage. They did not wish even to impress on him a sense of duty. They merely desired that he understand.

Men would seek him out, they said, in another year or two. Men who worshiped false gods. They would seek his help. Would seek to make him one of their own. To place a bracelet on his wrist, which could never be removed. They would tempt him with dark promises. He might refuse to listen. Or he might join them and serve their cause. Or . . .

He understood.

And for him—as it had been for a handful of others like him down through the centuries—that understanding was enough.

While he lay in a hospital bed with electrodes taped to his skull, while nurses looked in on him and pitied his dreamless sleep, Martin Drake took his vows.

He guided the Fiat along the highway winding through the San Gabriel range, looking for something he could not quite define, letting his instincts lead him where he must go. A few miles past Crystal Lake Road he turned off onto a dirt trail cut through the chaparral. It seemed right. He couldn't say why. He followed the trail to a dead end. He parked and got out. He continued on foot, trudging slowly up the sloping mountainside, pausing now and then to catch his breath. The sun beat down.

Two miles and an hour later, he stopped in a forest

glen ringed by stands of sumac and scrub oak. Sunbeams slanted through gaps in the canopy of interlocking branches. He surveyed the clearing.

Yes, he thought. This will do.

He did not know how he knew. He just did. This was the place.

He walked to the center of the clearing. He did not kneel or bow his head. His gods did not demand it, did not even desire it. They did not seek the obeisance of those whose allegiance they had earned.

He stood with his feet planted wide apart, his hands at his sides, his head lifted. He gazed up at the patches of cerulean blue caught in a net of shimmering green. He began to speak, quietly at first, then louder, remembering the words which had been given to him so many years before, as he lay in darkness. Words he had never forgotten but had never before been called upon to use.

"Kanos para notras asti ren asatras tull . . ."

He had communed with his gods only that one time. Never again had he felt the need of their guidance. Anyway, they did not guide. They did not see men as sheep to be led or as cattle to be herded. They did not look for excuses to impose their will on other minds. They did not wish to interfere in human affairs at all, if interference could be avoided. Their sole exception had been the war with the dark gods of Antarok, and that had been a battle joined as a last resort.

In college, Drake had studied Aristotle's theory of God, a God who was an immovable mover, perfect, self-contained, majestically indifferent to the world of men. Perhaps, he had often thought in more recent years, Aristotle had known the gods he served.

". . . esar unamas das res rentas relas roth thurren tos . . ."

Wild lilacs and mustard plants rippled languidly, stirred by a sudden breeze, a cool breeze laced with droplets of moisture, faintly fragrant of spices. It was not a wind born of the mountains. It smelled of Babylon, of Sumer, of the Nile delta, of ancient places and peoples, of other lands and other times.

Perhaps, too, the followers of druidic religions, the worshipers of elemental nature in all its myriad forms—perhaps they also had known his gods.

A coyote stole out of the manzanita fringing the glen. It paused, nostrils twitching, then padded forward. A family of rabbits hopped at its heels. They showed no fear. They seemed to sense that they were safe from harm, protected by that scented breeze and by the greater power which had summoned it.

". . . tabash altor seth seti saros heth omos nar . . ."

Antarok's dark gods were known by many names. Ragnaaroth, the Spider King. Dasharoom, He Who Eats Souls. Garnarlit, the Stealer of Light. Bethshul, the Screaming Woman. Toth, the Wind That Hungers. And more, many more, a confusion of names and mythic imagery.

Drake's gods were nameless. They did not need such crude symbolism to inspire awe. They were unutterably old, inconceivably vast, immeasurably powerful. If they used their full strength, they could never be defeated. They did not choose to do so. They chose only to match their enemies, strength for strength, to balance evil with good, then leave it up to man to tip the scale—one way or the other.

Billie, he thought as his prayer went on. It all depends on you now.

". . . paras nos sutras esah soth ramesh tash atim emas . . ."

The sky was brightening with a glow that was not sunshine. From the clearing came a matching luminescence, bright as a flurry of fireflies, ephemeral as mist, rising in sparkling waves from the ground itself.

The grass was alive with tiny forest creatures. Inch-long lizards scurried out from under rocks. Field mice skittered through the wildflowers at the verge of the glen. Horseflies and darning needles buzzed each other, dogfighting playfully. Blue jays darted from branch to branch.

A black-tailed doe stepped daintily through the scrim of trees, nudging her fawn into the clearing. They joined the coyote and the smaller animals that ringed Drake, gazing up at him, their ears pricked as if listening in respectful silence to his low, metronomic chant.

". . . soor naran antas astar aman teras surtan sar . . ."

Then the glow in the sky flashed down like a fork of lightning, merging with the ground cover of light.

Drake caught his breath, the words of the prayer abruptly cut off.

Light enveloped him. It flowed over him and through him. It was as white as molten steel, but cool, as cool as a cataract of foam splashing down a mountainside in the Sierras. It washed over him, but it did not cleanse and purify, it was no healing ablution. Instead it seemed to take its purity from him, its purity and its strength.

He looked at himself in silent wonder. He could see the bones of his hands, printed like an X-ray image, but in color and motion. Blood coursed through his veins and arteries and capillaries, a living and life-giving net. His heart pumped gently in his chest in graceful counterpoint to the slow expansion and contraction of his lungs.

He raised his head to gaze around him. The shaft of light had ripped open the sky to flood the clearing. Into its streaming radiance flocked the animals. They were drawn to it, as living things, uncorrupted, were always drawn to light and life. Squirrels, opossums, and muskrats scampered out of the bushes. A garter snake glided like a blue-green ribbon through the grass. Butterflies danced in the light, dust motes in a sunbeam. The blue jays wheeled, wings glittering angelically.

Drake closed his eyes and addressed his question to

the nameless forces whose presence he felt around him and within him.

The Door, he thought. Where is the Door?

And just like that, with no fuss at all, he knew the answer.

20

Gresham Avenue had once been a pleasant thorough-fare on the outskirts of downtown L.A. That was be-fore the population soared, and with it the crime rate and the level of fear. Now Gresham Avenue was de-serted, abandoned by the locals who had been rolled and raped there too many times. Stray dogs picked at trashcans at the backs of warehouses. A burned-out building, condemned but never torn down, stood at one corner. The only sign of life was the rush of traffic whistling along the Hollywood Freeway, which swept over Gresham between Market and Cortez.

The walls of the dank tunnellike passage below the freeway overpass were scarred with twisted hiero-glyphics of graffiti and sunbursts of dried blood. The graffiti had been left by the local gangs that hung out there, spray-painting over each other's markings, each wishing to lay claim to this turf. The blood spots were from the bums.

Every year, during the rainy season, which stretched from November through March, the bums came to the overpass, seeking shelter. Then one of the gangs would find them and beat the shit out of them and plug the louse-eaten bastards just for the hell of it. Their heads would explode like smashed cantaloupes under the im-pact of .44 Magnum shells. Blood would spatter the wall and drip down, drying in colorful patterns.

There were places in the city meant for death. This was one of them.

Frank Lancett sensed the presence of death as he guided his Lincoln Town Car down Gresham Avenue in the broiling midafternoon heat. It was out there, all right. It was waiting for him.

His groin still burned with agony. Intermittent shock waves of pain shot down his thighs and up his abdomen. The bitch had done one hell of a job on him. He'd used up a whole roll of paper towels blotting up the blood and urine and come. Finally he had bandaged himself with some gauze from the medicine cabinet. He did not think he would ever be getting it up again.

And the worst part of it was that the bitch had beaten him. He hadn't even burned her. Hadn't even put one little hole in that ugly freckled face.

He shook his head, putting the thought out of his mind. He had other, more pressing matters to deal with. He had an appointment to keep.

He pulled the Lincoln to a stop fifty feet from the overpass, killed the engine, and sat waiting. He was two minutes early. He was not going in there any sooner than he had to. There was a chance, a good chance, that he would not come out alive.

He had been assigned by the Director to kill Billie Lee Kidd. He had failed. And now, here he was, called to his first meeting with his faceless superior. The kind of meeting that was both an introduction and a farewell.

He knew the penalty for failure, just as Reynolds had known. But unlike Reynolds, he would not go without a fight. He had taken precautions, years ago, for just such an eventuality as this. He had his own private insurance policy, tucked away in a safe-deposit box. It ought to save his ass. Sure. It ought to.

Frank Lancett took a long, slow, steadying breath. He glanced at his watch. Three o'clock.

It was time.

He got out of the car. He walked toward the passageway beneath the overpass. The August air steamed like a sauna, but without a sauna's moisture. He looked up. Traffic rumbled on the freeway. Car windows caught the sun like mirrors flashing signals. A truck blasted its air horn. It barreled past in a thunder of wheels.

He reached the darkness of the underpass. He paused at the threshold, peering inside.

The passageway was narrow, dirty. It echoed with the roar of vehicles overhead. Unrhythmic vibrations rang through walls made of concrete and reinforcing steel struts. The pavement was littered with old newspapers the color of piss, glittering shards of beer bottles, and excrement. The place stank.

And it was empty. Utterly empty.

Lancett stepped under the freeway, into the tunnel, leaving daylight behind.

The Director was supposed to be here. Now. But there was nobody. Nobody except . . .

He froze.

Huddled on the sidewalk, halfway down the passage, was a human figure.

Lancett moved forward. He squinted. It was a man. A raggedy old man in Salvation Army clothes—grease-spotted tennis shoes, baggy clown trousers, a patchwork coat. Dirt-matted hair sprouted from his soiled shirt collar like a thicket of black weeds. He lay face-down, asleep, with his head in a pool of yellow filth that was his own vomit.

There was no one else in sight.

"Fuck," breathed Lancett. "The son of a bitch didn't show."

A whisper rose in answer like the slow, patient hiss of a fuse.

"Oh, yes, Lancett. Yes, he did."

Lancett lowered his gaze to the man at his feet. Very

slowly the ancient bum raised his head and smiled up at him with vomit-crusted lips.

"Greetings, my brother," he said.

Lancett swallowed.

That voice—it was the voice on the telephone, the mystery voice always half-obscured by the rush of traffic in the background. But it couldn't be. The Director was an important man. A man of power and influence. This had to be some kind of disguise. Yes. That was it. That must be it.

"No," whispered the papyrus face. "I know what you're thinking, Lancett. It's what they always think. But you're wrong. This is no act, no clever ruse. This is me. The real me."

Lancett found his voice, tucked away at the back of his throat, and summoned it with effort.

"You live . . . here?"

"I live everywhere. I roam the city. No one sees me. No one wants to see." He tittered, a low, lunatic sound. "The perfect cover. Except, you see, it's not."

"I've called you on the phone . . ."

"Pay phone. I hung an out-of-order sign on it. Nobody uses it now. It's not very far from here. I sleep in an alley within earshot. When it rings, I answer."

Lancett blinked, thinking of the traffic noise on the line. He had always assumed that the Director had an office facing a busy street. He had always assumed so many things.

"How did they recruit you?" he asked, still unable to make the situation real.

"Long story." The man's lips barely moved when he spoke. His face was a wrinkled mask. His eyes lay deep in the hollows of their sockets like the eyes of an actor peering through slits in cardboard. "I was a different man then. Society man. Businessman, like you. Only much smarter than you. Smart enough to see beneath the surface of things. And once you've seen too much, you can't go on, not their way. Not once you've seen the maggots." He leaned forward intently, squinting up at him. "Have you seen them, Lancett? Have you ever seen them? Even in your dreams?"

Lancett shook his head uncomprehendingly.

"I did. I saw. So I had to quit. Give up. Roll in the gutter with the rest of the trash. Eat out of garbage cans. Drink dog piss. Sometimes I catch rats in here and eat 'em raw."

"And you . . . I mean . . . you run everything . . . ?"

"Damn right I do. Director of the whole operation in the southern half of the state. And I do it for free. Don't get a fucking dime. They'd pay me if I asked. But I don't want it. I don't want anything."

"Why not?"

"Because it's all a crock." He raised himself to a sitting position, perching on the curb with his knees stuck up and one hand on his unshaved chin. "What good is luxury, anyway? Limousines and oil paintings. Fuck 'em. They rust and rot. Get eaten by the maggots. Everything gets eaten by the maggots. Know what I mean?"

Lancett shrugged. His mind was numb.

"Of course you don't. Because you've never seen."

The rheumy eyes rolled up in their sockets, studying the ceiling. Spittle glistened on prune lips.

"What's the real essence of things, Lancett? Ultimate truth? Universal reality? What's the stuff the world is made of? Heraclitus says it's fire and Spinoza says it's monads and the scientists say it's quarks, but they're wrong, all of them. Maggots. That's what it is."

A pale purple tongue flicked at rotted teeth, lizard-quick.

"The universe is a maggoty hive, nest of larvae, womb of worms. They eat holes in space, black holes. They vomit up quasars. They get in through your nostrils and your mouth and your asshole and they eat you up from the inside out. Like tapeworms, they infest your bowels. Like earwigs, they crawl into your skull and devour your brain. I can feel them, Lancett. They're in there now, slithering and chewing, feeding on my gray matter, swallowing my thoughts, killing me. But soon, very soon, they'll feed no more. Soon they'll have eaten their fill. Soon. Soon.'' He was laughing.

Lancett took a step backward. One word reverberated in his mind like the echoing vibrations of the traffic overhead.

Insane.

The man was insane. The man who had given him orders, who had been entrusted by his still-more-mysterious superior with the power of life and death over every Department Head, every staff member, every free-lancer, every outsider who might get in the way. Unlimited power. Unquestioned authority. And he was as crazy as Hitler in his bunker, as crazy as any other homeless derelict who lived in a gutter and slept in his own regurgitated breakfast.

''You think I'm a lunatic,'' said the Director, eyes narrowing, laughter abruptly cut off. ''Sure. That's another thing they always think. Well, maybe I am. You would be too, if you knew the whole truth. If you saw the reality I see. If you saw.'' He smiled, his teeth making a sickly crescent moon in the darkness. ''But you will not. You won't live long enough. I'm going to sing to you, Lancett. I'm going to sing at your funeral.''

Lancett's heart thudded in his ears. He fought to stifle his panic. He had some kind of escape plan— didn't he? He couldn't remember. Everything was confused.

''I tried my best,'' he said, knowing it was useless to explain. ''I went there, just like you said. But she was gone. She'd gotten a phone call and gone off someplace. Those three hick banjo players of hers were there by themselves. So I figured, what the hell, let them do it. Three against one. No way she can beat those odds." He swallowed. "Only . . . Only . . ."

"Only, you were wrong." It was a death sentence. Lancett knew that.

The bum opened his mouth to sing.

"Wait!"

Lancett's shout echoed in the darkness. The Director shut his mouth and waited, sitting cross-legged on the curb, a vomity Buddha.

"Listen." He had remembered now. He knew what he had to say. "There's something I have to tell you." He took another step backward. His mouth was so dry. His tongue was chalk. "Everything I know about the organization—all my operatives, the initiation rites, the meeting places, the whole enchilada—it's all written down." This wasn't going to work. The Director was crazy. He wouldn't listen to reason. Lancett retreated another step. "In a notebook. Hidden in a safe place." He kept moving, one step at a time, toward the distant semicircle of light framed in the archway. "If I die, it will be opened and made public. I've arranged for that. I've arranged everything."

He stopped, ten feet from the Director, ten yards from escape. He waited, his body tensed, poised for flight.

The bum drew back, studying him. An endless moment passed, punctuated by the irregular drumbeat of the traffic overhead.

"So," he said finally, his lips pursed. "Most prudent, Lancett. I'm impressed."

Lancett expelled a breath. He relaxed a little. It had worked. He had done it. He had saved his precious ass.

"Unfortunately for you," the Director went on, "one of my personal operatives has already looked through that safe-deposit box of yours. The one with the notebook." He reached into his tattered coat. "This notebook."

Lancett swayed with sudden faintness.

He was a dead man.

His only hope was to run. Get away. Now.

He turned. He stumbled toward the distant, beckoning street. His shoes pounded on the pavement. He was halfway there when he heard the song.

At first he did not know what he was hearing or where it came from. He was conscious only of a low humming sound that seemed to rise from the pavement, the walls, the roof, surrounding him, drowning out the freeway roar. Then he understood that the Director was humming a song and the concrete structure had caught the melody and amplified it, projecting it back in echoey waves from every corner.

He felt the first crippling pain. It shot up his right leg. He collapsed, screaming.

His trouser leg swelled up like a balloon. He lay on his back, staring at it in helpless horror. How could it do that? How could it inflate like that? What the Christ was happening?

The cloth, strained to the breaking point, burst at the seams. It fell away in tatters to reveal his leg. Only—oh, shit—it was not his leg anymore. It was some kind of grotesque goiter, impossibly swollen, expanding with some hideous internal pressure. His skin was stretched taut as a condom in a cathouse. And worse still, it was . . . shifting . . . rippling slowly with the scurrying movement of something within. Lancett had seen an ant farm once. It had rippled like that.

The song went on. His stomach was bloated with a lunatic pregnancy, nine months compressed into as many seconds. His shirt and jacket came apart in a drumroll of popping buttons, exposing his naked belly, rising like yeast in an oven. His navel elongated to a vertical slit. More small, skittering bodies shimmered under his skin. They were fighting to get out. To erupt into the open. To spill out of him like candy out of a piñata.

And now—Jesus!—the flesh of his face was bulging tumorously, shifting, swelling. He could feel things growing in there, taking form and multiplying, and as their numbers grew with dizzying speed, his skin kept on stretching, rubberlike, threatening to burst.

And suddenly he knew what they were. Of course. He knew it from their squishy softness, their eellike wriggling. He knew it from the greenish-white spaghetti strands curling out of his nostrils like runners of snot. He knew it from the mush of living mucus at the back of his throat.

Maggots, the bum had said. Everything is maggots. And they eat you from the inside out.

His leg exploded in a spray of wormlike bodies, showering him.

Lancett gibbered helplessly. The things writhed on his bare flesh. Thousands more poured out of the shattered remains of his calf and thigh. They streamed over his body, parasites feeding on a fresh corpse. Only he was still alive. The song would not let him go. It held him anchored to the earth, to feel it, to feel every last moment, to the end.

Once, as a child, Frank Lancett had had a bad nightmare. In his nightmare he was buried alive. He stared into the darkness of his coffin. He hammered on the lid with his fists. And then he felt the brush of an insect on his face, then another, and another. They were all over him, seething and writhing, eating him alive, and he was screaming and screaming and screaming, until finally he woke up, wrapped in sweat-soaked bedsheets, still shivering with multiple aftershocks of panic.

In the years since, he had forgotten all about that dream, that childish fantasy. He remembered it now.

The song went on. Lancett's belly split down the middle. Clouds of steam rose from his entrails. Maggots flowed forth in a living tide. They swarmed over his bandaged genitals, seeking blood. His underwear crawled. He had an unbearable urge to scratch himself. He could not. His hands were swelling up like cartoon gloves, Mickey Mouse hands. His manicured nails shivered and popped off. Insect larvae flooded out. His fingers deflated, leaving bloody stumps.

He had some vague thought of begging for mercy. He tried. No use. His mouth was clogged. The things were spilling out of him like popcorn overflowing a frying pan. They just wouldn't quit. There were always more of the things, and still more, and more and more and more.

Fucking bastards breed faster than Sambos in Niggertown, he thought incoherently. Shit, there goes the neighborhood.

His eyelids puffed up, squeezing his eyes mercifully shut. His eardrums burst, cutting off sound. His nostrils were pinched and useless. His mouth swallowed itself. He could not breathe. His mind was spiraling away like water down a drain.

In the last moments of his life, Frank Lancett had a thought. A funny, pointless kind of thought. He remembered that chink whore who had been his first kill, the one he'd smothered in a hotel room in Frisco. And suddenly he wondered if it had felt like this for her. If she had known this terror, this helpless anticipation of the end. If she had felt this kind of all-consuming pain. If she had suffered quite this much.

It would have been going too far to say that he was sorry. He just wondered. That was all.

Then his mind was gone, overloaded by shock and terror, and when in the next moment his head burst like a bubble of chewing gum, spraying pink skin tatters in all directions, he was no longer alive to know it.

21

The old man sat in his wheelchair at the corner of Olympic and Normandie, smoking his pipe, watching the cars go by. He was there every day, come rain or shine. Nobody in Koreatown took the slightest notice of him anymore. When he had first appeared, uncounted years ago, the neighborhood kids had teased him, their high, squealing voices raised in a mixture of English and Asian epithets, but soon they had grown tired of that game. The old man had been left alone to sit and smoke and stare, just another fixture of the corner, no more deserving of attention than the traffic signal or the bus-stop bench.

But had any of the passersby paused to look closely at him today—and none did—they might have noticed something in those narrowed eyes and pursed lips, a peculiar shade of expression on the weathered, liver-spotted face, a hint of unnatural intensity, of concentration not normally found there. Today, unlike all the other days, the old man was not merely gazing with sightless eyes at the traffic streaming past. Today he was watching.

The word had gone out in midafternoon, shortly after Frank Lancett called the Director to inform him of his failure. The Director, frustrated, had ordered a citywide sweep, a procedure that had been rehearsed only twice in twenty years and which had never before been implemented.

Throughout the city and its suburbs, phones rang. Orders were given and acknowledged. The men of the Brotherhood—who had awoken to find a change in the bracelets on their wrists and had spent the better part of the day staring at the blood-red stones with a mixture of hope and fear—those men learned the story at last.

They were told to watch the crowds, cruise the streets, look everywhere for a red-haired woman in a blue-black Lamborghini Countach, a woman whose face was nearly as recognizable as her voice. And if they saw her, they were to call in their report to the central switchboard set up to handle the crisis. With luck, someone would spot her and narrow down the area in which she might be found, and then the Brotherhood would move in with its army of spies and comb the streets and alleyways till Billie Lee Kidd was caught and that famous voice was stilled once and for all.

And so the old man, who wore a red bracelet on his left wrist, watched the rush of traffic with dark, brooding, desperate eyes. And the crowds, unseeing, passed him by.

Tony Alvarez was cruising in his RX-7, checking out the beach bunnies strolling Main Street in Venice, his favorite pastime on a summer Sunday, but this time his hobby had a sharper edge to it, a nasty, bitter edge which Tony liked.

Lamborghini, he thought coolly, scanning the rows of parked cars, looking for a fine set of wheels that belonged to a lady singer of some renown.

Well, shit, she had to be somewhere.

He had been out in the hot sun for two hours now, which was good, real good, because he needed to stay active. When he was alone in his bachelor shithole down on Washington Boulevard he got nervous, looking at that bracelet, which had been winking at him all day like a bloodshot eye. He knew, not just from the bracelet but from his bones, that it had gone down, yeah, last night it had gone down real good.

Repent, he thought wryly as he passed by a strutting

muscleman with two string-bikini'd bimbos on his arms, for the end is nigh.

Tony had never been much of a swinger, despite his fancy car and his fifty-dollar suntan and the aroma of Aramis that clung to him like a second skin. Women just got turned off by him for some reason. Maybe it was the anger he carried with him, the heavy load of hostility weighing him down. Of course, their attitude only made the load that much heavier, only made him more angry and—if he were honest enough to admit it, which he wasn't—lonely too.

The Brotherhood had been his salvation. It had kept him from buying a Winchester down at the gun store on Centinela and blowing his fucking brains to egg salad. But he had never expected their crazy prophecies to come true, and when he woke up from his solitary Saturday-night drinking party to see that the Bloodstone had turned, he was scared—no, he was more than scared, he was just plain bullshit with fear.

So he had been grateful for the phone call, for the excuse to leave his apartment and cruise, just cruise, and maybe even catch himself a country queen in a blue-black—

Jesus.

His breath froze in his throat. Up ahead, gliding out of a diagonal parking space, was a Countach, as sleek as a barracuda and as darkly blue as a midnight sky.

Tony resisted the urge to accelerate, to pull around the three cars between him and his prey. He had to avoid being noticed. He squinted, trying to see if the driver was a woman, a redhead. He couldn't tell. But, shit. It had to be her. How many of those frigging hundred-thousand-dollar cars were on the road, anyway?

He motored along, breathing hard through clenched teeth. The Countach swung onto Venice Boulevard. He followed. He was now only two cars behind. The Countach turned again on Lincoln. No problem. He was right behind her now.

He wondered if she knew he was in pursuit, if she were trying to shake him off her tail. He hoped not. He hoped the stupid bitch—they were all stupid bitches, every cockteasing one—didn't even know he was there.

Six blocks farther on, the Countach eased into a curbside space by a liquor store. Tony, heart pounding, pulled to a stop three spaces past it.

He had done it. Oh, man. And there was a pay phone right here so he could call it in. Christ, he had better have a quarter.

He was digging in his pants pockets for change, glancing compulsively in the rearview mirror, when the door of the Countach swung up and the driver got out.

Tony's jaw dropped, just like in the comic strips.

"Fuck," he said aloud, his voice thick with disgust.

It was not Billie Lee Kidd. It was some old guy, pushing fifty, with a mane of gray beard and a potbelly bulging out of his Le Tigre sport shirt. He lowered the car door, then pressed his remote-control and heard the answering chirp of the burglar alarm. Satisfied, he walked up to the liquor store and was swallowed by the clanging screen door.

Tony lowered his head and nearly cried, he was so bummed out.

Women, he thought in a wave of bitter hatred. God damn, do I ever hate their guts.

Russell Garrett guided the chopper around for another pass over the Hollywood Freeway. Normally, on his day off, he liked to put his feet up, put some music on, and maybe smoke a little reefer. But today he had some business to attend to, up here in the friendly skies.

Not the usual crap of ferrying well-heeled commuters across town to beat the morning and afternoon rush. Uh-uh. He had performed that particular service for what he fervently hoped was the last time. Never again would he have to play chauffeur to a bunch of goddamn rich bastards who smiled and made polite conversation with him, like slumming aristocrats who chummed with the hired help to prove how broad-minded they were.

Russell Garrett hated the rich. He had always hated them, ever since he was a kid. He had never been poor, had in fact enjoyed a fairly comfortable middle-class upbringing; but he had never been rich, either, and never expected to be. He didn't even particularly want to be. He did not want what others had. He merely wanted them not to have it. He wanted them not to exist at all. He wanted no superiors anywhere on earth. The world as it was presently organized would not permit him this small indulgence. But a new world was coming. And those who had been nothing, thought Russell Garrett with satisfaction, would be all.

He swung down, buzzing the freeway a tad lower than FAA regulations, strictly enforced, would permit. Even so, most of the cars tended to look pretty much the same. But a Lamborghini was a standout model, with a shape distinctive enough to be identified even from an altitude of two hundred feet. He had, in fact, spotted a Lamborghini an hour ago, on the Santa Monica Freeway, but it was red, so that particular sighting was a non-starter.

He didn't see anything this time. He kept looking anyway. He might find it. Somebody had to.

For approximately the twenty-fifth time that afternoon, Walter Gelbard paused with a tray full of luncheon entrées in hand, staring out the window of the Hamburger Palace at the traffic passing by on Ventura Boulevard.

Then a soft voice, a depressingly familiar voice, buzzed in his ear. He turned to see his supervisor standing there.

"Judas Priest," Chester Dickman was saying in that lit-fuse hiss that no paying customer ever heard. "What is it with you today? You developing a window fetish or something?''

Walter shrugged. ''Just a nice day, is all.''

''Yeah. And we got a lot of real nice customers in here. That tray was headed for table twenty-nine. The food is hot. Correction. *Was* hot when it left the kitchen. What it's like now, I decline to speculate.'' A pudgy index finger jabbed Walter in the shoulder. ''So try paying attention to the clientele, will you?''

Walter swallowed his reply and his pride, as he had done so many times in so many shitty part-time jobs over the past seven years. He had come to Hollywood to be a star, because all the girls in his hometown of Ferris, West Virginia, population eight thousand, had told him that he looked like Tom Cruise. Which maybe he did, a little, but that fact hadn't seemed to impress the talent agents and casting directors, whose doors, like their faces, were habitually closed to him. To pay the rent, he did this shit, hating it not merely because it was demeaning—after all, he had a high-school diploma, for God's sake—but because it was . . . well, dammit, such a cliché.

Struggling actor works as waiter in Hollywood. I mean, you haven't heard that one before?

He hated the mundanity of it, the TV-movie awfulness of it, almost as much as he hated the work itself, all the smiling and taking orders on his little pad and being careful not to mix up the hamburger platter with the hot-dog plate. Most of all, he hated Hollywood, for denying him not just success but, as he saw it, even a fair chance. And since Hollywood was his world, his only world, he supposed he hated the world too. Which was why the prospect of a new and better world, ruled by someone very much like, say, himself, was not unappealing to him. Which was why he wore a bracelet on his left wrist and why he kept looking out the window.

He delivered the tray to table twenty-nine, and—what do you know?—he really did mix up the hamburger platter with the hot-dog plate, but he got that straightened out, and he even remembered to smile. He was on his way back to the kitchen when his gaze was again drawn to the window, this time by a jet-black aerodynamic streak. He followed it with his eyes. But no. It was only a Fiero.

"Gelbard." Dickman had materialized, pixielike, at his elbow. "I'm warning you, pal. You look out that window one more time and you're history."

Walter considered the matter. If the prophecy did come to pass, then he wouldn't need this job or any other, because all the bastards who used to order him around would be working for him. If, on the other hand, the prophecy turned out to be a crock, as he sometimes half-suspected, then he wouldn't want this job anyway. He wouldn't even want to be alive.

He threw the empty tray against the wall, drawing stares and screams from nearby customers.

"Fuck you," he said loudly, liking the sound of that, wishing he had spoken his lines with the same kind of drama at casting calls.

He left the restaurant before Chester Dickman could reply. He emerged into the furnace heat, heading—he hoped—for a better world.

All across Los Angeles and its outskirts, singly or in pairs or in tight clusters of three and four, men watched.

They sipped Perrier in sidewalk cafés in Brentwood Village. They munched hot dogs at the Tail-o'-the-Pup. They lunched on French-dipped roast beef at Philippe's. They loitered in Palisades Park in Santa Monica, under the marble gaze of an art-deco saint. They scanned the rows of white sails at Marina del Rey. They strolled down Hollywood Boulevard, with one eye on the golden stars lining the Walk of Fame, the other eye on the crowds. They patrolled the Beverly Center and the Westside Pavilion and the Sherman Oaks Galleria and the Woodland Hills Promenade and

Santa Monica Place, bustling mazes of tile and neon and glass. They drove along winding roads in the Hollywood Hills. They cruised Artesia Boulevard and Melrose Avenue and Moorpark Street. They waited at L.A. International Airport, at Avis and Dollar and Budget rent-a-car, at Union Station. They hawked maps to the stars' homes, standing on the curb at Sunset and studying each passing car. They wandered among the surfers and the volleyball players on Zuma Beach.

They were everywhere. And they were watching. Always watching.

They would find her. They would not be denied.

22

Billie had driven only half a dozen city blocks after fleeing the penthouse before she realized she had made a mistake.

The Lamborghini was drawing stares, as it always did. Even in L.A., where fancy cars were as ubiquitous as suntans, the Countach stood out from the crowd. She was enough of an exhibitionist to enjoy that kind of attention most of the time. But at the moment it was distinctly unwanted. Had she been thinking clearly, she would have taken K.C.'s Mustang as she had done before. But she could hardly double back and pick it up now. She needed new transportation and she needed it pronto.

She could buy a car, she supposed. Any dealer would accept the Countach, $135,000 retail, in exchange for the clunkers and junkers on the lot. She shook her head. No good. A maneuver like that would attract too much attention. People would talk.

She had to do it some other way. Some less legal way.

She pulled off Sunset, motored on down to Melrose, and hooked east. She scanned the rows of parked cars, thinking vaguely that she could hot-wire somebody's ignition and take off, just like in the movies. Except she had no idea whatsoever of how to hot-wire anything. She had enough difficulty finding the dipstick to check her oil.

Then, hallelujah, she saw her chance.

The car ahead of her, a dented Chevette painted dog-puke orange, put on its brakes and came to a stop, blocking traffic. The yellow flashers strobed. The driver, wearing a jacket emblazoned with the logo SPEED MESSENGER SERVICE, hopped out. He left the car double-parked, engine running, and vanished into an art-supplies store to make a pickup or delivery.

Billie said a silent thank-you to whatever gods there be.

She pulled onto a side street, parked at a red curb, and pocketed her keys. She abandoned the Countach with only a brief wistful backward glance. A moment later she was behind the wheel of the Chevette. She hit the gas. The car shot forward, leaving its rightful owner behind.

Mission accomplished.

Now there was another problem to take care of.

She drove till she found a supermarket, took a deep breath, and went inside.

It was a calculated risk. Somebody, like that girl in Westwood, might see her, ask for an autograph, draw a crowd. Fortunately the place was nearly empty. It was too damned hot, she figured, to go grocery-shopping in the middle of a Sunday afternoon.

She found the pharmacy section and scanned the shelves. She grabbed a bottle of hair-coloring gel, a bronzing lotion, and a pair of kitchen shears. On the way to the checkout she passed a carousel loaded with sunglasses. She took a pair. She waited nervously in the express lane, her face buried in a copy of the *National Enquirer*. The checker passed the handful of items over the price-code scanner without looking up. Billie paid in cash. She left the store, her heart thumping.

She looked around the outdoor mall and spied a fast-food place. She entered, the grocery bag tucked under one arm. The aroma of barbecued chicken rose in hot, greasy waves over the blare of salsa music. It made her hungry. She had eaten nothing all day except a few forkfuls of her breakfast with Drake. Well, to hell with it. She would eat later. Right now she had a make-over to do.

She found the rest room. She closed and locked the door, then plopped the bag down on the counter. She tugged off her bloodied corduroy pants and cut them down to shorts. Next she smeared the bronzing lotion over her face, arms, and legs. Then the scissors went to work on her hair, followed by the hair-coloring gel. As a final touch, she pushed the sunglasses up on the bridge of her nose. She studied her reflection in the mirror over the sink.

Jesus, she thought, mildly astonished by the total effect. Who is this lady?

Her hair, once red, was dyed to a rich mahogany, cut short in a Dutch-boy style, marred by traces of punk in the spots where her hand had slipped. Her skin was olive, almost Hispanic in tone. Her freckles, companions since childhood, were gone. Even her telltale green eyes were concealed behind the shades.

She was certain that she could not be identified now, even by the most devoted autograph-seeker. She dumped the miscellaneous articles back in the bag, along with clumps of cut hair and the remnants of her trouser legs, and stuffed the whole mess in the garbage can.

Then, because you always should when you've got the chance, she used the toilet.

Her duty done, she left the rest room, looking

around warily to see if anybody noticed the transformation. Nobody did. Nobody seemed to be paying her the slightest attention. Which was just the way she liked it, thank you very much.

Okay, she thought as she pulled out of the lot, now I'm officially in disguise.

The next step was to get the hell out of town.

She pulled onto the Hollywood Freeway, southbound, and sped through the downtown area to Route 10. She headed east. Her plan was unchanged from three hours ago. She would drive as far as possible, find some two-bit motel in some two-bit town, and hide out.

The thought of going back to the police had crossed her mind only briefly. She knew that K.C. and Gary would not back up her story. They had probably already disposed of Bobby Joe's remains and returned the apartment to normal. She would be left with another Case of the Vanishing Corpse. No, thanks.

She wondered, for approximately the billionth time, what the hell had been done to the three guys. "You played with my head," Bobby Joe had told the man named Lancett. And Lancett had responded by humming a tune. Why would he do that? And why had it frightened her so much? What had she almost remembered in that moment?

She shook her head. She didn't know. She turned on the AM radio to drown out her thoughts. Lyle Lovett was singing cheerfully about death in L.A. County. She couldn't stand it. She switched to the all-news station. Heddy Lynne Hertes was reporting on a fire in Compton. Rhonda Kramer provided a traffic update. Then, at four o'clock, as she passed West Covina's city limits, the hour's top story came on. An all-points bulletin had been issued for famed country-western singer—

She hit the brakes and skidded onto the shoulder. She slammed to a halt. She hugged the steering wheel. She listened.

". . . reported hearing screams from a penthouse apartment. Police found three men later identified as members of Billie Lee Kidd's backup band. All three were declared dead at the scene. . . ."

"No," she said, very simply. "Oh, no."

Lancett, she thought as her mind reeled under numbing waves of shock. He killed them. Because they knew too much. Or maybe just for the hell of it. Oh, Gary. K.C. I'm sorry. It was all my fault. Sort of. I'm so sorry, guys.

She was crying.

". . . witness saw a woman resembling Billie Lee Kidd run out of the building and speed off in a navy-blue or black Lamborghini Countach. The singer's own car matches this description. . . ."

She wiped her eyes dry. She had to get hold of herself. She was wanted for murder. For three murders. She was in worse trouble than before. If that was possible.

". . . has learned that Kidd created an incident at the Malibu Police Department early this morning, when she reported a dead body in her home. Officers dispatched to the scene found no evidence of wrongdoing. There is speculation that the attempt on Kidd's life at a concert last night may have triggered a delayed shock reaction. . . ."

She snapped the radio off. She lowered her head.

After a minute, she put the Chevette in gear and drove on. She took the first exit, then got back on Route 10, heading west. Back into L.A.

She couldn't run away. She couldn't hide in a motel. Not with the police looking for her, not with this story leading every TV and radio newscast in the country and making headlines tomorrow from coast to coast. No matter where she went, no matter how greatly she altered her appearance, she would be recognized eventually, caught, taken into custody, transferred back to L.A. by paddy wagon, and then . . . then . . .

She would be locked up in a cell, surrounded by cops and criminals, any of whom could be one of *them*.

Christ. She exhaled a long shuddering breath. What the hell do I do now?

23

It was after five o'clock when a bright orange Chevette pulled off Tigertail Road and came to a stop before the gated entrance to Harve Medlow's home in Brentwood Park.

Billie cranked down the driver's-side window and pressed a button on the intercom. She waited for what seemed like an endless stretch of time. No answer.

Oh, please, Harve. It's Sunday. You've got to be home.

Sometime during the long drive back into town she had decided to seek help here. She couldn't quite say why, except that it seemed like the right thing to do. Harve had brains and connections and street smarts, and all those things could be useful to her now. But even more than that, he had a shoulder she could cry on. That was what she was really looking for, she figured.

After all, he had nearly shed a few tears himself on the phone this morning. He had told her that she was more than just a client to him. She was, he said, a friend. Well, dammit, this was just the sort of thing that friends were made for. At least, she hoped it was.

The intercom crackled to life, breaking into her thoughts.

"Yes," said a shaky voice. Harve's voice.

She took a breath. She tried to speak. No words came out. Suddenly she was afraid. What if he believed the news reports? What if he thought she'd really done it? He wouldn't let her in. Instead he'd call 911. Cop cars would descend on this neighborhood like horseflies on a meadow muffin. She could never get away in time. She would be finished.

"Hello," said Harve. "Who is it?"

She forced herself to answer. She had to take the risk. She had no choice.

"Harve. It's me. It's Billie."

Silence.

Her nails dug into the steering wheel. The engine throbbed, vibrating through her. Her heart pulsed in answer.

Please let me in, she begged silently. Please. Please. Please.

Slowly the wrought-iron gates parted, swinging open with a whir of gears. She stared at them, unmoving, as if afraid to believe she could really go through.

"Well, hell," squawked the intercom, "what are you waiting for?"

The curving driveway led to a one-story Spanish Colonial. Lilies, marigolds, and white roses bloomed in the central garden of the colonnaded courtyard. Birds flitted from the marble fountain, unused for years, to the vines trained along the stucco walls. An elm spread its branches over the red tile roof, brilliant in the late-afternoon sun.

Billie pulled up to the archway framing the entrance. She parked alongside Harve's gleaming Mercedes sedan, killed the Chevette's engine, and got out. She was still trying to decide what to say when the front door opened and Harve Medlow appeared.

The news must have hit him hard. He looked as if he had aged twenty years in as many minutes. He had never been a particularly attractive man—middle-aged, overweight, with a round, flushed face and thinning hair, badly dyed—but now he resembled a walking corpse, and like a corpse he was decked out in his

Sunday best, a pin-striped Giorgio Armani sport jacket and open-collared shirt. She had time to think that he must not have bothered to change after his flight from New York this morning. Too much had been happening, she guessed. Too much for both of them.

He stared at her, blinking. She remembered her disguise.

"Harve," she said with what was almost a smile, "it really is me."

"Billie. Jesus. What the hell . . . ?"

"It's my new look." She shrugged. She took a breath. "Harve. You've got to believe me. I didn't kill anybody. I swear. And I'm not crazy, either."

"Hey." He seemed surprised, almost embarrassed. "I know that."

"Do you?"

"Of course." He closed the distance between them. He touched her cheek. His hand, she noticed, was trembling. "Take it easy, Rockabillie."

She sniffed back a tear. "You haven't called me that in a long time."

"Too long." He lowered his eyes. "I know you're innocent. You don't have to prove anything to me."

She tried to answer. She could not find her voice. She was shaking. Abruptly tears were rippling down her face in bright rainwater streaks. She threw her arms around him and buried her face in his chest. He embraced her awkwardly and rocked her back and forth on her heels while she cried herself out.

"Damn," she said finally. "I'm sorry."

"It's okay. It's okay."

She lifted her head to look at him. "I'm so . . . so damn grateful to you. For this. For everything."

He pulled away self-consciously. "Don't say that," he whispered.

"Why the hell not? It's true. You're the only friend I've got left." She took his hand. "Thank you."

"Please, Billie."

"I guess you're just not too good with sentiment,"

she said, patting his hand, stroking the knuckles tenderly. "Well, that's okay. I normally don't . . . don't . . ."

Her words trailed off. She hitched in a breath. She stared down at Harve Medlow's hand . . . his hand . . . oh, my God . . . his *hand* . . .

Suddenly she was back on the terrace of a restaurant in Westwood in the morning sun. Staring at a bracelet worn by a man named Drake. A bracelet with a blood-red stone. She had thought it looked familiar. She had been almost sure she'd seen it somewhere before.

"We all wear one," Drake had said, his voice low and mysterious. "The stone was blue until last night. Then it turned. That was the confirmation. All around the world, at that precise moment, the Bloodstones turned."

"Bloodstone," she whispered now, gazing in detached horror at Harve's left wrist, at the bracelet he had worn ever since she'd known him, just an ordinary bracelet with a fine metal chain and a blue stone.

Only now the stone was red.

Harve drew back slowly. Billie raised her eyes to his. He held her gaze.

"How could you know about that?" he breathed.

"So it's true?"

He swallowed. He did not answer.

"Harve. What the hell's going on?"

"If you know about the stone," he said slowly, "then you must have a pretty damn good idea."

"I don't have any damn good ideas about anything." She took a breath. "You . . . you're one of them?"

He shut his eyes briefly in a way that signaled assent.

"Did you . . . ? Oh, God, did you know they were trying to kill me?"

"Ever since this morning. When I got back to

town." He hesitated, looking away. "Why do you think I called you?"

"Jesus."

She stared at him, numbed by shock. Her voice was a lifeless monotone.

"You called just to track me down?"

"Yes."

"Then you told them where I was?"

"I had to."

"And they did something to Bobby Joe and Gary and K.C.?"

"Apparently."

"You were ready to let them kill me. Kill all of us. Just like that?"

"Goddammit, Billie." His voice was strangled. She remembered how he had sounded on the phone. "I didn't want it to be you. But it was. So I had to." He forced himself to look at her. "I . . . I still have to."

She caught her breath. Her heart was a slab of ice freezing her rib cage.

A beat of time passed. On the road outside, a car hummed past. Somewhere a bird was singing.

Abruptly she turned. "All right. I've had enough of this shit. I'm going to turn myself in and take my chances. And, mister, you can't stop me."

She was halfway to the car, walking briskly, struggling not to look back, hoping she could bluff it out—come on, Rockabillie, just a few more steps—when a hand closed over her arm and suddenly the ground spun out from under her and she went flying headfirst into the pavement.

She landed in a tangle of limbs. She looked up at Harve Medlow, standing in semisilhouette against a cloudless sweep of sky. He reached into his jacket.

His hand was almost steady as he aimed the gun at her.

24

The house was a study in parquet, wicker, and glittering crystal. Sunbeams slanted through the wide windows looking out on vine-wrapped columns. Billie remembered Harve telling her how meticulously his wife had decorated the place. He had changed nothing in the ten years since becoming a widower.

The door swung shut behind him. Billie stood in the middle of the living room, her eyes on the gun in Harve's hand. She moistened her mouth and tried her best not to sound afraid.

"So what happens now? Do I get a blindfold and a cigarette? Maybe a last request?"

"Don't joke about it, Billie."

"That's what you said this morning, on the phone. Only then you were all choked up."

"Just shut the hell up, will you?"

"It was a pretty good act. I even believed you. That's why I came here."

His mouth twisted in a snarl and she stiffened with the sudden certainty that he was going to squeeze the trigger and blow her away right now. Then, in the next second, all the anger seemed to hiss out of him like air escaping from a punctured balloon. His face was suddenly empty, his voice low and faraway.

"It wasn't an act. I didn't want to do it. I had no choice."

"Didn't you have a choice about joining this loony-tunes outfit in the first place?"

"It was right after Celia died," he said softly, contemplatively, as if there were no gun trained on her, as if the two of them were simply old friends sharing a quiet reminiscence on a summer afternoon. "I was all alone. And scared. Not of her death. Of mine. Suddenly it was real to me. I thought about my bank accounts and my deals and this house, everything I had, and none of it could save me. Then they came. They offered me a chance to live forever." He looked at her, his eyes dark and pleading. "Never to die. Never to face that darkness out there that's always waiting. Have you seen that darkness, Billie? Have you felt it?"

"Yes," she breathed, unable to say otherwise.

He shook his head. "I don't think so. You're too young. Too innocent. Doesn't it sound crazy—calling a born hell-raiser like you innocent? You are, though, in some funny way I can't quite figure. And I'm not. I'm getting old, Billie. Old and scared. I'm afraid of the dark, the night. You ever see how an old hound dog cringes under the sofa during a thunderstorm? I'm like that now. As you get older, death starts to feel so close. Oh, hell, you don't know what I'm talking about."

"Let me go, Harve," she whispered.

"Dammit. I can't."

"You won't."

"You haven't heard a thing I've said."

"I heard it. But you're wrong. I'm not so innocent. And I'm old enough to be afraid of the dark." She sighed. "Only, I'm still fighting it. You gave in. You surrendered."

He shrugged heavily. "Maybe I did." His voice hardened. "But it looks like I made the right choice, doesn't it?"

He raised the gun a few inches, targeting her chest. She stared into the small black hole of the muzzle, a hole no bigger than a coin, yet large enough to swallow her up in its lightless emptiness. She thought of the abyss. It was here. She sensed it. It was huddled in some dark corner of this room. Waiting, watching, enjoying the show. When Harve Medlow pumped six rounds into her heart, there would be a witness. But not to worry, Harve. This witness would never talk.

"You can't shoot me," she said softly, desperately. "You've never killed anybody in your life."

"There's a first time for everything." He steadied his shaking hand. "I'm sorry, Billie."

"Harve," she said quietly, desperately, "you can't do it without at least telling me why. What's going on here? What's it all mean? Why me?" She forced a smile. "Inquiring minds want to know."

"It won't work, Billie. Playing for time."

"Dammit, it's my life!" She hitched in a breath. "Please, Harve. Please."

He hesitated. He lowered the gun a half-inch.

"You must already know some of it."

She swallowed. "I know a little," she said carefully, picking each word like a precious flower, fragile to the touch. "But what I know . . . it doesn't make any sense."

"Don't be so sure."

"You're asking me to believe there are some kind of ancient gods who want to take over the world? And their whole plan depends on me? And this song?" She shook her head. "Come on, Harve. We're two moderately intelligent grown-ups. This is comic-book stuff."

"I wish it was. They exist, Billie. I've felt their presence. Their ageless energy. They aren't like anything on this earth. They're things from some other plane of existence. And they have such power. Such utter contempt for life."

"If they're so powerful, what do they need me for?"

"There are other gods," he whispered. "They have power too. There is a balance, a precarious balance, between them. Like the balance between dark and light, night and day. All of mankind's oldest myths reflect their constant warfare, their struggle for supremacy."

"Good versus evil. Just like in the movies."

"You got it."

"And you chose evil?"

"I chose the winning side." He smiled. A bitter smile, drawn in lines of contempt and weary self-hate. She had never seen him smile like that before.

"And," she prodded, "these two sides are at war? Is that it? With the human race caught in the middle?"

"Not exactly. The war was fought four thousand years ago. The battleground was Antarok. You've heard of it?"

She nodded.

"A war of the gods. And when the final battle was done, Antarok was in ruins. The gods of Antarok and their enemies had fought each other to a standstill. Neither side would concede victory to the other. But both sides knew that the war could not go on. They were too evenly matched.

"So there was an armistice. An agreement. And out of that agreement came the prophecies, revealed to the high priest, Kuruk. Prophecies of what must come to pass before the final battle between what you call good and evil would take place. A battle to be decided by human action, with human casualties. And with the universe itself as the prize.

"In the meantime, the dark gods, Ragnaaroth and his legions, retreated into another world and were sealed behind the Door. And they waited. Waited with inhuman patience. Waited for the moment when the last of the prophecies would be fulfilled and they would return."

"And then, last night, I came along and sang the golden oldie everybody's been waiting to hear?"

"That's about the size of it."

"Well, shit. Why me?"

"You were chosen by the gods we're fighting. I don't know why." He shrugged. "Whatever the reason, they wanted you, Rockabillie. You should feel honored."

She closed her eyes. Under other circumstances she

might have burst out laughing. But it was bad form to laugh at funerals. Especially your own.

"Harve. You remember, last year, when that little junior college in Busted Elbow, Arkansas, or wherever the hell it was, handed me an honorary sheepskin? Then I felt honored. Right now, all I feel is scared. And pissed off in a really major way. I mean, according to you, the fate of the universe was riding on this nag. And she didn't even make it down the stretch."

"Don't take it too hard. The odds were never in your favor. There are thousands of us and only one of you. And, of course, we have the songs."

Her eyes flicked open. She stared at him, feeling the first hint of hope, stirred inexplicably by that word.

"Songs?" she whispered.

"You mean you don't know about that either?"

"Enlighten me."

"That's our power. The songs. Sacred songs, revealed to the high priests of Antarok centuries ago. Preserved, handed down, kept alive by the Brotherhood. We can kill with song. Kill or wound or inflict pain."

"I've heard some garage bands that were pretty painful."

He managed a smile. "It's not quite the same thing, Rockabillie. Our songs are like voodoo spells. They can alter reality, twist the mind. I figure something like that must have been used on Bobby Joe and the other guys. They tried to kill you, right? And you got away?"

"How'd you know?"

"It's the only way I could make sense out of the news reports. There's a song that hypnotizes people, makes them to do anything they're told. That's what got into the guys. They never really wanted to hurt you, Billie. They didn't know what they were doing."

"Too bad I can't say the same about you." A low blow, but what the hell. She would take what she could get. Anything to keep his mind off that gun and keep him talking. She had to keep him talking. Because she was onto something here. She didn't know what. But the things he was saying seemed to connect with some half-glimpsed memory at the back of her mind and point the way to a plan. A chance. "So what other songs are there? Any with commercial potential?"

He tried to chuckle. It came out like a dry cough. "Not too many possibilities for airplay, I'm afraid. There are some that put the victim in a trance. He comes to and doesn't remember a thing. Or he remembers what you want him to."

She thought of Chet, slumped in his chair in the gatehouse. The memory she was seeking almost came into reach, then receded again.

"There are songs that make your skin flake off like dandruff. Turn your bones to marshmallow. Burst your heart like a water balloon."

"How sweet." She had to keep him talking. "Care to hum a few bars?"

"I don't know any of those. If I did, I guess I wouldn't need a gun. The deadly songs are reserved for the higher-ups."

Her palms were wet. Her heart was racing. She forced herself to stay outwardly calm. She almost had it. Almost remembered. Almost understood.

"Well, are there any you do know?"

"Sure." He was bragging now, pleased at the opportunity to share his secret knowledge, kept to himself for too long. "There's one that acts like an aphrodisiac. Care to hear it?"

"Talk about a fate worse than death." Come on, Harve. I'm almost there. Almost there.

"There's one that can poison you and another that cleans poison out of your system, just like that." He snapped his fingers. "Guess you could have used that one when you got snakebit, huh?"

"I don't remember telling you that story." She was close now. So damn close. "Tell me more."

"There's a song for inflicting blindness, another for insanity. And there's one that induces suicide . . ."

Bingo.

He was still talking. She no longer heard him. She was lost in thought, replaying a mental tape that had been lost to her conscious mind until now.

The bathroom mirror, smashed to glittering shards. The senseless, mindless urge to take her own life. And all because of a phone call in the middle of the night. And a mystery voice, humming a tune. A song.

"Christ," she hissed. "Jesus H. Christ."

Harve's eyes narrowed.

"Billie? Hey. Billie."

She still did not hear him.

They had tried to kill her with a song. And it had nearly worked. If her willpower hadn't been quite so strong—if she hadn't seen her reflection in the glass—she might have gone through with it. Wasted herself, to the disappointment of her many fans.

For the first time, she began to be afraid, really afraid, not afraid of death, not afraid of some bunch of crazies with a psychotic fixation on her. No. Afraid that Drake had been right. That there really was a Door and she had opened it. Because if this much was true, then maybe the rest was too. Maybe . . .

She pushed the questions out of her mind, replaced by another, far more urgent thought. A life-and-death kind of thought.

The song had worked.

And it could work again.

She remembered every note. And she was a singer. She even had a Grammy to prove it.

Softly, with quiet intensity, she began to hum.

The song was easy. Only four notes, endlessly repeated in a haunting melody. It was a sad song. No, more than sad. A song that spoke of lost love, hopeless longing, and the endless loneliness of life.

Harve listened. For a moment he was too stunned

to react. Then slowly he lowered his head to stare at the gun in his hand. He touched the barrel. Stroked its glossy smoothness. Like a boy feeling himself for the first time. He was intrigued. Fascinated.

In the next moment he blinked, coming partly out of it. He raised his head, fighting visibly for control.

"It . . . it's no use, Billie." The words were broken up, like beats of a radio voice punctuated by static. His lips quivered, spastic with the effort of forming articulate sounds. "You . . . you can't make it work."

She did not reply. She kept on humming. Her fingertips tingled with electric tension. Her body was taut with the unnatural stillness of summer air before a storm. She had never felt this way before. Wrong. She had felt it once. Last night. When she sang the Deathsong.

Because I did sing it, she told herself.

She could no longer pretend otherwise.

Harve licked his lips. His face was pale. "You . . . you can't do this," he stuttered. "You're not trained. Didn't go through . . . the initiation rites. Didn't . . ." The gun writhed in his hand like a living thing. "Just singing . . . it's not enough." He made a last desperate attempt to convince her, or perhaps himself. "You need . . . to have . . . the power."

But I do, she thought with a blinding rush of clarity.

She had the power. She'd always had it. The power to see that looming abyss where others could see only air. To sense its presence. And to fight it. To fight and win.

Then she was singing. She did not know the words to the song, if it had words. She sang them anyway. She found the words, just as she had found the words to the Deathsong. Ancient words of a dead language. The language of lost Antarok.

"No," Harve said as his hands fought to turn the gun on him against his will. "No. Jesus. Stop."

She did not stop. She could feel that power surging through her like electric current, energizing her, turn-

ing each breathless trill of her voice to a red-hot needle stabbing at Harve Medlow's brain.

The gun jerked like a dowser's rod seeking blood.
He fought it with the last of his power of self-control.
Part of him was yielding to the song. Another part still
resisted. His body was at war with itself. He twitched
and shuddered, a puppet on snarled strings. He was
screaming.

"Stop!"

She was on a lighted stage, singing into a microphone, her voice at full strength. She breathed in
through her mouth and felt her diaphragm expand like
a bellows with the rush of air, and she transformed
that air into clean, pure notes that rushed out in a fury
of sound.

The gun, clutched in two shaking hands that had
turned traitor to their owner, inched toward Harve's
sweat-slick face. He stared at it in helpless terror. He
shouted to be heard above the violence of the song.

"Goddammit. You bitch! You fucking *bitch!"*

Her voice resonated in the room. The sheet of glass
framing an Ellenshaw seascape burst into spiderweb
cracks. A chandelier swayed pendulously. The pages
of the Sunday *Times,* lying discarded on a table, flut-
tered with a sudden breeze.

"Please," said Harve as his hands pressed the muzzle of the gun to his forehead. "Please don't make me.
Don't make me."

Her voice rose to a crescendo. Windows exploded
in rapid-fire sequence. Glass shards rang like cymbals.
Tables teetered, then tipped over. A potted rhododen-
dron withered to brown dust. Distant dogs bayed like
choruses of wolves.

She was on fire. She felt it. She was alive with an
energy transcending her own. She had been chosen for
a purpose. Chosen to tap this inner strength she had
never fully suspected. It was her mission. Her destiny.
She could not deny it. She could not escape it. Not

now. Not ever. She believed. She believed. She believed.

She did have power. Such power.

Harve moaned, a low animal sound. He stood frozen, unable to move, staring into space, his eyes unfocused and bright with panic. Slowly his index finger tightened on the trigger.

"The dark," he whispered, half-coherently. "I'm afraid, Billie. I'm afraid of the dark."

In the next instant the back of his skull disappeared in a thunderclap of blood and gray matter.

He swayed. The gun slipped out of his hand and clattered on the floor. He stood there for a moment longer, his eyes and mouth open wide, as if in mute astonishment at the fact of his own nonexistence, and then his knees buckled and he folded up in a boneless heap.

She stopped singing. The last echoes of the song died away in ululating waves.

She stared at the remains of Harve Medlow, crumpled on the parquet squares like a toppled figure on a chessboard. She lowered her head. She felt the waves of power still rushing through her body, the tingling of her nerve endings, the racing drumbeat of her heart. She had never been so alive.

She closed her eyes. She made a vow.

They had seduced Harve with their dark siren songs—Harve, who had been, whatever his transgressions, her mentor and friend. They had bewitched Bobby Joe and Gary and K.C., turned them against their better natures, programmed them to kill and to be killed. They had murdered a young man in her bed, a man whose name she would never know. They had tried to kill her by every means at their disposal, and they would keep on trying. And all of it because they sought a new world, a world that would be a photo-negative of this one, where darkness would swallow light, where death would reign over life.

You can stop them, Drake had told her. You—and only you.

She had the power.

She would not fail.

25

He sat in the window seat, gazing without interest at the control tower of Los Angeles International Airport as the DC-10 taxied toward its destination gate.

Things had been moving very fast since the moment, nearly eighteen hours ago, when the blue stone in his bracelet had turned a brilliant red. Shortly afterward had come the phone call from his aide-de-camp in this city, the man known to his underlings as the Director. And he had learned all that he needed to know.

He had booked a first-class seat on the next available flight. His housekeeper, one of the deaf-mutes he preferred, gave him an inquiring glance. She was an attractive olive-skinned woman, her black hair tied in a bun, her small breasts poking at the thin cloth of her shirt. He had grown almost fond of her in the twenty years she had served him in the kitchen and in bed. He was almost sorry to have to kill her. But she would be of no further use to him now. He sang a lilting song. Her eyes rolled up in their sockets. She walked obediently into the garden, down the steps of the swimming pool, and kept on walking till the water rose over her head.

He left the house forever without looking back. He had no feminine sentimentality about the place, or about any of the places he had lived. He had spent time all over the world. He felt at home everywhere and nowhere. The island of Sri Lanka had been pleasant enough, but it was merely one more way station on a road to a distant goal. A goal which was, at last, within reach.

The plane took off on time but encountered headwinds over the Pacific. The turbulence was bad. An amusing thought occurred to him as cocktails flew across the cabin and the other passengers moaned and gripped their armrests and said their useless prayers. After all his years of waiting, he might die in a plane crash en route to his destiny. He dismissed the idea. He was not, despite everything, a superstitious man.

The plane survived the rough weather. The passengers recovered such wits as they possessed. Things returned to normal. Except for the child. An infant in its mother's arms, alarmed by the disturbance, squalling fitfully. He endured the bedlam till his patience was exhausted. Then he got up, feigning an interest in the rest room, and as he passed the child he sang a song in that high-pitched timbre that only children, with their sensitive ears, could detect. The child gazed up at him with round, frightened, helpless eyes. It stopped breathing. Its pudgy face turned blue. Its tongue swelled out of its gaping mouth. The best efforts of the mother, the flight crew, and an earnest passenger who knew CPR failed to revive it. The mother, of course, was hysterical with grief. They always were.

He settled back in his seat, shut his eyes, and listened with pleasure to her sobs.

A short time later he made a discovery. Flipping through the in-flight magazine, he came upon an article about a country-western singer named Billie Lee Kidd.

He stared at her photograph, printed in full color on the glossy page. She looked very young, almost childlike. But her eyes were not a child's eyes. They burned with green fire.

He studied the picture for a long time, memorizing

every detail. This was his enemy, his last obstacle. The only person or thing on earth still standing in his path. Unless, he thought hopefully, she was already dead.

He had spent the rest of the flight thinking of Billie Lee Kidd, contemplating her as a lover might contemplate his love.

Now he waited with unaccustomed patience as the female passenger and her dead child were helped off the plane. After a decent interval, he and the others disembarked also. He strode through the main concourse of the airport to an endless moving sidewalk which carried him to the exits. He had no luggage to pick up. He disdained suitcases. He had wandered far, and never had he required more than the clothes on his back.

A limousine was waiting at the curb. The driver nodded curtly, then opened the rear door.

"Greetings, my brother," said the man, stammering a little, as they often did in his presence.

"May you hear the song," he answered in his rumbling baritone, his voice clipped with an unknown dialect.

The limousine whisked him away from the airport.

"Have there been any developments?" he asked the driver.

"One of our operatives found the woman's car," said the man, speaking too quickly, the words tumbling out in a breathless rush. "Abandoned. We towed it to the house and searched it for clues. There was nothing."

"And the woman herself?"

"She still eludes us."

He slid up the glass partition, forgoing further talk. He watched the scenery glide by.

He had not been to this part of the United States in years. Los Angeles had changed a great deal. He remembered it as little better than a small town, a spread of dirt roads, steaming shacks, and palm trees wilting

in the desert heat. The heat, of course, was unchanged. It lay over the land as thick and stifling as a
wool blanket on a summer night. He liked it. He had
always liked the desert, the alien harshness of it, the
grim monuments of weathered stone rearing against
the brittle sky.

He caught a whiff of sea breeze as the car shot up
the San Diego Freeway. He wrinkled his nose in dis-
taste. The sea was soft, like a woman. It had none of
the desert's stoic purity, its hard, masculine indifference. The sea, he thought, cajoled. The desert merely
scorned.

The car left the freeway and melted into the stream
of traffic choking Wilshire Boulevard. It passed a
crowd of people demonstrating in front of a government building. Hand-lettered placards proclaimed
the protesters' opposition to the African dictator Usu
Ndamos.

He smiled, a dark, secret smile, thinking of that.

The car traveled on. It reached Hollywood. The giant sign spelling out the city's name hung over a blight
of pornographic movie theaters and hustling street
people like a memory of past glories.

The driver headed north. The car climbed the smog-
wreathed hills to Mulholland Drive, the ribbon of road
on the spine of the Santa Monica Mountains, and
pulled at last into a gated driveway, where armed
guards materialized out of the surrounding trees, in-
spected the car and driver, then hastily let it through.
The car pulled down the curving drive, and the mansion swam slowly into view.

It was one of many great old houses in the Hollywood Hills, a French Colonial palace put up when the
city was young, when groves of Valencia orange trees
and fields of lima beans stood where Hollywood and
Beverly Hills could now be found. It had been a place
of luxury once, of dancers twirling on the marble floor
of the grand ballroom, of giddy revelers splashing in
the moonlit swimming pool, of elaborate topiaries and

manicured lawns. But for many years the ballroom had been silent, the pool drained and empty, the once-proud grounds untended, the house crumbling in disrepair. It had been put on the market a dozen years ago for the value of the real estate it sat on. The Brotherhood had purchased it. It was of use to them.

No attempt had been made to restore the faded grandeur of the house. Beauty and luxury were matters of indifference to the men serving his cause. The house had been wired for electricity, but the wiring was shot. Very well, candles and torches would do. The walls were rotting; flakes of plaster fell from the ceiling; rats could be heard scurrying under the floorboards. No matter. Nearly every window had been shattered long ago by vandals who had crept inside to loot the place and scrawl obscene graffiti on the walls. Well, let the dust-dry Santa Ana winds gust through the hundred empty rooms and corridors, let the walls be littered with filth. The Brotherhood had endured far worse hardships and had been strengthened by them.

The car eased to a stop outside the front steps.

He got out at once, then stopped, observing a blue-black sports car parked under the fronds of a royal palm at the side of the house. The woman's automobile, he gathered. He approached it. He ran his fingers over the smooth steel. He studied the car as he had studied the photograph in the magazine, as if seeking some clue, some insight hidden there. He found none. He turned away with a shrug and mounted the steps to the front door of the house.

He entered the foyer, glancing up at the chandeliers veiled in cobwebs, noting the word FUCK scribbled in huge, contorted letters across faded wallpaper in which the designs of columbine and ivy were still faintly visible. The house stank. Vaguely he recalled reading in one of the Director's monthly reports that the toilets did not work. The men who worked here often emptied their bowels by squatting in hall closets. Yellowed newspapers, candy-bar wrappings, and fast-food containers covered the floor like scum on the surface of a pond. He kicked the stuff aside.

"Sir."

He turned.

The driver stood in the doorway, nervously shifting his weight. "The study has been prepared for you."

"Take me there."

The man led him down a maze of corridors lit with shafts of sun. They entered the vast ballroom, ringed with six massive carvings in dolomite and oolitic limestone, ranging in height from ten feet to thirty. They glared down from their pedestals, malevolent as gargoyles, but inexpressibly more ancient—artifacts salvaged, he knew, from the subterranean tombs that were all that remained of Antarok. Many statues had been unearthed there in secret excavations, then transported to the far corners of the world to decorate meeting halls like this one.

He paused in the middle of the room, under a crystal chandelier, and swept his eyes over the statues, taking in each one in turn.

Bethshul, the Screaming Woman. A hideously twisted female figure, all bulging eyes and twisted mouth, the physical form of a shriek of deathly terror.

Toth, the Wind That Hungers. A limbless confusion of shapes, formless as a breeze, rising out of a litter of human skulls.

Dasharoom, He Who Eats Souls. An octopuslike mass, all lamprey suckers and leech mouths.

Garnarlit, the Stealer of Light. Bat wings and scimitar fangs.

Narantos, the Hidden One. Humpbacked, ferret-eyed, crouching down on goat legs and grinning mirthlessly.

And at the far end of the room, looming over them all, the Spider King, Ragnaaroth. It rose to the high ceiling, a monument in unglazed marble, exquisitely carved, grotesque, beautiful. It was caught in an impossible pose, standing erect on its two rear legs, with the other six multijointed legs and the twin feelers extending into space in what might have been an imperious gesture of command. There was a suggestion of hair on the bulbous abdominal sac, a hint of malignance in the eight glassy eyes, and a promise of poison on the knifelike fangs.

He knew the Spider King well, as he knew them all and dozens more like them, gods of suffering and torment, of grief and guilt, of death and loss, all the dark gods of Ragnaaroth's legions.

The gods which soon would claim their ultimate prize.

Below the pedestal of the Spider King, a dozen men were erecting a wooden dais. His pulpit for the services tonight.

"Have our brothers been called?" he asked the driver.

"The calls are being made now," the man answered with pathetic eagerness. "Every man within a hundred miles."

They left the ballroom. A few doors down the hall, they found the study. It was a large room, hastily furnished and repaired. An easy chair, a sofa, and a desk gave the room at least the illusion of habitability.

"Will there be anything else?" asked the driver.

"Leave me." His voice was bored.

The man departed hastily.

He surveyed the room, satisfied. It was merely one more way station, but it had, to him, a special quality, because it was the last. The final stop on a very long journey. A journey which would be assured of a successful conclusion, once he had eliminated this singer with the ridiculous name of Billie Lee Kidd.

He pursed his lips, faintly annoyed. He stroked the black ropes of beard framing his high cheekbones. His hand moved, as it often did when he was lost in thought, to the jagged white scar bisecting the left side of his face from eyelid to mouth.

A woman. It seemed somehow unfair to have been

provided with an adversary so patently unworthy. He would have preferred a more even match, a greater challenge.

He moved his huge shoulders. It was not his place to engage in such baseless speculations. Not his place, nor his purpose. His only purpose was to see the woman dead. He would not fail.

He had waited four thousand years for this day. He had fulfilled every vow he had made in a farmhouse in ancient Sumer as he gazed down at a tablet inscribed with prophecies.

In just a few more hours his long wait would be over. He and the gods he served would achieve their final victory. And his faithful ones, the humble, smiling, genuflecting fools like the man who had chauffeured him here, would receive their final reward.

Kuruk smiled.

26

The sun had arced lower in the sky and the hand of his wristwatch had just touched six o'clock, when Martin Drake returned to his house in Topanga Canyon.

It was a small, one-story bungalow set well back from the road, squatting on the parched hillside. He had bought the place five years ago. He had told himself that it was a good deal, a fixer-upper to be had for cheap, convenient to the Malibu precinct, and that he liked the privacy it offered. But he had known he had a deeper reason than that. There was something about the house, an air of isolation, of withdrawal from the larger world, which struck a chord of kinship with him. He had moved in, then rebuilt the house nearly from scratch with his own hands over a long stretch of lonely weekends. When he looked at it now, its windows shut tight and curtained against the sun, its stucco walls screened by trees and veiled in shadow, he saw his own face, gazing back at him, tight and closed, all its secrets locked inside.

There had been a time when he had kept no secrets, because there had been no secrets to keep. But once he had sworn his allegiance to the gods he now served, all that had changed. Then he had learned to be afraid of growing too close to another person and seeing that other life drawn unknowingly into the web of danger in which he lived. His infiltration of the cult was risky business; he could be found out at any time; and he knew that if he were exposed, the Brotherhood would take out their vengeance not merely on him alone, but on his wife and family.

And so there had been no wife, no family. He had never come home to the smell of dinner on the stove or the sound of children's laughter in the yard. He had eaten solitary dinners with only the TV news for company, smiling at the weatherman's feeble jokes, then had gone to work to sit at a desk under the flicker of fluorescent lights which mimicked sunshine. On his nights off, when the other cops he knew were out with their wives and girlfriends, he had taken long, aimless drives, rolling the top down on the Fiat to feel the wind on his face, while the seat beside him mocked him with its emptiness. He had driven along Sunset Strip and Melrose Avenue and Westwood Boulevard, where the sidewalks streamed with youth and life, where music poured from stereo speakers, where women with short skirts and long legs smiled at the men who had won them, and then he had driven on, alone, always alone, into the night.

He had never admired martyrs or envied them. And yet he supposed that in his devotion to his cause, he had martyred himself, in his own way. The thought did not make him happy.

He shook his head. None of that mattered now. All that mattered was to stop the Brotherhood, to cheat them of their bloody prize. If he could play any role in their defeat, if he could help Billie find a way to win—then all the years of loneliness and danger would have been worth it. And he would have no regrets.

He pulled the Fiat off the road, onto the brown lawn, and parked. There was no driveway or garage. He got out and moved swiftly to the front door. As he fumbled with his key, he found himself listening for the ring of his telephone. He heard nothing. But that didn't matter. He had caught the news reports on the radio about the APB. Everyone in the city would be looking for her now. She would have no place else to turn. She would have to call.

He opened the door, stepped into the living room, and stopped.

The house had been ransacked. Tables and chairs were overturned. Wastebaskets had been emptied, their contents pawed through. The sofa cushions, slit open, drooled clumps of foam rubber. Paintings, yanked off the walls and razored out of their frames, littered the floor. Every book he owned had been pulled off the shelf and cut to confetti.

He stood just inside the doorway, staring at the mess, while two words echoed in his mind: They know.

They had found him out somehow. They had come here looking for him, and, finding no one home, had hunted for clues—for a directory of names and addresses, perhaps, or for a codebook hidden in the seat cushions or in the picture frames or in the leaves of a book, or for some other spy-movie prop which he didn't have. Or perhaps they had simply been angry at his absence and, like children, had taken out their frustration on inanimate objects.

He shut the door behind him. He moved through the living room, looking around warily.

"Greetings, my brother."

Drake whirled. He stared into the curtained darkness of the far corner of the room. A man was there, all but invisible, lost in shadow.

He let a moment pass, then completed the ritual for what he knew would be the last time.

"May you hear the song."

A chuckle, as dry as the scrape of a dead leaf, answered him.

"But we both know it is too late for that. Don't we, Drake?"

He did not answer.

The man moved forward slowly, into the light. An old man, Drake saw. A patchwork, raggedy man, limping with the creaky dignity of age. He stopped, a yard away. His eyes locked on Drake's own.

"Do you know who I am?"

"No."

"I am called the Director."

Drake did his best to betray no reaction. He failed. He knew it from the sudden smile on the old man's face and from the malice in his eyes, sparkling like droplets of some rare wine.

"What do you think of that?"

"I think"—Drake took a breath—"you could use a bath."

The Director threw back his head and laughed.

"Very good, Drake. Excellent. I had you pegged as a less amusing fellow, rather somber and serious. I'm pleased to see that you are able to appreciate the lighter side of your situation. Nothing matters that much, does it? It's all maggots. Maggots and maggot food. So laugh. Laugh at your funeral." His smile faded. "Where have you been?"

"Out."

"Where?"

"Nowhere."

"You try my patience. That's not wise."

"Fuck off."

"My, my. Aren't we testy? You don't want to be

testy with me, young fellow. Uh-uh. You don't want that at all.''

He sang.

Drake hissed breath through clenched teeth, in time with a dizzying shock of pain in his right hand.

He grabbed it, a reflex action. The fingers of his left hand sank into his palm, swallowed in its sudden spongy softness, vanishing up to the middle joints. He stared, unable to react, as his right hand began to lose its shape, liquefying. Skin dripped like molten wax. Bone melted to marshmallow. Fingers ran together in streams of goo. He fought to free his left hand, still embedded in the slime like an animal in a tar pit. He wrenched it loose. Ribbons of pink taffy stretched from his fingertips. Droplets of liquid flesh pattered on the floor.

He collapsed on his knees, gasping, as the remains of his right hand oozed and puckered and bubbled away.

"Jesus," he gasped. "Jesus."

"Come now, Drake," said the Director. "We both know you worship older gods than that."

Drake clutched the stub of his wrist. He made no reply.

"You may be wondering how I found you out. It was quite simple. One of my employees, now deceased, told me that our quarry left her friends' apartment this morning after receiving a phone call. This prompted me to wonder who had made that call. Only a handful of people would have known to reach her there. And only someone with the most urgent information to impart could have persuaded her to go out in public at that time. Then I thought of you. You have always been such a reliable man, Drake. Too reliable. Too perfect. Of course, I wasn't certain. Not until I had a man in my service, who works at the telephone company, check to see what calls were made from this number today. His report confirmed my suspicion. And now here we are.''

Drake lifted his head. "So what are you waiting for?" he said, teeth gritted. "Go on. Finish it."

"Brave talk." The Director smiled. "But I am not prepared to end your life quite yet. You have been busy, my brother. You have made contact with the woman we seek. And since that time, you have been out for hours. I believe that you were communing with your false gods. I believe that you summoned their help and located the Door. I want to know where it is."

"So you can send an army of men to stand guard over it and shoot anybody who comes close?"

"Precisely."

"Go to hell."

"You enjoy pain, then. Well, I can oblige you. You have several more appendages to lose."

Drake sucked in a lungful of air, steeling himself for whatever would come next, as the Director opened his mouth to sing again.

A single bell-like tone rang out in the stillness. Drake flinched, thinking for a wild instant that it was the first note of a song. Then he realized that it was merely the telephone ringing.

The Director stared at the phone, then at Drake.

"That's her," hissed the old man. "Isn't it?"

"I don't know who it is."

"Answer it."

"No."

"You amuse me, Drake. Do you really think you have a choice?"

Then the Director was singing again, and Drake, against his will, was listening.

27

At the other end of the line, the phone was ringing.

Billie waited tensely, huddled in the phone booth, looking out at the snarl of traffic where Bundy met Wilshire in West L.A. The service-station attendant was filling the tank of Harve Medlow's Mercedes, her latest acquisition. She figured the more frequently she switched cars, the more she would confuse her pursuit. And one thing was for certain: she had plenty of pursuit.

She did not know how long she had stood motionless in the living room, staring down at Harve's body and trying to decide what to do next. Then, in the distance, sirens rose. Long ululating wails of distress attacked the late-afternoon stillness. Growing louder. Closer.

The neighbors, she thought. They had heard the gun go off. They had called the cops.

She was already suspected of murder. Somehow she didn't think that being found with a fresh corpse would go a long way toward establishing her innocence.

She stooped. She dug in Harve's pants pocket for his keys. Her fist closed over the key ring.

Then she was running out the door, down the terrace steps, past the litter of glass from the windows that had exploded under the impact of her voice. The sirens were close now, perhaps two blocks away. She leapt behind the wheel of the Mercedes, gunned the engine, and tore around the curving driveway to the front gates. She leaned out the window and mashed the button on the control box with her fist. The gates swung apart slowly. When they were halfway open she sped through, scraping the sides of the car with a sickening tear of metal.

She cut down a side street. She pulled up to the curb and waited, breathing raggedly, as three black-and-whites shot past on the main road, domelights flashing, sirens howling. They hadn't seen her.

Slowly, warily, she pulled back onto Tigertail Road and drove on.

Ten minutes later she was in West L.A., getting a tankful of premium gas, listening to the slow, maddening ring of a telephone.

"Hello?"

She caught her breath. She knew that voice. Drake's voice.

"It's me," she said simply.

It took him a moment to answer. "Billie."

"I have to talk to you."

"I . . . I know."

His voice was slow, the words halting. She frowned. "Hey. You okay?"

"Sure." A chuckle, which did not sound quite right. "Never better. Now that you've called."

"I need your help. I need to know the rest of what you started to tell me this morning. I . . ." She hesitated, then said it. "I believe. All of it. I know it's true."

She heard a long, slow exhalation of breath, which should have been a sigh of relief, but wasn't.

"Okay," he said softly, his voice still unnaturally torpid. "Where are you now?"

"Gas station."

"Stay there. I . . . I'll be over."

There was something in the way he said it, some hint in the catch of his voice—and suddenly she knew. He was not himself. He had been taken over. He was on their side now. He was fighting it, the remnant of his conscious mind struggling against the spell they

had put on him, the same spell that had mesmerized
Bobby Joe and K.C. and Gary. Struggling, but losing.

"I can't stay here," she said quickly. "Too many
people around. There's an APB out on me, you know."
She fought to keep her voice normal, not to betray
what she knew. She was forming a plan even as she
spoke. A strategy. "I need to get out of town. Away
from all these cops. There's a park out in the high
desert, about an hour north of L.A. The Vasquez
Rocks, it's called. Can you get there?"

"Yes. I . . . I'll meet you as soon as possible."
Another hitch in his voice. In the gap between words
she heard a shout of warning, a plea not to listen, to
run away. She ignored it. She was setting herself up,
sure, she knew that. She was walking into another
death trap. But this time she knew what she was up
against.

And this time she had the power.

"Okay, Drake," she said, fighting for calm. "See
you there."

28

The desert hung in the windshield, framed like a photograph, the distant horizon immobile despite the
headlong rush of the car.

Billie eased the Mercedes up to seventy-five. She
swung into the opposing lane and flashed past a
wheezing pickup loaded with three would-be cowboys
and a dog. She glanced at her wristwatch. Seven
o'clock. The sun would be setting soon. Midnight was
drawing nearer. Too near.

She looked around her as the white strip of highway
unrolled under her hood. The faraway mountains were

a lusterless shade of purple merging in tone with the dull mat finish of the sky. Rearing up from the roadside, strobing past her like the pickets of a fence, were stark projections of rock, jagged shelves jutting out at bizarre angles from the naked earth. Scraggly desert plants crawled over the rocks like twisted traceries of veins, bluish-green in the dying sun.

A sign swam into view, announcing the turnoff for the Vasquez Rocks. Billie hooked right with a squeal of burning rubber and swung onto a two-lane road that swept her past horse farms and frame houses. A farmer stared openmouthed as she shot by. Then the entrance to the park expanded in the windshield.

The place was closed for the night, the gate chained and locked. She pulled off the road, bypassing the gate, and crawled in low gear over the crackling brush. In five minutes, at three miles an hour, she reached the main parking area, a spread of sandy soil encircled by great slabs of angular rock upthrust from the desert floor, looming imperiously against the twilight sky.

The place was deserted. Good. She had arrived first, and that fact might, just might, make all the difference.

She pulled to a stop behind a grove of tired-looking shrubs, which served to camouflage the Mercedes from the road and the parking lot. She got out.

The heat, undiminished even at this hour, hit her like a furnace blast. She staggered a little. Already her forehead was measled with sweat. She wiped it away with the back of her hand.

She moved away from the car, her boots crunching on the dry soil. A lizard no bigger than her little finger scurried out of her path, onto a boulder, and froze there, nearly lost to sight against the matching texture of the rock. A triangular shadow passed over her. She looked up and watched a crow wheel slowly in the air, a living mobile. It cawed once, a low, mournful sound, like the cries of the gulls on the beach outside her Malibu home.

Who knows? she thought grimly as she scanned the natural arena in which the coming battle would be fought. Maybe I'll even get to see the old homestead again someday. Yeah. Maybe.

But she wasn't taking any bets.

She knew that her plan was a long shot of suicidal proportions, but with limited time and still more limited options, she did not see any alternative. Drake had told her this morning that her only hope was to locate the point of access called the Door, then confront it, sing the Deathsong in reverse, and undo the spell. But where was the Door? How could she find it, with the clock ticking down? Drake was of no help to her now. Which left her exactly nowhere.

Unless she could find the answers from somebody else. Somebody in the Brotherhood. Somebody, perhaps, who was on his way here right now.

It was a trap—but a trap could work both ways.

In the city, she would have had no chance. Even if she could have outmaneuvered her enemy, she would have called undue attention to herself while doing so. If the cultists hadn't gotten her, the cops would've nabbed her. But out here, alone in the wilderness, it was a different story. Here it would be a contest of wits and skills, perhaps an unequal contest, one which she would be doomed to lose, but a contest, nonetheless. Here she had a fighting chance. At least she hoped she did.

She had no idea what man or what army they might send. She doubted they would use Drake to do their dirty work, even though he was now under their control. She had sensed that he was fighting them with every word. He would not make a reliable assassin. So it would be someone else. Someone dependable. An expert. A pro.

He would have skills of some kind, and cool nerves. She would have the advantage of surprise. And she had the power. She had to count on that.

During her drive, she had practiced the song she

planned to use. Not the song which induced suicide.
Her enemy would be no good to her if he was dead.
No, it was the song she had first heard from Frank
Lancett's mouth, when Bobby Joe advanced on him,
knife in hand. The song which Lancett must have used
to mesmerize the three of them, make them slaves to
his will.

If he could do it, she could too. She could turn her
enemy into a zombie and make him yield whatever
secrets he knew.

That is, if he didn't kill her first.

The silence was broken by the low, distant whine of
a motor. She listened. She heard the bite of tires on
the pitted surface of the dirt road leading into the park.

She took her position behind one of the larger rocks,
in a shadowed recess under a jutting overhang, where
she could crouch, unseen, with a clear view of the
parking lot. She waited.

A cloud of dust rose from the road in shimmering
waves. Out of the cloud swam a big car, a Lincoln,
streaked with dust. The car swung off the road into the
parking area. The engine died, then ticked fitfully,
cooling down.

She stared at the car. The windows were tinted,
opaque from the outside. She couldn't tell who was
inside or how many of them there might be. She
crouched lower, drawing deeper into shadow. She
waited.

The door swung open on the driver's side. A man
got out.

No way, she told herself. It can't be.

Billie tried to figure out what the hell was going on.
She couldn't believe they would have sent such a pitiful specimen of humanity to waste her. A wheezing
geriatric, a vomit-spattered bum, all baggy clown pants
and creased parchment skin, a skid-row reject who
didn't look like he had enough of the killer instinct to
polish off a decent-size roach with a full can of bug
spray.

But appearances could be deceptive. She had to be careful, not leap to conclusions. Here, she told herself warily, there be tigers. Or, to put it in the vernacular: boss lady, watch your ass.

The old man stepped away from the car, limping slightly, and stopped. He stood motionless in the middle of the parking lot. Then slowly he looked around, studying the rocks that hemmed him in. His eyes passed over her hiding place without stopping.

He didn't know she was here. He didn't suspect a thing.

Okay, then, she thought as her heart hammered in her ears. It's showtime.

The Director was ten yards from Frank Lancett's car, walking aimlessly, waiting with practiced patience for Billie Lee Kidd to arrive—when he heard the song.

It rose in the twilight stillness like a sudden eruption of insect chirruping. It seemed to come from the rocks themselves. He whirled, scanning the rocks, looking for the source of the song. He saw only inkspot shadows.

But she was here. Somewhere. She had turned the tables on him. She had chosen to play the huntress rather than the prey. And she had learned to sing. She had discovered her secret gift, activated her latent powers.

Resourceful, this one. And daring. But foolhardy. To think that she could defeat him with this simple tune.

He knew the song, of course. He had used it himself, in his younger days, before he had been entrusted with the stronger stuff. It was the song which erased will, blanked mind, smothered self. The song which turned men into puppets dangling on their masters' strings. The song which lifted from their shoulders the crushing burden of self, which set them free, free . . .

He shook his head, fighting for control. The song

was strong, stronger than he had ever heard it sung before. It seemed to gain added power from her voice. And yet why was that surprising? This was the singer of the Deathsong.

He fought to block it out, to fight off the waves of sound which were so oddly soothing, each one rolling in like a breaker on the beach, inviting him to dive into the surf and let that cold, clear water wash over him, wash him clean. . . .

He slapped himself hard with the back of his hand.

"Damn you," he said aloud, not knowing whether he meant the woman or himself.

He had to fight back, stop the bitch, shut her damn mouth. If only he could see her. If only he knew where to direct his attention and his powers. But she was hidden in the shadows, in the rocks.

The rocks.

He knew what he must do.

The low, ominous rumble was the first warning sign.

Billie kept on singing as the distant thunder rose in volume and intensity, shaking the earth, loosening a cataract of quartzite which peppered her head and shoulders like a rain of hail.

In the next instant she became aware that the old man, too, was singing now.

The rocks groaned, splitting the twilight with dinosaurian bellows. They shifted, shuddering fitfully. A huge chunk of sandstone snapped off the overhang and crashed at her feet, sending up a cloud of dust. More rocks cascaded down, thudding around her on all sides, missing her by inches.

She gave up on her song. She had to get the hell out of here before she was buried alive. She tried to crawl backward out of her hiding place. Rocks showered down, bouncing like papier-mâché props in a bad movie. They piled up with dizzying speed, forming a jumbled moraine that cut off escape.

She could not retreat. She had to go forward. She

scrambled on hands and knees through the riot of falling rocks. The ground vibrated wildly like a happy-fingers bed in a cheap motel. The rumbling seemed louder. Dimly she remembered that the Vasquez Rocks were an outcrop of the San Andreas Fault. Was his voice reaching down into the depths of the earth to trigger action along the fault line itself? Could he bring on the big quake, send L.A.'s skyline tumbling to the ground like a pile of broken toys, with nothing but a song?

She reached daylight. She dragged herself out from under the overhang. She half-staggered, half-crawled into the parking lot. She fell on her knees, gasping. She knelt, unable to get to her feet, aware that she was helpless, that he could go for the kill in that moment and she would have no strength to put up any resistance.

Behind her, the rockslide slowed to a trickle as the song died away.

She raised her head to look at him. He stared back, his eyes flicking from her clothes to her hair to her face, taking in the alterations in her appearance. Then he smiled.

"Greetings, Miss Billie Lee Kidd."

She said nothing. She took a breath. Slowly she rose. She faced him across the empty parking lot.

"I see you were expecting me," he said.

"Not exactly." She tried to smile. "I was expecting somebody who could put up a fight."

He laughed. "Such spirit. I like that." He met her eyes. "A duel, then? To the death?"

She stared him down.

"Uh-uh," she said with all the courage she could find. "I'm taking you alive."

"No, my dear. You are not taking me at all."

The two songs rose at the same instant and clashed like swords in the summer air.

* * *

At first, the Director did not understand what was happening. He had steeled himself for another assault of hypnotizing waves. Instead, a new song warbled in his ears. He required a second to recognize it.

Of course.

She was singing the same tune he had used just moments ago, the melody that had set the earth shaking. But that was a bad strategy, a suicidal miscalculation. There were no rocks where he stood. There was no danger. She could sing as long as she liked, to no effect, and all the while he would be focusing his own song on the sky above her head, where already a black cloud was taking shape like a jet of ink shot from a squid.

The ground shifted under him.

He looked down, startled, and saw a long jagged crack snake through the sandy soil directly between his feet. The crack split into a mosaic of twisted lines as the ground broke apart under a sudden internal pressure.

He was pitched off his feet. He fell sprawling in the dirt. He kept on singing. He had already grasped her plan—not to bury him under an avalanche, but simply to throw him off balance, break his concentration, so that she might use her other song to rob him of will.

And it could work, he realized with a rush of fury. This witless bitch might beat him, after all, and cheat history of its proper climax.

He sang louder. The thunderhead redoubled, its black edges tinted pink by the sun's dying rays.

The ground shuddered. One jagged crack opened wide, exposing a chasm that descended into darkness. Dirt and pebbles streamed into its yawning mouth. It expanded as the earth buckled, exploding into a webwork of fragments like a mirror shattered by a blow.

He clung to a six-foot chunk of ground. Slowly it tilted up at an angle. He began to slide backward, toward the open maw. Streams of dirt rushed past him. He sang to the sky. His hands scrabbled for purchase on the slippery slope.

He glanced at Billie Lee Kidd and saw that she was smiling.

Billie was pretty damn sure she had the old bastard where she wanted him.

He'd been expecting her to try the same song again. Well, that was his mistake. She'd learned long ago, in musty barrooms and sold-out concert halls, that you always kept your audience guessing.

She watched him as he slithered helplessly toward the gash which her voice had opened in the earth. She couldn't let him fall in and plunge to his death. She had to hope he stopped singing before things got that far. Then she would switch to her original number and bring him under her control before he could find the strength to resist.

Concentrating on the song and the scene before her, she had barely even noticed the unnatural darkening of the sky. But she noticed it now, along with a light patter of rain.

She glanced up, startled, and saw a huge black formless mass materializing out of nowhere to overshadow the sky.

The abyss, she thought in sudden terror.

Then in the next instant the thing began to crackle with purplish-blue veins that were electrical discharges, and she realized that it was not her old enemy, no, it was only a stormcloud, a cloud that had taken shape at the command of the old man's voice.

A forked tree of lightning shot out of the cloud and struck the earth a yard away. She screamed. Her song was silenced. She backed away, staring alternately at the sky and at the smoking patch of earth where the bolt had hit. Thunder cracked like a bomb-blast. Wind howled. And rising above the sounds of the storm was the old man's song, louder now, triumphant.

She looked at him. He had taken advantage of her lapse of concentration to leap free of the patch of shifting earth. He stood watching her from thirty feet away, his ragged clothes streaked with dust, his eyes fever-bright, his mouth twisted as if with laughter. He sang and sang and sang.

Lightning flashed again. Instinctively Billie hurled herself to one side. An instant later, the spot where she had stood was ripped by a high-voltage stream. Another eruption of thunder rocked the sky. Rain cascaded down, turning the earth to mud.

Twin ladders of lightning descended, winding through the sky like traceries of neon tubing, to strike at her from both sides. She took cover under a rocky overhang. A tendril of electricity zapped the rock, disintegrating it. She ran, her boots kicking up a spray of mud and rainwater. Lightning pursued her, cracking like a whip at her heels.

She forced herself to think straight. She had to fight back, had to take the offensive again. She glanced over her shoulder at a dagger of lightning, terrifyingly close. Then her eyes moved to the old man, barely visible through the mist of slanting rain. He stood watching her, still singing.

Singing.

Well, hell, she thought with a burst of clarity, two can play that game.

She opened her mouth and sang the same song, the song that controlled the lightning. Around her, the storm seemed to pause, as if listening.

She looked up at the twisting thundercloud. She arrowed her voice at it, willing it to obey her command and only hers.

A streak of lightning burst out of the black heart of the cloud, then instantly broke apart into a thousand splinters shooting everywhere at once. Thunder barked and growled.

She sang louder. She called up the last reserves of her energy. She ordered the lightning to bend to her will, to her purpose.

Then, with a ripple of thunder, a bluish-white ball of fire shot out of the cloud, flamed to earth like a meteorite, and struck the ground inches from the old man's feet. He threw his hands over his face and staggered backward, his face suddenly ashen, his voice silenced.

Billie smiled. She had him. She had him now.

She stopped singing. An instant later, the rain died out and the last echoes of thunder died away. Already the sky was clearing as the stormcloud broke up into wisps of dirty cotton. She ignored it. She sang the song that would mesmerize the old man and bring him, finally, under her control.

The Director felt the first piercing trill of Billie Lee Kidd's new song like an icicle in his heart. He reeled backward, fighting to force air and melody out of his throat. He had never encountered an adversary with such power.

What a force she would have been, he marveled dizzily, on our side.

He forced all such thoughts out of his mind. He had to concentrate on the task at hand. To fight off the deadly narcotic now buzzing in his brain.

He needed a song so powerful that even the singer of the Deathsong could not resist it. He searched his memory.

He found it.

At first Billie did not know what the hell had hit her. She kept on singing, still trying desperately to bring the old man under her spell, as spasms of pain shot up her sides.

Strobe lights flashed over her field of vision. Her head swam. Her stomach heaved. She doubled over, her body contorted in a gargoyle pose. She pressed her hands to her belly. Inside, she felt something growing tumorously. She did not know what it was. She did not want to know.

She had to keep singing, had to fight back. She couldn't let the goddamn bastard win, not now, not when she had come so close. But the pain—Jesus, the *pain*—it was just too much. She couldn't stand it. She forced a few last feeble notes out of her throat, then gave up, unable to continue.

The killing song went on. It filled her brain. The earth itself seemed to vibrate in harmony with it. The rocks rang like cymbals. The wind screeched like woodwinds. The world was singing to her, singing her to death.

She stumbled backward and thudded blindly into a rock wall. She ground her palms into the naked sandstone. She moaned. Tears splashed down her cheeks.

The thing inside her grew, an unwanted pregnancy. Tiny claws scrabbled at her insides. Her stomach was growling—really, for Christ's sake, growling like a junkyard dog. Oh, God, what the hell was inside her and what would it do to her once it got out?

She tried once more to sing. What came out of her mouth was a spray of vomit, spattering her muddy cowboy boots, dyeing them red.

She staggered away, trying to put as much distance as possible between herself and his voice. She found a crevice in the rock wall and backed inside. She retreated into the shadows, into the cooler darkness, like a wounded animal seeking a corner in which to curl up and die.

The thing twisted and squirmed in her gut. She slapped her palms to her ears to block out the song. No use. She heard it anyway.

She had thought that she could beat him. She had been wrong. She had no power. She had no destiny. She had nothing. Nothing.

She took a final backward step. Her hands brushed against something soft and delicate and papery, like a Chinese lantern, incongruous in this place. She glanced at it.

And then she knew that there was still a chance.

* * *

The Director was certain of victory, so certain that he let down his guard for just one moment, and in that moment Billie Lee Kidd stumbled out of the shadows and hurled a bomb. It hit the ground by his feet and exploded.

Wasps sprayed out, humming angrily, rising toward his face.

Not a bomb, he realized. A hive. A nest.

He had perhaps one second to defend himself. And in that second, he knew that Billie had just made a mistake, a major mistake, her final mistake.

He sang the song the woman had intended to use on him, the song which controlled the will—but he sang it to the wasps.

The buzzing cloud seemed to pause, frozen in the instant of attack, hovering in midair. Listening.

His voice rose higher, keening.

The wasps whirled into a flurry of motion, dancing and twirling giddily.

Hear me, my lovelies, he told them with each crystalline note. Hear and obey.

They received their final instructions, then streaked like a hail of living buckshot directly at Billie Lee Kidd.

For one brief moment Billie was ready to celebrate.

The maneuver with the wasps' nest had taken the old man completely by surprise. His song was silenced, his spell neutralized. The thing in her stomach vanished. She felt it wink out, heard the muffled pop as air rushed in to fill the sudden vacuum. The pain was gone and she felt ready to do battle again—and this time, to win.

She took a step forward, readying herself for one last round, and that was when she saw the wasps turn, swarming in her direction.

Shit, she thought with a sinking sensation in her gut.

She covered her face with her hands. Instantly the wasps—yellowjackets, thousands of them—were upon her. Stingers sank into her exposed flesh. Shocks of pain rippled up her legs and arms. Insect bodies tangled in her hair. Her ears buzzed. She was screaming.

She collapsed on her side in the dirt. She slapped frantically at herself. She kicked and flailed. Wasps plastered her bare legs. They gloved her hands. Already her skin was puffing up. Humps of flesh rose like golf balls.

The old man sang, driving the wasps to frenzy. They whipped around her, buzzing furiously, singing their own deadly song.

She had to fight back. Had to sing the song of hypnosis, the song the old man was using, and turn the wasps against him, just as she'd done with the lightning.

She sang. Nothing happened. Wasps flew inside her shirt collar. They stabbed like needles at her breasts. She sang louder, nearly screaming the notes. The wasps would not listen. Would not obey.

The Director smiled as his song went on. He had instructed his insect assassins well. His final orders had been that they must disregard this song, this hypnotic lullaby, should they hear it from the woman's lips.

There would be no turnabout this time. There would be only the certainty of death for his adversary. Slow death by slow poison. The poison already pumping through her veins.

Billie gave up on the song. For some reason it wasn't working, it had no effect. She couldn't figure out why. She had no time to think about it. She had to escape somehow. Had to get away before the damn things killed her, as they had been ordered to do.

She twisted onto her stomach. Wasps swarmed over her skull, a living hairnet. Her scalp burned with the needle jabs of stingers. She peered through the web of fingers cupping her face. A few yards away, huddled against the rock wall, lay a clump of bushes. If she could reach them, pull herself inside the protective folds of branches, she might still survive. She tried to crawl. She dragged herself forward a yard or two. The wasps pursued her, stinging her again and again and again.

She collapsed in the dirt. She could not make it. She was too weak. She had lost. Goddammit, she had lost.

She lay on her belly, helpess, while images flashed in her mind, images of a ten-year-old girl on a desert trail, a girl who kept on struggling for life till strength failed and consciousness faded and the abyss closed in. She had survived then. But now she felt that same black cloud stealing forward once more, spreading its inkspot tendrils over her like the lengthening shadows of the rocks swallowing the desert floor, and there was no way to fight back, no way to win.

Her legs were numb. Her arms tingled, losing all sensation. Waves of faintness washed over her. The insect buzzing became distant, unreal, the faraway murmur of a crowd. She was so warm. Her forehead burned. Even her eyes were hot, as hot and dry as the desert itself, the desert which had claimed her at last.

Somewhere a radio was on, tuned to the *Grand Ole Opry Hour*. A woman was singing. She could not quite make out the voice. A familiar voice, one she liked. She listened more closely.

It's me, she thought in dim astonishment, as her mind flickered on the brink of darkness. It's my voice.

She smiled a little, thinking of how much she had always loved to sing.

29

Later, what the Director remembered best was the look on Billie Lee Kidd's face when she saw the wasps coming at her and knew that she was going to die. He supposed she had not realized that the songs which mesmerized human victims could work their witchcraft on the lower animals as well. But she had learned.

He drove slowly down the Antelope Valley Freeway in the darkness. It had been years since he had handled a car, yet he drove effortlessly, enjoying the feel of the steering wheel under his hands and the rush of the road streaming past. For once, he understood why people liked luxury, why they were willing to sweat and kill merely for the sake of possessing fine cars and fine clothes and fine homes, all the lovely things which, come midnight, only three hours from now, would be theirs no more.

But it was not the car that made him feel so very good inside. It was the knowledge that he, alone of all the Brotherhood, had been blessed with the opportunity to destroy the singer of the Deathsong and to wipe out the last remaining obstacle in their path.

He had sung beautifully tonight. He had been in excellent voice. He could have gone on singing for hours without strain. He had in fact continued to sing for some time, keeping the wasps at their work, as Billie stiffened with the first wave of paralysis, then was racked with shudders, then lay trembling fitfully, like a tuning fork vibrating to the pitch of his song.

Still singing, he had approached her. He stared down at her through the droning cloud. He kicked her in the

side, nudging her with the toe of his shoe onto her
back. He wanted to see her face.

Her eyes were open, staring. She gazed up at him.
Her face was twisted in a grimace of pain so extreme
it bordered on caricature. Her tongue lolled out of her
mouth.

He could not tell if she were alive or not. He reached
down, brushing wasps away. He found the carotid artery at the side of her neck. He felt her pulse. It was
weak, irregular, but not yet stilled.

He let his song die away. The wasps inflicted a few
more petulant stings, then rose in a mass and glided
off slowly into the last rays of the sunset.

He knelt by her side.

"Billie," he breathed. "I don't know if you can
hear me. But if you can, I wish to tell you something."

He waited for some flicker of acknowledgment, perhaps a moan or a flutter of eyelids. There was nothing.
He went on speaking anyway.

"You have lost, my friend. You had to lose. Life
always loses. Death wins in the end. Death is the essence of things. Maggots feed on corpses. Death feeds
on life. Everything is maggots. Everything is death."

He took her hand, puffy with poison. He squeezed
it gently.

"Nothing matters," he whispered. "There is no
good or evil. There is no purpose. There is nothing.
Nothing but the maggots, feeding till they've had their
fill."

He leaned close to her. He put his mouth to her ear.

"Fools believe that a new Antarok will rise tonight.
They must believe it. They do not know the truth. No
one knows. No one but the master. And me." He giggled. "And now you, Billie. Now you know too."

He sat by her, holding her hand, listening as her
breath came more slowly, then did not come at all.

He felt for a pulse. There was none.

He got up. He looked down at her. Her skin was a
mass of blue-black humps. Her eyes were glazed and

sightless. Where there had been life and thought and energy, now there was nothing.

He looked up at the sky, bright with the first sprinkle of stars. He looked at it for a long time. He thought about the death which feeds on life. He thought about maggots. He thought about the dark gods of Antarok, who had waited so long.

Then he walked slowly back to the car. He stopped with his hand on the door. He looked back at Billie. Soon the maggots would feed, yes, feed on everything. But somehow it did not seem quite right to let them feed on her. She had shown such spirit. She had been nearly his equal. He did not wish to leave her there, unburied and exposed.

He smiled at himself, amused at this touch of sentiment, so unlike him. Then he shrugged. One more song would do no harm.

He sang. Three lilting notes danced in the air.

And Billie Lee Kidd, or whatever might be left of her, had become dust, and the dust, borne on a current of wind, had been scattered like ashes across the desert wastes.

30

Drake awoke to a nightmare.

He was lying faceup, arms and legs splayed, staring up at the night sky. He was in a hammock. Yes, a nice, relaxing hammock, like the one in the backyard of the bungalow he'd rented for the one timeless summer of his youth, the summer spent loafing and chasing girls in the Florida keys. The hammock trembled, swaying slightly. He imagined the warm breeze off the gulf

caressing his face, stirring his hair, rocking him to
sleep.

Gradually he became aware of pain, a dull, throbbing pain in his right hand. Pins and needles shot
through his fingers. He flexed them. They seemed stiff
and unresponsive. He turned his head slowly, to look
at his hand. His hand . . .

He had no hand. It was gone, melted away at the
wrist, leaving only a fleshy, puckered stub, like the
remnant of a candle.

Then he remembered.

The Director had sung to him, robbing him of will,
forcing him to answer Billie's call and say the things
which the old man whispered his ear. Then he had
been left in the hands of other men, the Director's
henchmen, stationed around the house. They took him,
blindfolded, to some secluded place. They tortured
him with songs, with drugs, with fists. They wanted
to know the location of the Door, so they could ring
it with guards and guns. He would not tell. Could not,
even had he wanted to. His gods must have imparted
the knowledge to him under the protection of some
mental block that resisted all efforts at coercion.

Finally he had passed out. And now here he was.
But where?

He peered into the darkness. He tried to move his
arms and legs. He could not. He was tied down. No.
Not tied. Glued. Pasted to some sort of net. It trembled again, and this time he knew that the gentle
rocking was not born of a Florida breeze.

There was something on the net with him, something moving, setting the gossamer strands quivering
like plucked harp strings. Something in the dark, beyond the range of his vision. Something coming this
way.

It crept closer. He squinted, trying to make out its
shape. Then the crescent moon swam out from behind
a ragged cover of cloud, painting the scene in a lu-

minous whitewash, spotlighting the thing which loomed perhaps fifty feet away.

Drake stared at it while his lips moved soundlessly, mouthing one word.

Ragnaaroth.

He remembered the night, eight years ago, when he was initiated into the Brotherhood—the torchlit ceremony in the grand ballroom of a crumbling mansion high in the Hollywood Hills. Dominating the room was a marble idol, twenty feet tall, mounted on a pedestal nearly as high as the figure itself. He had gazed up at it, awed despite himself, taking in the stylized likeness of the darkest of Antarok's dark gods, the symbol of that consummate evil to which he made his lying vows. The Spider King.

And now here it was, as big as life, three times the size of a man, crawling slowly toward him over its monstrous web.

His eyes moved from the immense, grossly distended abdomen, a leathery sac spiked with paintbrush bristles, banded in bright green and gold, trailing a gossamer dragline from its rearward spinnerets—to the eight walking legs, their joints working mechanically, hauling the thing forward in a series of shudders and jerks, clambering with gingerly slowness over the web—to the serrated feelers, twitching fitfully, like lobster claws—then, finally, to the head, that shapeless, hairless black bulb studded with eight glassy eyes and tapering to twin fangs wet with poison.

Below the fangs, Drake knew, was the mouth, a toothless orifice designed to draw him headfirst into its gullet, where the sucking stomach would go to work, dissolving skin and bone in a bath of digestive juices, draining his body fluids, consuming him whole.

The spider scuttled closer.

He turned away. He took a breath, fighting for control. He forced himself to study his surroundings, to try to determine where the hell he was and what was going on.

He craned his neck, looking down through gaps in the web, and saw a concrete floor, faintly greenish with moss, fifteen feet below. A mosaic of a mermaid riding a giant seahorse was painted there in colors once garish, now faded. A small skittering shape—a rat—passed by, squeaking, then vanished into shadow.

A swimming pool, he thought. An old one, drained, abandoned, left to crumble and rot.

He had seen it before. He was sure of that. He tried to think.

Of course.

He was on the grounds of the mansion. He remembered how, as he had waited for the initiation rites to begin, he happened to look out a window and see this pool, nestled in a secluded garden well back from the house, screened off by trees.

Well, that made sense. The mansion was the base of operations for this chapter of the Brotherhood. But he could not help thinking it was ironic, in a way, that his captors should have gone to such fruitless lengths to learn where to find the Door, when a ten-minute drive through these hills would have taken them there, and when the location itself was plainly visible from the grounds of this estate, as it was from nearly all points of the city.

He dismissed the thought. He turned his attention to the web. It was a wheel-shaped net of symmetrical lines radiating from a central point, suspended over the pool, anchored at regular intervals to the pool's concrete border. He tugged at the ropelike strands of spun silk. The web quivered crazily. His bonds held.

The spider was now less than thirty feet away. It paused once to lower its abdomen to the web and secure the dragline there. It advanced again.

Drake felt the pounding of his pulse in the veins of his forearms. He listened to the irregular rhythm of his breathing. He concentrated on the pain where his right hand had been. He flexed his ghost fingers. Anything to keep his mind off that slow, relentless, spider crawl.

Then, from out of the darkness enveloping the pool on all sides, a voice rose in song.

Instantly the spider seemed to freeze up, like a movie strip stopped on a single frame. It sat there, caught and held like a fly in a cube of amber, twenty-five feet away.

Drake turned, searching for the source of the voice. For a moment his brain whirled with the crazy certainty that it was Billie—she had told him she believed, so she must have the power—yes, and somehow she had tracked him down and now she was singing, singing to save his life. . . .

Then he made out a distant figure, all but invisible against the shadows of the trees.

"Billie?" he whispered.

The figure moved forward. Its face swam into focus. Drake felt a small, brief stab in his chest which was the death of hope.

It was not Billie Lee Kidd. It was a man. A tall, massively muscled man in a dark business suit. His face was hard, angular, crusted with black beard, scarred by a gleaming vertical slash.

"Who are you?" asked Drake softly, tonelessly.

The man smiled. The curve of his teeth made a brilliant scimitar against the darkness.

"Your executioner," he answered in a low, rumbling baritone.

Drake took a breath, then jerked his head in the direction of the spider. "Did that thing come through the Door? Is that it? Is it after midnight?"

Laughter answered him.

"You are such a fool, Drake. Such a blind fool. You do not even comprehend the nature of that which you have sworn to fight."

"What do you mean?"

The man shook his head, dismissing the question. "The thing before you is not a god, but merely the image of a god. Its earthly replica, carved in marble, which once stood as one monument among dozens in the underground tombs of lost Antarok. Look at it, Drake. Take a close look.''

Slowly Drake turned his head. He gazed at the spider, motionless on its web.

It had changed. He saw that now. It was no longer black and lustrous with a brittle, metallic sheen. Instead it seemed oddly pale, almost alabaster white. The multiple eyes were dull, lifeless. The fur fringing its legs looked curiously unreal, like detail carved in stone. In marble.

"It was real," whispered Drake. "It was alive."

"Yes. It was. And it will be again. I need only sing my little song and I can bring it to life once more. To hunt. To feed.''

Drake looked at the man. "No song can do that."

"Mine can.''

"No singer has that power.''

"I do.''

"Who are you?''

"Kuruk.''

Drake let a long moment pass. He said nothing. There was nothing to say.

"Yes, Drake," said Kuruk finally. "My gods gave me the gift of immortality, so that I might fulfill the task they had set for me—four thousand years ago.''

Drake thought of this man, the high priest of Antarok, a man as ancient as this statue and as ageless, wandering the world while civilizations rose and fell, directing the operations of his private empire from behind the scenes. A mystery man, a figure of legend, nestled—like a spider—in the center of his own monstrous web.

"Is it midnight?" he asked in a low, beaten voice.

"There are two hours yet to wait. Two hours, after four thousand years. It seems so little. And yet I find the minutes do pass slowly.''

"You think you've won. Don't you?"

"I know I have."

"You're wrong. You don't know what you're up against. Billie will beat you. She'll find the Door somehow. She's stronger than you think. She sang the Deathsong. She has power. And she believes now. You hear me? She believes. That means she can't be stopped."

"But she can be, Drake. She has been." Kuruk smiled. "She is dead."

Drake shut his eyes. He listened to the echoing hammerblows of his heart.

"Bullshit," he said after a long moment.

"Do you want proof?"

"There is no proof."

"Oh, but there is. And it is so very simple." Kuruk smiled. "If she were still alive, I could hardly permit you to die without having revealed what you know. But now, you see . . . I can."

He sang again, a brief tuneless air.

The spider shimmered, white stone dissolving liquidly to jet-black flesh and fur. Its eyes, alive once more, caught the moonlight. Its feelers twitched. Its fangs dripped death.

It began creeping forward again.

Kuruk nodded, satisfied, then turned away.

"Good-bye, Drake."

He vanished into the darkness of the trees edging the pool.

Drake was left alone with the spider as it advanced, dragging its bloated body over the web, remorselessly closing the distance between itself and its prey.

So he was finished. There would be no last-minute reprieve, no rescue in the nick of time, not for himself or for the universe. Good would not triumph in the final reel. Billie was dead, and soon he would be dead too, and then the clock would strike midnight and the true Spider King and his dark minions would pour forth to claim the world as their prize.

Kuruk had laughed at that idea. But why? He didn't know. He couldn't think. The spider was closer now.

He shut his eyes. He tried to shut out the thoughts whirling in his brain. He could not.

He was thirty-two years old. He had dedicated his life to the service of his gods. He had lived in solitude and secrecy, hiding his innermost self from all others, forsaking friendship and love. He had made himself a martyr to a cause. And what was it all for? What had he gained?

His cause was lost. His gods were beaten. And he was tied down, helpless, sentenced to death.

Something harsh and bristly brushed against the side of his face. One of its legs, he realized as a slow shudder ran over him. It left his skin scraped and raw.

The web creaked. It did sound so very much like that old hammock of his. He had put up the hammock in the backyard of the bungalow he had rented in Key West for the summer, twelve years ago, when life was still before him and anything was possible. He had not carried any heavy burden of secrecy then. He had not been concerned with saving the world. He had merely wanted to live. He had almost forgotten how that felt, to want to live, not for any larger purpose, not to save anybody or anything, just to breathe in the clean air of a summer morning or taste the honey of a woman's lips.

The web stopped shaking. He knew, without opening his eyes, that the spider was looming over him.

He heard a low hiss. Instantly his legs were blanketed in a thick, heavy coat. He understood what was happening. The spider had raised its abdomen over his own midsection, and from the multiple spigots of its spinnerets it was spewing out a mist of silk to wrap him in a gossamer cocoon.

He didn't want to die. Maybe he'd never realized, until this moment, how much he loved his life.

His heart raged in his chest like a cornered animal. The web trembled in sympathy with the jolts of terror and fury shaking his body. He shook his head violently from side to side, fighting to break free. No use.

The spider shifted its weight. Another leg scraped his ribs. The coarse needles of hair shredded his shirt. In the next moment the spider was binding his arms in silken ropes. Each strand was threadlike, as fine as copper wire, but sticky, elastic, and incredibly strong. The webbing tightened, hardening.

Then the spider stopped spinning, leaving his chest and his face exposed.

Drake opened his eyes. He stared up at the eight-legged horror looming over him, blotting out the stars. The two rows of eyes gazed down without expression, reflecting multiple caricatures of his own face, like the distorted mirror images in glassy Christmas ornaments. Its feelers quivered in anticipation of a kill. Its fangs were poised, ready. Its mouth dripped.

The web sagged, groaning ominously. The spider bent over him, smacking its toothless gums. It lowered its head slowly, lovingly, like a lover bestowing a kiss.

"Go away," Drake whispered. "Go away, God damn you."

He wanted to strike out, to kill it somehow, to smash it with his fist the way he could have smashed a spider on the wall. He could not move.

The twin fangs tested the skin of his chest, poking at his rib cage. He hissed breath in through clenched teeth. The fangs dug in deeper. Slowly, almost gently, they sank into his flesh. He felt a surge of agony as poison shot into his bloodstream.

He stiffened with sudden paralysis. His brain hummed. But he did not die. Not yet.

The spider withdrew its fangs. The feelers scrabbled at the web, dragging its bloated body forward. He gazed up at it helplessly. He wanted desperately to scream. He could not find his voice.

The huge mouth closed over his head. He was drawn inside, into a hot, dank darkness reeking of acid, the stench of the digestive juices which bubbled and simmered like a witch's caldron somewhere nearby.

Eaten alive, he thought dizzily. I'm being eaten alive.

His forehead burned, bright with fever, the effect of the poison or of simple animal terror.

His shoulders came next. He felt the mouth widen to let them through. He slid on his back, inch by inch, down a long, wet, narrow tunnel glossy with slime. The reek of acid became stronger. In another few seconds he would slide headfirst into that pool of stomach acid and his flesh would melt away. He remembered how it had felt when his hand turned to streams of taffy. This would be worse. A thousand times worse. The only saving grace was that it would not last long.

He waited. There was nothing else to do but wait. To wait, and then to die. To die for nothing. Nothing at all.

As the spider continued its slow, patient work, drawing him ever deeper inside, he thought of Billie Lee Kidd. He wondered how she had died. He hoped it had been quick.

Then his face tingled with the first droplets of acid, sizzling like grease on a skillet, and Martin Drake had no room left for thoughts of anything but pain.

31

In the grand ballroom, men waited. More than three hundred men, of all ages, all races, all backgrounds. Men with nothing in common save the black hoods framing their faces, the black robes draping their bodies, and the black wells of bitter anger in their eyes. They had come from all points within the area under the Director's control, from Los Angeles and Long Beach, from Newport and Oceanside, from San Diego and San Luis Obispo. They had come, abandoning jobs, homes, families. They had come, knowing that the hour for which they had waited was finally here, and that the lives they had led in unspoken frustration and resentment could now be discarded as gratefully as a snake discards its skin.

They crowded the vast room, overspilling its confines, waiting to see and hear, for the first time, the nameless mystery man who was their master. They had arrived in business suits, in tennis shorts, in dungarees, but, once here, they had donned their ceremonial costumes, the clothes they had worn in the rituals which were their initiation into the faith, clothes they had kept in secret hiding places in the expectation of this day.

And they carried torches. That, too, was part of the ceremony tonight, as it had been part of the initiation rites. In ancient Sumer and Babylon and Assyria, in Egypt and Persia and Nubia, the members of the Brotherhood had always carried torches when they met in the moonlight to chant their songs and commune with their dark gods.

They waited, arrayed in neat rows, torches upraised in their right hands, bracelets glittering on their left wrists. Torchlight flickered on walls painted with faded flowers. Hooded shadows danced among the columbine and ivy. Massive carvings worn by weather and time gazed down on them from high pedestals—statues of Toth, Bethshul, Dasharoom, Garnarlit, Narantos. Only the Spider King, Ragnaaroth, was absent. The pedestal behind the dais was empty.

There was no sound from the crowd, not even the murmur of breath. They stood silent, moveless, like ranks of corpses risen on Judgment Day.

Among their number was Tony Alvarez, who liked to cruise the streets in his RX-7, but who had no luck with girls. A van had picked him up two hours ago and whisked him here with a dozen others. They had sat in silence, clutching the bundles of black raiment in their laps, till the van rumbled through the gates into the driveway of the mansion, patrolled by black-uniformed guards carrying Uzis and M-16's. Tony and the others had been directed to a room on the ground floor, where they cast off their street clothes and assumed a new and more ominous form.

Now he stood in the very last row, near the huge double doors at the rear of the room, clutching his torch and thinking how glad he was that no women were allowed in this privileged company, because all women were whores and cockteasers, and when the new world came and he had power, he would find the girls who had scorned him and he would make them pay.

Elsewhere in the ranks was Russell Garrett, who flew a helicopter for affluent passengers he despised. He had often gazed down at the manicured lawns of Beverly Hills and Brentwood, hating each swimming pool and tennis court, wishing that his chopper carried a load of bombs which would blast those fine houses to twisted rubble and litter the streets with charred corpses. Soon he would not need bombs.

And there was Walter Gelbard, who had wanted to be an actor but who worked mostly as a waiter instead. He gazed at the flickering fireglow on the cowled heads and shoulders of the men around him and thought of Chester Dickman, his supervisor until earlier today, and of the casting directors who had turned him down, the talent agents who had not taken his calls, all the people in positions of authority and influence who had ignored and humbled him. He thought of them and he smiled. Their power would be his, soon.

Look out, world, he thought grimly. Here I come.

* * *

In a corner of the room, an old man sat in a wheel-chair, unnoticed by the crowd around him, as he always went unnoticed. But people would notice him tomorrow. Yes. And for all the tomorrows after that.

The Director, standing near the dais, looked out over the rows of faces, the faces drawn in lines of bitterness and hate. He read the thoughts in their eyes. He smiled, a slow, sad smile of hidden meanings.

He thought of maggots. He thought of death.

32

Kuruk paused in the doorway, surveying the crowd.

They waited, breathless with expectation. Waited for the ritual he was now to perform. Waited for the new world, that better world that had been promised to them.

He looked down at his body, draped in a ceremonial robe, a sheet of velvet as black as pitch. His cloak flowed behind him like the train of a black wedding gown. He raised his left hand into the torchlight. The Bloodstone sparkled like a pool of red wine.

From somewhere in the maze of corridors at his back, a clock chimed eleven, signaling his entrance. He strode into the ballroom. He passed by the Director. The two men exchanged a knowing glance.

"One hour left," whispered Kuruk, "to the dawning of a new world."

"Yes." The Director smiled, exposing yellow, rotted stumps of teeth. "A new world."

Kuruk ascended the steps of the dais. He stood before the crowd, his hands at his sides, his huge body casting a contorted shadow on the wall at his back, where the statue of the Spider King had been.

"Greetings, my brothers," he intoned.

A murmur of voices rose in unison. "May you hear the song."

He inclined his head gravely, acknowledging the completion of the ritual which was so very meaningless now.

"You know why you have been summoned here," he said softly. "The climax of history has been reached. Two hundred generations of men have come and gone before you, men who waited in vain for the miracle which tonight will come to pass."

His audience listened, spellbound, three hundred pairs of eyes fixed on him. The men assembled here had not been told his identity. They did not know that the high priest of Antarok was addressing them. They knew only that the tall, black-bearded man on the dais was the superior even of the Director himself. That was enough.

Kuruk raised his voice. It rumbled like thunder through the vast room.

"Our last obstacle has been swept away. The only voice which might have stopped us has been stilled forever. The singer of the Deathsong is dead."

A babble of shouts and breathless whispers answered him. Torches bobbed like buoys in a rough sea. Kuruk stood, watching impassively, letting his faithful ones savor this moment. He himself felt no triumph, no elation. He felt nothing. He had never known that state of being which men called joy.

"Come midnight," he went on, speaking louder, "less than one hour from now, this universe will receive its proper masters. We who have been laid low will be raised up on high to torment our tormentors. We who have been trod under hoof and heel will rise to crush our oppressors into dust. We who have been denied will be denied no longer. We will have power. We will have riches. We will have life everlasting."

The words rang through the hall. They were good words. They named the hopes and longings of his audience. But not his own. No. He, who had served at the right hand of tyranny, had never sought power. He, who had lived in luxury on tropic isles and in castle keeps, had never aspired to wealth. He, who had achieved immortality, had never yearned for everlasting life.

"We have waited four thousand years for this day. Now our long wait is ended. Let us bow our heads. Let us sing, my brothers. Let us sing."

He closed his eyes. He hummed in his dark baritone. He sang the song of obeisance to the dark gods.

The Director was first to join in. Then one by one, other voices rose in the stillness, coming in at random points in the song, a tremulous alto here, a warbling tenor there, some voices clear as crystal, others flat as dust. But each voice was charged with the energy of a purpose larger than itself, each man transfixed by the awareness of the powers to which the song paid homage.

Kuruk's voice boomed like cannon fire, the loudest in the hall, ringing out in praise of Ragnaaroth and his black legions. The crowd chanted the words of a dead language which he alone, among all the peoples of the earth, was still alive to know. The song rose to a crescendo, a hundred voices blending in a seamless chorus, a hymn to chaos, a celebration of destruction, a perfect harmony of discord.

Then the purity of tones was shattered by a drumroll of thunder.

Gunshots.

Kuruk's head snapped up. The song died away in a confusion of voices. The shots went on, splitting the night. They came from outside, from somewhere on the grounds of the estate. Then they were cut off as abruptly as they had begun.

The sea of hoods swirled and eddied noisily. The

glow of the torches danced on faces twisted by fear into twitching, ratlike masks. Some faceless figure in the hall panicked and ran screaming through the crowd.

"Silence!" shouted Kuruk above the din.

Instantly the room was quiet.

"Fear not, my brothers," he said softly, his whispery voice reaching to the room's far corners, soothing the crowd with the hypnotizing persuasiveness of a python's hiss. "I have told you that our last obstacle has been overcome. Nothing can stop us now."

Footsteps pounded through the house. The double doors at the rear of the room swung open. The crowd parted before a contingent of guards. Into the glow of the torches they dragged a prisoner clad in a black robe and hood. His body was limp, unresisting. They shoved him up against the dais with an M-16 pointed uselessly at his back.

Kuruk glanced at the Director.

"Do you know this man?"

The Director shook his head.

"Lift him up," rumbled Kuruk.

A pair of strong arms raised him off the floor. Kuruk found the carotid artery and felt a pulse. So he was still alive. Good. He could be made to suffer, then, for whatever futile treason he had planned.

He studied the face half-concealed under the hood. Something about it struck a low warning tone in his mind. He could not say why.

He touched the man's forehead. His fingertip came away stained with oil, a cosmetic lotion of some sort. The man must have darkened his complexion to disguise himself. But why? Was he afraid that someone might recognize his face?

His face . . .

Kuruk stiffened. A magazine photograph flashed in his mind, as soundless as a burst of heat lightning.

Slowly, almost hesitantly, he reached out with one

hand and peeled back an eyelid to expose the eye. A green eye. Darkly green.

"This is no man," Kuruk whispered. He raised his head, looking into the vast darkness around him. "This is the singer of the Deathsong."

A low breathless sound rose from the crowd.

Kuruk turned with infinite slowness to look down at the Director, standing at the edge of the platform. "The woman whose voice had been forever stilled."

The old man gazed up at him with helpless, senile, pleading eyes.

"I *did* kill her," he breathed. "I did. I saw her die."

"You saw what she wanted you to see."

The Director took a step backward. He raised his shaking hands as if to ward off a blow.

"No," he said. "Don't."

Kuruk parted his lips to sing.

The Director whirled to face the crowd. "It's a lie!" he shrieked. "There is no new world! No power! No glory! There's nothing! Nothing but maggots! Maggots and death!" He was laughing, the last of his sanity gone. "Nothing," he cackled. "Nothing. Nothing. Nothing."

Kuruk sang one note and the Director exploded, head and torso and limbs flying apart in all directions, spattering the crowd with a hail of blood and brains.

Black robes milled in confusion. Fresh waves of panic rippled through the room. Kuruk paid no attention. He looked down once more at the woman named Billie Lee Kidd.

"And now, my dear," he said softly, "you, too, will receive your reward. And this time, there will be no illusion."

33

Billie had almost died in the desert, but as was the case in horseshoes, darts, and sexual conquest, almost didn't count.

She certainly wouldn't have bet the farm on her chances of survival as she lay on her stomach in the dirt, her eyes squeezed shut, her face shielded by her hands from the wasps' multiple stings, while her mind flickered on the brink of darkness and a faraway voice sang to her. Her own voice, she realized. She smiled a little, thinking of how much she had always loved to sing. To sing. . . .

Then her eyes opened in time with a light-bulb flash in her brain.

The wasps would not respond to the song that hypnotized its listeners. The old man had steeled them against it with some magic of his own. But there were other songs. The song that had taken Harve Medlow's life, for instance. Maybe they weren't immune to that. Or maybe they were—but, hell, it was worth a try. It was the last ace she had up her sleeve, and if she didn't play it, the house was going to cash her out of this game for sure.

She opened her mouth behind the protective webwork of her fingers and sang the song that induced suicide.

The wasps seemed to hesitate, as if confused by conflicting signals. She sang louder. Abruptly they rose in a humming cloud. They buzzed wildly, tracing crazed half-circles in the evening air, and then in one mindless mass they spun into a reckless kamikaze dive, hurled themselves at the rocks, and smashed their fragile bodies to glittering dust.

She looked up through the net of hair plastered across her face. The old man, taken by surprise, took a split second to react. Into that momentary opening she thrust her voice. She sang the song that would harness his will to hers. He staggered backward, caught off-guard. He tried to find his voice. He made only a dull clicking noise, the sound of his tongue against his teeth. Already her song was taking effect.

As she watched, his eyes slowly narrowed to slits, his eyelids drooping heavily. His body swayed in time with the rhythm of the song. She sang louder. He shook his head with sudden savage energy, a final desperate attempt to tear free of the song's influence. Then he seemed to sag, his body going limp, the last of his willpower drained away like the dying sunlight.

She let the song trail off. She waited, watching, still expecting a trick or a trap.

There was none. He was out. She had done it. She had won.

She got halfway to her feet. She could rise no further. The pain in her legs was too great. Her whole body was on fire, burning from the inside out. She felt the stiffness in her joints, the itching of her skin, the agonized swelling where the dozens of stings had gone to work. Light-headedness passed over her like a wave of nausea. She sank to her knees once more. She lowered her head, fighting to stay alert.

The wasps had done their job well. Poison pulsed through her veins. Without treatment she would pass out. Or die.

Need antivenin, she told herself half-coherently. Have to get back to the ranch.

She realized that she was seeing herself on a desert trail with a rattlesnake bite on her arm.

Then, out of context, the memory of Harve Medlow's voice, disembodied and sourceless as the whisper of a ghost, came back to haunt her.

"There are songs that make your skin flake off like dandruff," he had told her in his sun-streaked living room a few hours and several lifetimes ago. "Turn your bones to marshmallow. Burst your heart like a water balloon. . . . There's one that can poison you, and another that cleans the poison out of your system, just like that. . . . Guess you could have used that one when you got snakebit, huh?"

Yeah, Harve, she answered silently. I could have used it when I got snakebit. And maybe, just maybe, I can use it now.

She looked up at the old man, still swaying in time to a melody playing only in his head.

"Can you hear me?" she asked.

He nodded.

She took a breath. "Okay, then. You're going to do whatever I tell you. Got it?"

Nod.

Another surge of dizziness sent the world spinning around her. She ground her palms into the dirt. She fought to stay conscious as her face was suddenly flushed with fever and her body stiffened with the onset of paralysis.

"Your little insect friends did one hell of a number on me," she said, forcing the words past frozen lips. "I need to check myself into a detox program pronto. You follow?"

Nod.

"Okay, handsome." The world was going gray, not with twilight. "You know the score. So hum a few bars."

He hesitated, his face drawn in lines of resistance, as some part of his mind still fought the spell.

"Come on." She was giggling as fireworks exploded in her brain and arthritis crept like slow death up her arms. "Play it, Sam. Play 'As Time Goes By.' "

His mouth trembled. The muscles of his neck stood out like cords of piano wire.

"Do it!" she screamed with her last strength.

He sang four notes. Instantly her mind and body cleared.

She touched her forehead. It was cool and dry. She looked down at her arms, her legs. Insect bites still peppered her skin like multiple pinpricks, but the itching and swelling were gone, along with the stiffness of her joints, the paralysis.

She rose in one swift, sure motion. She inhaled deeply.

I'm healed, she thought wonderingly. Healed.

"Well, say hallelujah," she whispered, "and pass the collection plate." She looked at the old man, standing motionless as if rooted to the desert floor. "Okay, pal. You did that real good. Now you're going to do Billie another little favor. You're going to tell her where to find the Door."

His words came slowly, paste squeezed from a tube. "I don't know where it is. Nobody knows. Nobody except him."

"Who?"

"Drake."

"You know where to find him?"

"Yes."

"Okay, Crockett. Let's roll."

"No. Can't."

"Sure, you can."

He shook his head. A ribbon of spittle ran down his chin. "Won't . . ."

She smiled for the first time in quite a while. "Oh, yes, you will. But first you just listen up, pal. Listen good."

It had not been difficult to implant a suggestion in the old man's mind. According to this new draft of the script, he had won the battle after all. She watched as he accepted the idea. Then slowly he walked to the empty patch of ground where, it seemed, he saw her expiring body. He knelt. He seemed to brush the non-

existent wasps away. And then he began to talk, while
she stood at his side, invisible to his clouded mind,
watching, listening.

"Billie," he said in a low undertone, "I don't know
if you can hear me. But if you can, I wish to tell you
something."

She waited, curious.

He told her that she had been doomed to lose. "Life
always loses," he said almost sadly. "Death wins in
the end." He uttered some incomprehensible non-
sense about maggots. Then he took the hand of the
dying woman who existed only in his mind. He leaned
down as if to whisper in her ear. She moved closer,
straining to catch his words. She heard him mutter,
"Antarok," and something about a truth which only
he and the master knew. She could not make out the
rest.

After a long while he rose to his feet. He gazed up
at the night sky. She wondered what he was seeing up
there in the empty spaces between the stars.

Then he walked slowly to the car. He stopped. He
looked back at the spot where he still saw her corpse.
He seemed to hesitate for just a moment. Then he sang
three high notes. A breeze stirred. That was all.

He got into the car. She realized that he was leaving.
Quickly she opened the rear door and climbed into the
backseat. He would not see her.

The car glided onto the main road, winding past
fields and farmhouses. Inside those homes, she
thought, people were settling down to watch TV, having already finished their Sunday supper and put the
younger kids to bed. They would relax, take it easy,
sip a beer or two, and think idle thoughts about what
they had to do tomorrow, on Monday, another Monday. And none of them would suspect that there was a
reasonably good chance that this world of theirs, this
ordered, predictable world that fit them as easily as
a faded pair of blue jeans, would end at midnight, to

be replaced by something else, something new and unimaginably different.

She checked her watch, the digital display glowing greenly. Nine o'clock.

Three hours left.

An hour later, she was curled up in a fetal ball on the floor of the Lincoln, hoping against hope that she could not be seen through the windows. She might be invisible to her unwitting chauffeur, but not to the guards patrolling the gates of the estate the car was slowly approaching.

She had kept track of their route, checking street signs and gauging miles as the old man drove. The estate was on Mulholland Drive, the winding two-lane strip of road that crested the Santa Monica Mountains, offering spectacular views of the city to the south and the San Fernando Valley to the north. It lay, by her estimate, perhaps a half-mile west of the Hollywood Freeway, which would put it midway between Cahuenga and Laurel Canyon Boulevard. Due north was Universal City, with its multiplex movie theater and the roofed amphitheater she had played on more than one occasion, always to a sellout crowd. Due south was Hollywood itself. Off to the east was the lighted HOLLYWOOD sign, barely readable from this angle, suspended in space like a bar of light.

Billie tensed as the Lincoln pulled to a stop. She waited. The driver's-side window slid down with a whir. Muffled words were exchanged.

Then the car rolled forward again, passing through the gates.

She let out a long shuddering breath. She was in.

She waited, still curled up on the floor. The car pulled off the driveway onto a rougher surface. It continued for a few moments longer, then slowed to a halt. The engine died. She heard the creak of the driver's door, then felt the gentle rocking of the car on its springs as the old man got out. His footsteps, crunching on what might have been dry grass, receded into the distance and were gone.

She lifted her head and peered out through the rear window.

The car was in a weed-strewn lot at the back of the house. Other cars and vans were parked nearby in disorderly rows. There was nobody in sight.

She took a deep breath, then opened the door and got out. She waited for a siren to sound or a pack of guard dogs to come loping out of the shadows. Nothing happened.

So far, so good.

She closed the door quietly and sank down on her knees, hugging the side of the car. She scanned the area, reconnoitering the field of battle before her.

The house was a big old rotting Manderley of a place, a pile of expensive lumber heaped up in a vague homage to the Queen Anne style. From inside came a murmur of voices, the sounds of a party, but devoid of laughter. The grounds curved around in a wide sweep of untended grass littered with dandelions, fenced in by high brick walls topped by iron spikes. At the back of the yard stood a line of trees, somber as sentries.

She looked around at the cars. A lot of people had come here tonight. Some kind of major shindig was going down. She counted two dozen vans before giving up. They must have trucked in houseguests from all over town. They . . .

She froze, her eyes narrowed, as she caught a hint of blue-black metal under the fronds of a palm tree.

Her car. Her very own car.

She got to her feet. She approached the Countach. It showed no outward sign of damage. With luck, it would still go. And she still had her keys. She could hop behind the wheel and take off.

Once she found Drake. If she found him.

She brushed stray hairs off her forehead and tried to

figure out how the hell to accomplish that minor task. The first step, she decided, was to get into the house.

She crept, as soundless as a shadow, across the wide lawn. She stopped once, certain that she heard someone coming. Then she heard the noise again and realized it was merely a scrap of newspaper rustling fitfully in the night wind.

She reached the house. She moved cautiously around to the eastern side, hugging the walls, listening to the murmur of conversation from inside. She stopped by a broken window, unshaded, with jagged glass teeth still clinging to its frame. She crouched down and peered in over the windowsill. Two men, latecomers to the party, stood in a cobwebbed room lit by torches. They were changing from street clothes into black robes and hoods.

"Won't be long now," said one man as he pulled a black cowl up over his ears. "Hey, what's the first thing you're gonna do?"

"There was a guy," said the second man, still in his underwear. His voice was low and thoughtful. "A guy who beat the shit out of me in the fourth grade. Emilio Lopez was his name. I know where he lives. I've been waiting. Waiting all these years." He laughed, a dry, mirthless sound. "I'm gonna cut off his balls. Make him eat 'em. With Tabasco sauce, maybe."

"Then what?"

"There are other guys," he said, his eyes dark and serious. "I've been waiting a long time."

Brave new world, thought Billie grimly.

The first man finished changing, kicked his abandoned clothes into a corner, and left without a word. The other man, the one who wanted to take revenge on every schoolyard bully who had haunted his sleep for twenty years, fumbled with the clasp on his robe. He cursed under his breath.

Billie sang to him, a sweet humming song wafted into the room on the night breeze.

He listened. Slowly his hands dropped to his sides. He stood motionless, awaiting orders.

"Okay, creep," she whispered. "Take off the drag-queen getup."

He obeyed. He stood naked except for his underpants and the bracelet on his left wrist.

"Hand it over."

He gave her the clothes through the window.

"Now sleep. Sleep for a good long time."

His legs folded under him. He sank down weightlessly in a corner, his head nodding.

Better than Sominex, she thought with satisfaction.

She pulled the costume on over her clothes. It was loose enough to conceal the anatomical details that made her ineligible for membership in the Brotherhood. Her hair was hidden under the hood. All in all, she figured she could crash their party without attracting undue attention to herself.

She was about to climb in through the window and put her theory to the test when, from the trees at the back of the yard, there rose a brief flurry of song.

She froze, listening. A moment later she heard footsteps approaching. She crouched down, hugging the wall of the house, losing herself in shadow.

A man took form out of the darkness. A huge man, powerfully built, wearing a dark business suit which seemed oddly inappropriate, as if his body had been intended for other, less civilized attire. His face was framed with spikes of black beard in a style alien to this age, a style reminiscent of those faces painted in distorted perspective on crumbling potteries and the walls of ruined temples.

Billie felt the short hairs on the nape of her neck stiffen with sudden fear.

The abyss, she thought. He knows it too.

Directly opposite her hiding place, the man stopped. He stood motionless, his head cocked, as if listening. She sat very still, her body taut, her heart hammering in her ears.

Then she began to breathe again as he moved on.
She watched him disappear around the side of the
house. She heard a door creak open and slam shut.

She huddled in the shadows, hugging herself and
thinking.

He had come out of the trees at the back of the yard.
He had sung to someone back there. But who? Who
would be hidden from sight, far from the mansion and
its guests?

She thought she knew the answer. She only hoped
she was not too late.

She got to her feet. She ran across the grounds of
the estate, the black robe rustling around her legs like
the slow-motion folds of a nightgown in a dream. She
found a break in the trees and ran through. She
emerged into a small hidden garden. She stopped at
the edge of a swimming pool. She stared.

At first she could not quite take in what she saw. A
huge, bloated, obscenely inhuman shape quivered at
the center of a net of silvery lines—a web . . . oh,
God Almighty, a spiderweb . . . a web strung like
streamers of cotton candy across the empty pool, spun
by the spider that crawled slowly forward, like a movie
monster, on immense hairy, multijointed legs—and directly underneath the creature, pinned down, helpless,
his body half-concealed in a silken cocoon, his head
and shoulders already disappearing inside the spider's
yawning mouth . . . Drake.

Billie sang.

Her voice rose in a low, almost tuneless warbling.
She sang the suicide song, softly, with quiet intensity,
not wishing to be heard beyond the confines of these
trees, singing for an audience of one, an audience that
regarded her with eight glittering black eyes.

The spider scuttled backward, disgorging its prey.
Drake, or whatever might be left of him, slid out of
its mouth like a fur ball out of a cat. His upper body
was coated in slime. She could not tell if he was alive

or not. She had no time to think about it. She kept singing.

The spider whirled, dragging itself in circles in a mindless quest for death. Its feelers twitched in sudden frenzy. The spinnerets splashed silk in foaming waves. The web bobbed crazily, vibrating like a trampoline. The spider twisted its head and dug its scythe-like pincers into its own underbelly. The soft flesh ruptured. A flood of goo rushed out. Its legs buckled. It collapsed on its side. It struggled weakly, the eight legs pawing at air. Its fangs, still seeking flesh, tore a gash in the fleshy bulb of its abdomen. Milky white fluid bubbled out, dripping through the net, spattering the floor of the pool. The abdomen deflated, a spent balloon.

The spider twitched and writhed on its back for a few moments longer, while Billie kept on killing it softly—as the saying went—with her song, until finally the eight eyes went dark, the legs drooped, and the thing gave a final shudder and lay still.

"Drake?" she whispered.

There was no answer.

Gingerly she stepped onto the web and tested its strength, then made her way across. She reached Drake's side. She knelt by him. She stared down, her mind rebelling against the reality of what her eyes insisted they saw.

There was almost nothing left of his face. His hair had been burned away in a bath of acid. A few pitiful strands clung to his scalp like stubborn weeds on a bulldozed hillside. His flesh was mottled with bluish-purple scars. His eyes were black hollows, empty and sightless, above the mangled cavity of his mouth.

She looked down at his body. His arms and legs were encased in silk. His right arm seemed unnaturally abbreviated. She wondered through a fog of shock if something had happened to his hand. She shook her head. It didn't matter. Nothing mattered.

"Drake," she said again hopelessly, expecting no reply, receiving none.

She forced herself to look at his face again, studying it with desperate intensity for any sign of life. Her attention was caught by a flicker of movement at the corner of her eye. She looked down with a stab of hope, then felt it die as she realized that what she had seen was only the slow trickle of blood from twin puncture marks above his collarbones.

The spider, she thought numbly. It bit him, injected him with poison . . .

Poison.

Slowly she raised her head.

Drake was dead. He had to be. But . . . but what if he wasn't? What if he was paralyzed, helpless, able to hear her when she called his name but unable to respond?

She pressed her ear to his chest. Faintly she heard the flutter of a heartbeat.

So there was still a chance.

She sang the song the old man had sung at her command, four magical notes with the power to sweep a poisoned body clean. She waited breathlessly, watching Martin Drake for some endless period of time, five seconds at least. Then his head moved and his mouth worked, pronouncing a single word.

"Billie . . . ?"

She forced a smile which she knew he could not see.

"You were expecting maybe Joan of Arc?"

"Billie." He spoke louder, with almost disbelieving wonder. He turned his head in her direction. The sightless face stared up at her. She could see his teeth too clearly behind the half-melted remnants of his lips. "Billie, oh, Jesus, Jesus. I thought . . . They told me you were . . ."

"That's what they're supposed to think."

"How did you get here? What . . . what happened?"

She knew there was no time to explain it all. He

would not last much longer. He had lost too much blood. No song—at least, none she knew—could keep him alive for long. She had to speak fast. She leaned close. She pressed her mouth to his ear.

"Martin. Listen to me. I need your help. I need to find the Door."

"Yes."

"Where is it? Tell me."

"The sign," he whispered. "Go to . . . to the sign."

She blinked, bewildered.

"You know," he said, "you can even see it from here. They've been looking for it so hard, and . . . and there it was, right in front of them the whole time." A sound like a chuckle escaped his ruined mouth. "That's a good joke on them. Isn't it?"

"What sign? What do you mean?"

"At the top of Mount Lee. You've seen it. Everybody's seen it."

She tried to make sense out of what he was saying. Mount Lee. She knew where that was. In Elysian Park. Only a mile from here. The old housing development, Hollywoodland, had been put up there back in the thirties. And at the summit of the mountain was the advertising gimmick of all time, a string of fifty-foot letters spelling out HOLLYWOOD against the night sky.

The sign, she realized with a click of mental tumblers falling into place. The HOLLYWOOD sign.

"I understand," she told him. "I'll get there. And, Martin . . . I'm sorry." She swallowed. She had to say it. "I should have believed you. I should never have run away. I knew you were telling the truth. I was afraid, that's all. Afraid to face it."

He coughed. A stream of pale liquid bubbled out of his mouth and oozed down his neck.

"It's all right, Billie. You've . . . you've done better than anybody could have hoped."

"You and me both," she said gently.

"Yes," he breathed in a soft, wondering voice, as

if the thought had occurred to him for the first time. "Both of us. We . . . we can still beat them . . . after all."

Then with a burst of strength he raised his head, staring blindly into the dark, his face twisted with emotion. "Billie. Promise me you'll stop them. Promise you'll shut that goddamn Door and keep it shut once and for all."

Tears burned her eyes. Her voice trembled. "I promise," she whispered. "I won't let them win."

Martin Drake smiled, and in that one last moment his face was almost human again.

"Then it was worth it," he whispered.

In the next moment his features smoothed out, as devoid of expression as a rubber mask, and as lifeless, and although Billie called his name again and again, she knew he could not hear her anymore.

The digital display on her wristwatch was flashing eleven o'clock when she emerged from the trees into the open expanse of the yard.

She had a plan. It might even work.

She would sneak up on the guards and sing to them, then order them to open the gates for her. She would climb behind the wheel of the Countach and make tracks. The Door was only minutes away. Then it would be time for one last performance.

Later, she would grieve. For all the people she had lost. For Bobby Joe. For Gary. For K.C. For a young man whose name she would never know. Even for Harve Medlow, maybe. And perhaps most of all for Martin Drake. Yes. Later. It would all come later.

Right now she had a world to save.

She stole across the yard, passing the parked cars, making a wide detour around the house. She reached the trees edging the front wall. She peered out from the shadows. Just ahead lay the driveway. Half a dozen guards, clad in black pajamalike uniforms and toting M-16's, flanked the gates.

No problem, she thought coolly, while jewels of sweat trickled down her forehead and her heart jumped through hoops in her chest. Hell, I can take out these clowns with one vocal cord tied behind my back.

She was just about to prove it when she felt a circle of cold steel kissing her neck and heard the click of a safety's release.

She closed her eyes. Billie, old gal, she thought hopelessly, this just ain't your day.

"Turn around," said a rough masculine voice.

She turned. The man—another security guard in black jammies—stood with an Uzi trained on her, its long barrel gleaming like polished chrome in the moonlight.

"Okay, mister," he growled. "What's your name and what are you doing out here?"

Billie blinked, momentarily confused, then realized that the costume had him fooled. The guy thought she was a man, a member of the Brotherhood. Which was good, real good. It had probably saved her from getting shot on sight.

The muzzle jabbed her in the throat.

"Come on," said the guard. "Talk."

She took a breath. She knew that what she was about to do was risky. If he resisted for more than a split second, he would have time to pull the trigger and blow her brains to oatmeal. She had to chance it. She had no choice.

She sang, trilling the song that mesmerized its victims.

His finger tightened on the trigger. For an instant she knew, just knew, he was going to fire. Then his eyes clouded over. His grip relaxed. Slowly he lowered the gun.

From the driveway came a shout. One of the guards had heard her song.

"Hey! What the hell's going on over there?"

Her concentration was broken just for an instant. The guard's eyes swam back into focus. His mouth

twisted in a snarl. He raised the Uzi, targeting her
chest. She lunged for the gun and jerked it into the
air. It went off, firing a volley of shots. She wrestled
with him as bursts of blue flame strobed over their
faces. Then the Uzi was empty and the night was silent
save for the raucous screeching of a scrub jay in the
tree branches above their heads and, from the direction of the driveway, a drumroll of racing footsteps.

She tried to sing. The guard kicked her legs out
from under her. She thudded on the ground on her
butt. He stood over her, blotting out the stars. He
gripped the Uzi by its barrel and raised it in a deadly
arc.

At the last second she found her voice. She sang.
Too late. Already the gun was sweeping down to crash
into her skull and set off an explosion of white light
inside her brain.

Her song was silenced as consciousness slipped
away.

34

Billie came to slowly, and found herself in a dungeon.

At least it looked like a dungeon, something out of
a medieval castle or a chamber of horrors. A dank,
windowless, shadowed room lit by a single torch
cupped in an iron holder on the granite wall.

Then she blinked, bringing the world into focus,
and saw that it was only somebody's basement. A perfectly ordinary basement, if you ignored that torch
casting its malevolent fireglow over the room. In the
far corner lay a heap of antique furniture, family por-
traits, and wooden crates piled up behind a scrim of

cobwebs. Nearby, a short flight of stairs rose to a closed door.

She looked down at herself. She was sprawled on the cold wooden floor, still draped in the black robe she had stolen. Her skull ached, a reminder of the gun which had crashed down out of the dark. Her eyes moved to her wristwatch—11:22. Less than forty minutes left.

The thought shocked her alert. She twisted around to a sitting position and lifted her head, and that was when she saw the man.

He stood watching her from a few yards away, his huge arms folded across his chest, inkspot eyes regarding her darkly. She recognized him at once. It had not been very long ago when she had watched, hidden in shadow, as he crossed the grounds of the estate. Then he had worn a business suit; now he, too, was clad in a black robe and peaked hood. A cape flowed like a black waterfall down his broad back to the floor.

The suit had looked wrong on him, she recalled. This new costume was right. She could not say why.

She thought of the song that had preceded his appearance in the night—the song which must have set the spider to work. Anger rose in her, a black wave. She got to her feet. She stood facing him from across the room.

"You killed Drake," she said quietly, her words evenly spaced and unnaturally distinct.

He studied her. He took a moment to answer. Then a rumble of thunder, his dark baritone, filled the room.

"And how might you know that?"

"Lucky guess."

"It is the only luck left to you." He smiled, his teeth like daggers. "Yes, I took his worthless life. He was the only man who knew the secret of the Door. Now he is dead and his secret has died with him. Which means that you have lost this game."

"Maybe."

"You have." He pursed his lips, almost sadly.

"When I first heard of you, I regretted that I had not been provided with a worthy adversary. Now I must offer my apology. You did indeed make a contest of it. I should have expected no less from you, Miss Billie Lee Kidd."

"You talk like you know me."

"I do. I have known you for years. Since long before you were born."

"Do I know you?"

"Perhaps."

"What's your name?"

"Kuruk."

She stared at him. "The high priest," she said after a long moment.

"The same."

She swallowed. Suddenly she knew why the ancient robe looked so right on him, and why modern clothes were wrong.

"You founded the cult," she whispered. "You started it all."

"And now I will finish it."

She took a breath. "Don't count on it, buddy," she said with all the bravado she could muster. "I've added a few new tunes to my repertoire in the last twenty-four hours or so. And I can sing 'em, too. I can sing 'em real good. I'm not fighting the feeling anymore. You understand what I'm telling you? I've got the power."

"Do you?" Kuruk shrugged. "Then use it."

She looked at him, bewildered. He spread his hands. The bracelet glittered on his wrist.

"Go on," he said softly. "Show me your great power. Sing to me. Turn my bones to water. Sentence me to death by my own hand. Make me your slave. Do what you will."

She hesitated, knowing that this must be some kind of trap. Then, because she had no alternative, she sang.

She chose the song she had heard in the desert, the

song that had birthed some kind of monster in her belly. She threw it at the high priest's face in tremulous waves. Kuruk stood motionless, offering no resistance, showing no expression save the hint of a smile.

She sang louder. Fragments of melody echoed in the room. The torch flamed more brightly. The floorboards shook. A webwork of cracks shot through the walls and ceiling. Chips of granite pattered down like hailstones.

And still Kuruk stood watching her with those cold black lifeless eyes.

Then, very softly, he trilled three notes.

White agony shot through her body. Her song was choked off. She collapsed. Pain ricocheted like a bullet from her stomach to her heart to her spine.

Kuruk sang again. Billie was hoisted off the floor on a current of song. She hung upside down, arms and legs flailing uselessly. Kuruk's voice rose up the scale. Helplessly she flipped over, turning somersaults, wheeling in dizzy circles through the air.

Kuruk stopped singing. Billie plummeted to the floor. She lay in a heap of twisted limbs. He gazed down on her.

"I have spent many lifetimes," he said, "learning the secrets of the sacred songs. You cannot harm me with their magic. While I, on the other hand, can kill you at any time."

"So why don't you?" she gasped.

"Because I want you to suffer. Cruel, is it not? But I have waited so long. I have earned this reward."

"Fuck you," she said hopelessly, because no other answer occurred to her.

He sang a note, a single note, and her hair came alive. It twisted and coiled and writhed, a nest of snakes, crusted with scales, hissing with forked tongues. She scrabbled wildly at her head. Vipers bit her hands, drawing blood. She was screaming. Then she heard a second note, an octave lower than the first, and the snakes were gone. Her hair, real hair, was back. For the moment.

She lay in a huddle of flesh on the cellar floor. He approached her. His shadow, cast by the torch, swallowed her up.

"You have lost, my dear. At midnight, mere minutes from now, the world will end." He smiled. "Everything will end."

She blinked, hearing something unexpected in his words, a clue to a secret she had not suspected. She looked up at him through the net of hair plastered to her face.

"Everything?" she whispered.

He nodded.

"Wait a minute. Hold the phone. What about this sequel you guys were planning? You know, the empire strikes back? The glorious new world?"

Kuruk laughed. "There will be no new world. No empire. No Antarok, reborn, to span the stars. The purpose of the gods I serve is not to build, but to destroy. To destroy worlds, galaxies, space and time itself. To reduce this universe to a gray spread of ash from which no phoenix will ever rise."

Billie stared at him while images flashed in her mind. Constellations flying apart. Suns going dark. Planets shattering like crystal globes. And in the depths of space, a door—the Door—opening to spew forth darkness and engulf the universe.

It was the vision she had seen when she sang the Deathsong. She had been baffled by it then. Now she understood.

The end of everything, she thought numbly. Not with a bang. Not with a whimper. With a song. My song.

Kuruk seemed to read her thoughts on her face.

"You see it now, do you not? The song to which you lent your voice was not a song of empires, of riches, of eternal life. It was a song of death."

"But why?" she breathed. "Why do this? What's in it for you?"

Kuruk smiled. "Nothing."

She shook her head, unable to understand.

"I have no interest in the wielding of power or the looting of nations or the building of empires. I seek only to wipe out. To destroy. To kill for the sake of killing. To put an end to life, any life, all life. To cancel out existence and leave a dead void.

"That is the goal I have sought all these long years. My promises of a better future were cheap lies, fables told to entice feeble minds with dreams of glory. The half-wits and cowards lured to my cause have never guessed my motive—or their own. Not even your friend Drake knew the whole story. Down through the centuries only one man, other than myself, ever dared to glimpse the darkest secret of the Brotherhood. The man known to his underlings as the Director. The man you bedeviled in the desert. He alone understood, many years ago. He grasped my purpose. He saw the truth.

"And it drove him insane."

She thought of the old man and his aimless mutterings about maggots and death. She remembered how he had stopped, looking up at the night sky seeded with stars. He had looked at it for such a long time. She had not known what he was seeing. She knew it now. He was imagining the moment when those stars would wink out, when those eternal flames would sputter and die, when the vastness of the universe would be left cold and dark forever.

Insane, she thought in dull horror. Of course he was insane. How could he not be insane?

"Now," rumbled Kuruk, "that man is dead. Soon I will join him. I will vanish into oblivion—and take all existence with me."

"And you're proud of that?" she said, her voice breaking with strain. "You're happy?"

"Pride and happiness mean nothing to me. I have

never known such a state of being. And soon"—his lips curved upward in a twisted mockery of a smile—"no living thing will know it ever again."

Then Billie understood. She knew the kind of hatred that had driven him for centuries.

She stared up at him helplessly. He stood less than a yard away. His hands, meaty slabs crisscrossed with blue veins, hung at his sides. The bracelet shone, blood-red, on his left wrist. The bracelet which, Drake had told her, could never be removed—under penalty of death.

"I have labored," said Kuruk softly, "for a hundred lifetimes to reach this day." He stared past her, his eyes narrowed, as if he were seeing a record of all those centuries painted on the walls in brushstrokes of flickering torchlight. "I have worked in secret, down through all the ages, to fulfill each deadly prophecy in turn. The history of the world is written in my hand. Written in blood."

She gazed up at the bracelet as if hypnotized. She could almost reach up and touch it. Almost.

"I rode with Attila. I sang for Nero. I whispered in Torquemada's ear. He thought it was the voice of God he heard. Alexander was lured from philosophy to conquest by my siren songs. Napoleon knew me. And Stalin. And Hitler. They all knew me. All the tyrants on throne or horseback. I sought them out in palace halls, in desert camps, in prison cells, in lonely exile. Sought them out, those men with dark eyes and darker souls, and bent them to my will. Helped them to disarm and crush their enemies. Urged them on to glory and destruction."

She pressed her palms to the floorboards. She dragged herself forward a half-inch, then a half-inch more, slowly, haltingly, bringing the bracelet within reach.

"Think of all the wretched millions, down through the centuries, who perished in war, in famine, in slavery. Their lives were had—one might say—for a song."

She tensed her arm. She would have one chance. Just one.

"You could never have defeated me, Miss Billie Lee Kidd. I have come too far. I have seen too much. I have honed my powers over the span of two hundred generations. I have been alive for four thousand years."

Billie gazed up at him.

"You've never been alive," she whispered.

Her arm shot out like a steel spring uncoiling. Her hand clamped down on the bracelet. She ripped it free.

He stared at his bare wrist as if unable to comprehend what he had lost. And then with a shriek of mingled agony and rage, Kuruk began to change.

Fur sprouted on his hands and face. His robe bulged with eruptions of muscle. The black velvet strained under the enlarging pectorals and biceps, then fell away in a cloud of rags. His cape, still fastened to his thickening neck, lashed behind him as he whirled, howling. His mouth was a muzzle. He wrinkled his snout, exposing canine teeth. He swayed, then dropped down on all fours. He was not a man anymore. He was some sort of ape-thing, huge, hulking, prehistoric.

Billie leapt to her feet. She backed away.

"You blew it, pal," she shouted. He had to know this. She wanted him to die knowing it. "You fucked up. Drake didn't die on schedule. I got to him first. You listening? *Drake told me where to find the Door!*"

Kuruk howled. He pounded his fist against his chest. Billie had time to smile, giddy with exhilaration, certain of victory.

Then, with astonishing speed, Kuruk came at her.

He swung out with one massive paw. She jumped back. His fist missed her by inches. It punched a crater in the granite wall. The room shuddered with a drumroll of echoes. He pulled free. He launched a circling blow with his right fist. She ducked. Air whistled over her head. Then his left hand shot out, catching her by surprise, and snatched the bracelet back.

Billie gasped.

Kuruk clutched the bracelet tightly. Instantly the transformation was arrested.

She stared at him, waiting for the next move.

Kuruk's snout worked desperately, slavering bright spumes of spit, trying to force out articulate sounds. A song, she realized. He was trying to sing a song. He could not do it. He produced only a series of animal grunts.

He lashed out at her with his fists. She jumped sideways, dodging the blows. He advanced on her, loping on his knuckles.

She looked into his eyes, human eyes embedded in an animal face, like the eyes of an actor in a mask. They caught the glow of the torch at her back and magnified it, burning with hatred, with blood lust, the lust to kill this woman who dared to challenge the high priest of Antarok in the moment of his triumph, the lust to take her weak, helpless body in his hands and drag her with him to his grave—and with her, the universe itself.

She backed into a corner, trapped. He gazed down at her, his face contorted in a fanged grimace that might have been a smile. His right hand closed over her throat. He lifted her slowly off the floor. His fingers tightened, viselike. Her breath was cut off. Her brain buzzed. Her legs kicked uselessly. She scrabbled at the wall behind her, groping blindly for a loose stone, for anything she might use as a weapon, and her hand closed over the stem of the torch.

She yanked it free of its holder and thrust it at Kuruk's face, setting him aflame.

Kuruk jumped back, releasing his grip, then spun, tearing out handfuls of burning hair. Flames spread to his cape. It blazed, twisting and writhing like a living thing. He beat at it with his fists. He ripped it free of his neck and flung it into the far corner, where crates

and pieces of old furniture were piled high in a tangle
of cobwebs. The dry wood caught. Jets of flame leapt
up, painting the basement walls in shades of orange
and red.

Billie grabbed the torch, sputtering on the floor. She
advanced on Kuruk. She brandished the torch like a
sword, sweeping it across his chest, cutting a wide
swath. He roared. He staggered backward. She followed, stabbing with flame at his legs and groin. He
blazed like a fireball. He stumbled into a wall. He
waved his huge arms helplessly, trying to shield his
face, his chest, his legs, every part of him at once.

She took a final step, closing the distance between
them. She thrust the torch at his left hand. He jerked
it away, his fingers splayed. The bracelet fell free. It
clattered on the floor. And before he could react, Billie kicked out and sent it spinning into the fire raging
in the corner of the room, lost to sight, lost forever.

Then Kuruk screamed.

It was a sound born of an animal throat, but it was
not an animal's cry. It was a scream of torment, of
frustration, of fury. A man's scream. A death scream.

Billie watched, unable to turn away, as the gorilla
form crumbled, dissolving to dust, exposing something smaller, shrewlike, something that squealed pit-
eously as its silver fur ignited. In the next instant that
too was gone, replaced by a wriggling eellike thing
that flapped its boneless flippers, sizzling like a fish
on a grill, its scales bubbling and streaming off in rivers of melted flesh. It shriveled, trout eyes bulging, as
something still smaller and more helpless scuttled
weakly inside the deflating bag of flesh, seeking to get
out, like a cat trying to claw its way free of a burlap
sack. The flames blazed brighter, throwing up a rainbow of red and blue and silver. Billie had time to see
a pair of twitching eyestalks peep out of the charred
carcass, and then she heard an awful hissing and
crackling, the sounds a lobster might make if it were
cooked alive in a dry pan, its shell popping like corn,

as the eyestalks withered, shrinking down to a milky puddle, to a speck, then finally to nothing at all.

All that remained of Kuruk was a rising cloud of greasy black smoke and the last fading echo of his scream.

35

The flames spread through the cellar. They marched up the stairs. Billie fought her way through the net of fire and the choking waves of smoke. She climbed the stairs, reached the door, and tugged it open. She stumbled into a hallway. She ran.

The fire raced after her. Flames hopped giddily down random corridors, igniting the dry wood like tinder, feeding on the litter and debris scattered everywhere, setting the ground floor of the mansion ablaze.

The men assembled in the ballroom had been given no instructions when their master departed abruptly with the guards and the singer of the Deathsong, and so they had not dared to leave. They stood as they had been told to stand, in ordered rows, holding their torches aloft, murmuring nervously and waiting. At first, nobody noticed the wisps of smoke curling up from the crack under the huge double doors at the back of the room.

Then Tony Alvarez, in the last row, wrinkled his nose and sniffed. He had caught a smell, the odor of pipe smoke, maybe, or some pretty good weed. He turned, curious, and saw billows of smoke rising directly behind him.

"Jesus," he breathed.

He took a cautious step sideways, then another, then

one more. He was thinking that he had to get to the side door, yeah, but nice and casual, without attracting attention, because the last thing he needed right now was a panic.

He had just taken his fourth step when somebody screamed.

Instantly the crowd became a mob. The neat rows of hooded figures disintegrated like a rack of billiard balls under the first stroke of the cue.

One man made the mistake of trying to get out through the rear doors. He brushed past Tony and flung the doors wide. Smoke and flame rushed in like water through a shattered floodgate. Tony looked back once as he ran away, and saw the dumb bastard blazing like a straw figure burned in effigy.

The crowd, retreating, stormed one of the side doors. The door was unlocked but it was designed to open inward. Against the sudden press of bodies it would not budge. More men piled into the mass. They were tangled up in screaming knots.

Walter Gelbard, who once had wanted to be a movie actor and who now wanted merely to survive, ran through the swirl of hooded figures, seeking an exit that did not exist. Smoke blinded him. He slammed into the pedestal of a statue and dropped his torch. It slithered down the front of his robe, leaving a trail of fire. Sudden heat baked him, singeing the short hairs of his chest and groin. His hands tore at the robe, trying desperately to pull it off. It clung to him like a jealous lover. The flames rose and his robe rose with them, climbing higher, hitching up around his waist and leaving his legs bare. Absurdly he was reminded of Marilyn Monroe on that subway grating, her skirt blown by a draft. He staggered sideways. He collided with other men, bouncing from one to the other, a pinball racking up points. Flames spread like a contagion. Black robes blazed.

Men climbed the dais, seeking safety in higher ground. The platform sagged under the mounting

weight. Still more robed figures fought to climb
aboard, with the mindless desperation of men pouring
into an overcrowded lifeboat. The wooden posts sup-
porting the structure groaned. The dais swayed drunk-
enly. The posts gave way. The platform collapsed with
an ugly splintering sound. Men were trapped in a
wreckage of broken lumber and smashed limbs. They
fought to tear themselves free as fire rippled over them,
setting the planks alight. Wood glowed like hot coals
in a barbecue pit. The stench of roasted meat rose in
sickening waves.

An old man in a wheelchair raced by. He was on
fire. His gnarled hands spun the wheels, propelling
him forward, as if in the hope of outracing the flames
lashing his back. The chair careened into a burning
body prostrate on the floor. The old man was launched
into space. He slammed down on the floor. Ribs
snapped. He groaned. He dragged his crippled body
forward, screaming shrilly for help. Racing feet tram-
pled his hands, his neck, his spine. Nobody helped
him. Nobody noticed him. Nobody ever noticed.

Smoke choked the room. Men fell on their knees
and crawled. They butted their heads against the walls.
They pounded senselessly at the plaster while the paint
bubbled and the faded columbine and ivy peeled off
in scorched strips.

Russell Garrett dangled thirty feet above the crowd.
He clung to one of the curving octopoid arms of the
statue of the god Dasharoom. His eyes watered from
smoke. His fingers ached. He hung on anyway. Here,
at least, he would not be crushed underfoot or set afire.
Here he had a chance. He could look down and watch
the frantic efforts of the men below him, as he had
often looked down from his chopper at the antlike figures of firefighters struggling to control a blaze.

The statue groaned.

He looked up in sudden terror. For one light-headed
moment he was sure the statue had come alive. Then

he realized the sound was merely the protest of the ancient limestone crumbling under his weight.

The statue bent at the waist as if taking a bow. Russell Garrett held on, paralyzed, as the massive carving lurched, teetered, then snapped free of its pedestal. It leaned forward, lowering like a boom. One of the ballroom's crystal chandeliers caught its head, topping it like a jeweled crown, holding it briefly suspended over the screaming crowd. Then the chandelier was ripped away from the ceiling in a rain of plaster, and the statue crashed down, smashing men like insects, pinning Russell Garrett under its mass.

His spine snapped like a breadstick. He lay helpless on the floor, listening to the moans of the half-crushed men writhing around him. He shut his eyes. He cursed the world.

Somewhere, in some far corner of the room, a man was singing the song of obeisance to the dark gods, as if beseeching them for help.

Other songs, less melodious, rose in the smoky darkness. High-pitched, ululating songs which climbed the scale to reach a screeching crescendo, then were abruptly cut off. Songs with no black magic to perform.

Songs that were only screams.

Some men escaped from the room. Tony Alvarez was one of them. He crawled over burning bodies. He shoved weaker men out of his way. His face was contorted, his eyes crazed. He found a side door and fled into the corridors, a shadowy labyrinth strobing with orange sunbursts.

Halfway down the hall, he stopped, frozen by the sight of a robed figure running in his direction.

Her, he thought with savage fury.

He seized a torch from the wall and ran, screaming obscenities, straight at Billie Lee Kidd.

Her eyes stopped him. They were not afraid. They were not angry. They showed no emotion at all. They gazed at him, and through him, as if he did not exist. The way women always looked at him.

She sang.

Tony thrust the torch into his own mouth, like a fire-eater at a carnival sideshow. He ate flame. He thudded on the floor in a spastic heap.

Bitch, he thought feverishly as flames scurried, insect-quick, over his face, consuming him. God damn you to hell, you bitch, you bitch, you bitch.

Billie ignored the man blazing on the floor, the man who had just heard a command performance of the suicide song. She had no time for him. No time for any of them. She had to get out.

She ran past a doorway framing a vast room lined with statues, one already toppled, the others threatening to fall. Smoldering bodies littered the floor like the victims of an air raid. She kept running. She veered down a side corridor, seeking an exit in this smoke-filled maze.

"There she is!"

She whirled in the direction of the shout. Three cultists came rushing at her out of the shadows. She had time to see their faces, pale ovals fringed by black hoods, their upper lips curled over canine teeth in a mindless snarl. Then her voice leapt up like a jet of flame. Instantly all three men were on the floor, twisting and writhing and jackknifing crazily as their stomachs swelled with unholy life.

She ran on. Smoke rolled down the corridor like a black fog bank. She tore off a strip of her robe and held it to her face. Her eyes burned.

She reached the end of the hall and came up against a blank wall. Dead end. She turned. Already the fire was advancing to cut off escape. Arteries of flame radiated over the floor and walls and ceiling.

Doors lined the hall. She ran to the nearest one and threw it open. A closet. She ran to the next door. Locked. She tugged uselessly at the knob, then stumbled to the third door in line. She pulled it open and looked in on a room with a window.

She ran inside. Flames raced after her in hot pursuit. She reached the window. She kicked out the glass, then brushed away the jagged shards clinging to the frame. She hoisted herself onto the windowsill. She climbed through and dropped lightly to the ground.

She was out.

An instant later, the window became a sheet of fire, billowing like a curtain in the night breeze.

She stumbled away from the house toward the blue-black Lamborghini Countach parked under a palm tree thirty yards away. She passed a blazing fireball that was a man rolling over and over on the lawn, trying frantically to put himself out.

Behind her came a sound like the roar of an explosion. She looked back in time to see the side wall of the mansion cave in. A shower of sparks shot up, pinwheeling dizzily in the night sky. Men fled the house, escaping through windows, through doors, through gaps in the walls. They ran past her in all directions.

The mansion swayed like a house of cards. The roof collapsed. The remaining walls sagged inward. The interior of the building was briefly revealed, like a cutaway of a doll's house. The stairway plunged down. The second story dropped away. The house flattened out as if crushed by a giant hand. The wreckage burned, a blazing funeral pyre.

The fire, fanned by the dust-dry wind, spread outward from the ruins. The parched grasses went up like so much kindling wood. Trees erupted into sheets of flame. Crisscrossing rivers of fire blazed across the grounds of the estate like twisting lava flows.

A stream of flame shot past Billie and engulfed the Lincoln Town Car parked a few yards from the Countach. The gas tank exploded. The Lincoln was lifted into the air in majestic slow motion. It hovered aloft, a dragon snorting fire and flapping the puny wings which were doors sagging on their hinges.

Billie reached the Countach. The door, thank Christ, was unlocked. It swung up at the touch of her hand. She sank behind the wheel and pulled out her keys. The engine roared. The high-beams flashed on.

Next to her, flames boarded a van and blew it inside-out in a hail of glass and shrapnel.

She shifted into first. The Countach shot forward in time with a series of deafening blasts rocking the night. She glanced in the rearview mirror and saw the rows of parked vans exploding like clay pigeons in a shooting galley, spraying the lawn with chunks of scorched metal and scraps of flame.

In the distance sirens rose, splitting the night like the answering echoes of screams.

Billie accelerated, arrowing the Countach at the driveway. The front gates expanded, filling the windshield. Twin rows of iron spikes rushed at her. She sat rigid in the driver's seat. She gripped the wheel. She stamped the gas pedal to the floor.

She hit the gates at sixty miles an hour. Metal screamed. The Countach's hood folded up like an accordion. The gates burst wide. She crashed through, leaving the fire behind.

The dashboard clock glowed greenly—11:50.

Ten minutes left.

36

She took a hard right onto Mulholland, heading east. The road veered into a series of tight turns. The Countach took the curves under protest, tires screaming. She pressed down harder on the gas, accelerating to eighty miles an hour.

Eleven-fifty-one. Nine minutes.

She rounded a corner. Taillights swam into view directly ahead. She swerved into the opposing lane and shot past the slower car. Another curve came up, too fast. She hit the brake. The Countach caromed off the guardrail, sending up a shower of sparks. It skidded across both lanes, fishtailing wildly. She turned into the skid and straightened out.

She glanced at the dashboard clock again—11:52.

She hit Cahuenga and veered south, a roundabout route but the only one that would get her where she had to go. She left the hills, racing into the outskirts of Hollywood. She hung a left onto Franklin.

Eleven-fifty-three.

It would be close. Very close.

She almost missed Beachwood Drive. She slammed on the brakes and swung left with a squeal of burning rubber. She took the gently rising street at a hundred and ten. Houses and parked cars flashed past.

Up ahead, framed in the windshield, hanging over the city like the symbol of glamour or the sword of Damocles, was the lighted HOLLYWOOD sign.

It looked so small, so near. It was not. It was all the way at the summit of Mount Lee, still a good two miles away.

Eleven-fifty-four.

She shot through the sandstone gates opening onto the Hollywoodland development, a cluster of modest homes hugging the corkscrew twists and hairpin turns of these mountain roads. She pumped the brake, slowing to sixty, and hooked a sharp left onto Ledgewood Drive. She climbed higher up the mountain. The sign flared up in a break between the houses racing past on her left. Bigger than before. Closer.

Eleven-fifty-five.

Not much time. Maybe not enough. But it had to be, dammit. She couldn't lose now. Not now.

Why not? asked a jeering voice in her mind. You've already lost everything else.

She couldn't argue. It was true.

She had lost Bobby Joe and Gary and K.C., her three friends who had made music with her, and never again would their four voices blend in seamless harmony in the last chorus of "I Ride an Old Paint," never again would she listen, spellbound, as Bobby Joe's skilled fingers negotiated the solo on "Restless." They had been with her almost from the beginning and now they were gone, as was Harve Medlow, the man who had believed in her when she had almost quit believing in herself, who had raised her up out of the obscurity of dingy back-alley bars and put her on the stage of the Opry for the whole world to see. Whatever his sins, he had been her friend too, and now she had lost him for good.

And there was one other friend she had lost. Maybe—she thought grimly—the worst loss of all.

She shook her head. She gripped the wheel tighter. She had to keep herself together.

Eleven-fifty-six.

She shot into a cluster of intersecting streets. She barreled straight through, onto Deronda Drive, a narrow, winding strip of road rising higher, still higher, up the mountain. She put the pedal to the metal, watched the speedometer struggle toward eighty-five. Each curve nearly wrenched her out of her seat with centrifugal force. The tires shrieked like animals in pain. The dashboard rattled crazily. She bounced up and down in her seat, buffeted by the rough road surface.

Distant lights on surrounding hillsides flashed into view through gaps in the screen of houses and trees. The sign was huge now. It loomed over the treetops, filling the sky.

"Come on," she breathed, talking either to the car or to herself. "Come on, baby. Move your ass."

Eleven-fifty-seven.

She could make it. She knew she could. She was almost there.

Without warning, the road ended.

It came to a stop in a dusty turnout and a steel barrier marked with a NO TRESPASSING sign.

She slammed on the brakes. The Countach spun out. Scenery whipsawed wildly around her. Her forehead slammed into the steering wheel. The horn blared. She thudded back into her seat with a whiplash snap of her neck.

The car twirled like a top toward the eastern edge of the turnout, where the ground fell away in a sheer drop to the canyon a thousand feet below. The right-rear tire swung over the edge. The car lurched backward.

Over the side, thought Billie with a rush of terror. I'm going over the side.

She scrabbled at the door handle. Her fingers, slick with sweat, could not get a grip on it.

The left-rear tire left solid ground behind. The Countach was perched on the edge of the mountain, half-on and half-off. It listed slowly toward the rear. It slid back an inch at a time.

Hoarse, ragged breathing filled her ears. With a final effort she grasped hold of the door handle. She tugged. The door swung up on its strut. She threw herself out of the car. She sprawled in the dirt on hands and knees.

The Countach's front wheels rose off the ground. The headlights swept up, lighting the sky. The car slid backward over the edge of the cliff and careened down the mountainside, a blue-black streak. It hit a ledge, flipped over, and began turning cartwheels. The headlights flickered, then died, and the car, still tumbling giddily end over end, vanished into the darkness somewhere far below and was gone.

Billie looked at her watch—11:58.

She got to her feet. She ran to the barrier, a structure of posts and crosswise poles low to the ground. She climbed over. She found herself on a fire road, a strip of cracked macadam bordered by scraggly brush. She ran up the road, gasping. Her legs trembled with exhaustion, threatening to fold up under her at any moment. She hoped to Christ she still had the strength to sing.

Eleven-fifty-nine.

Fifty yards up the road, she stumbled onto a sandy ridge studded with cacti and wildflowers. She ran to the edge of the cliff. She stopped.

The sign lay before her, spread out across the southern face of the mountain, on a slope perhaps a quarter-mile from where she stood. She could see it clearly. It was huge, fifty feet high, nearly five hundred feet long, the giant letters supported by metal scaffolding sunk into the earth, braced by cables, lit by white floodlights. Its glow seemed to wash out the mountain, leaving the sign suspended in space, a word written in the sky.

Below her feet, lights twinkled in the canyon—the lights of homes clinging to the naked rock like hardy desert plants. On a faraway summit the glow of the fire, still raging, lit up the night. Off in the distance, Los Angeles was spread in a glittering panorama of multicolored lights from the desert to the sea.

And looming over it all, suspended in space midway between the sign above and the city below, was a patch of darkness, an inkspot splotch, like a black hole in the universe, a rip in the fabric of existence, twisting, expanding, opening wide.

The Door.

She stared at it. Her breath froze in her throat.

You, she thought, past numbing waves of shock. It's you.

The cloud on the horizon. The shadow stealing over a desert trail. The half-glimpsed shape lurking in every dark corner.

The abyss.

Hello, Billie, it seemed to say. We meet again.

An ill wind stirred the mountaintop. The wildflowers and cactus plants shivered. A clump of weeds was ripped loose. It wafted through the air, into the thing's open maw, and winked out instantly, as if it had never been.

Billie shivered. Gooseflesh rippled over her arms. Her heart hammered in her chest.

She stared at the abyss. She fought the urge to turn away. She forced herself to look. To confront it, face it, as Drake had said she must. To peer into its lightless depths, into that bottomless pit seeking to extend its black tendrils and ensnare the universe and swallow it whole.

This was her enemy. This was the monster that had haunted her sleep, the nameless nemesis that had pursued her all her life. She had run from it. She had tried to hide. She had sought protection in the comfort of a spotlight or a stranger's arms. Because she had been afraid. So afraid.

You don't scare me, she told it silently. Not anymore.

The readout on her wristwatch flashed 12:00.

Billie sang.

Seven notes rose like a flurry of birdsong in the night air. Seven notes reversed from last night's performance. The Deathsong, backward.

The Door howled. It throbbed and pulsated. Shapes flickered in its recesses. Contorted, inhuman shapes. They writhed and squirmed and bared their rodent teeth. She saw them. She knew them somehow. Perhaps all mankind knew them and always had—the primal forces embedded in human consciousness, the deeper truths underlying myth and metaphor, the ageless evil forever posed in opposition to the good.

There was Toth, the Wind That Hungers. And Bethshul, the Screaming Woman. Garnarlit, the Stealer of Light. Narantos, the Hidden One. Dasharoom, He Who Eats Souls. And others, so many others, devils without name or number. And lording over them all, the Spider King himself, Ragnaaroth, vast and formless and shrieking in impotent rage.

She sang louder. Her voice stabbed at them. They

screeched in agony, impaled on each bell-like note. They scrabbled with ragged fingernails at the edges of the Door, seeking without success to pry it open as it shrank, folding in, threatening to seal them up forever.

Now the Door was a mere portal, a window looking in on another world, some trackless purgatory where things unfit for existence were exiled, to bide their time and nurse their mean hopes and scheme for the day when they would be set free again to wipe out the living world they hated. A day that now would never come.

Her song rang out in the night, waves of sound traveling high above the city, waves which would reach in widening ripples to the stars, to distant galaxies, to the ends of the universe, where light and life must die.

But maybe—Billie's thoughts whirled—maybe there is no end. Maybe the universe goes on forever. Maybe life does too. World without end, she thought giddily. Amen.

She let out a final burst of sound, and the Door contracted to a speck, to a pinpoint, and was gone.

She lowered her head as if taking a bow.

My greatest performance, she thought with a rush of faintness, and, wouldn't you know it, I played to an empty house.

She sank to her knees, gracefully, weightlessly, her body folding up like the petals of a flower as the last of her strength ebbed away. She lay there unmoving for a long time.

I did it, she thought numbly. I did it. I did it. I did it.

She did not know whether to be happy or sad. She was too tired to care.

Sometime later, perhaps a minute or an hour or a year, Billie raised her head. She looked at the city, as if to reassure herself that it was still there. Then she gazed toward the distant fire, raging on, consuming the last of the estate that had been the Brotherhood's secret lair.

She listened. Sirens wailed fitfully in the night. Sirens which seemed, oddly, to be growing louder. Closer. Too close.

Slowly she got up. She made her way back down the road. Up ahead, red lights strobed, cutting the darkness. Ambulances and police cars ringed the turnout. A police chopper swam into view, aiming its searchlight at the canyon.

The car crash, she told herself without surprise. Somebody reported it. Called the cops.

She supposed she ought to hide in the brush till the cops had gone. Then she could run. But . . . run where? Could she hide out for the rest of her life? Did she have the strength even to try?

She shook her head wearily. It was over. One way or the other.

Besides, she thought with a hint of a smile, I saved the whole fucking world. They ought to reduce my sentence considerably for that.

She shrugged off her robe and tossed it into the bushes. In street clothes once more, she walked to the steel barrier dividing the fire road from the turnout. She hoisted herself over it in one easy, almost lackadaisical motion, and walked swiftly into the circle of men and vehicles. She stopped before the nearest cop and held out her hands, palms down, fingers spread.

"Slap the cuffs on, mister," said Billie Lee Kidd. "You just nabbed yourself a desperado, for sure."

37

The cell was damp. Billie could not figure out how that was possible. Like the song said, it never rained in Southern California in the summertime. Maybe, she thought idly, some places are always damp. Just part of their charm.

The cops had escorted her here, to the Hollywood precinct house, after her impromptu surrender. She used her one phone call on Dial-a-Joke. She wanted to be cheered up. It didn't help.

She had no intention of calling a lawyer. She had no intention of answering any of the damn-fool questions the cops kept asking. She had no intention of uttering so much as one syllable. Quite frankly, she had no intention of doing anything ever again. She was tired. She was finished.

Eventually they gave up on the interrogation and put her in a holding cell while they tried to figure out what to do next. She sat on a bench against the rear wall, ignoring the people around her, a ragged collection of pimps, hookers, junkies, and drunks, shadow figures which barely registered on her conscious mind. One of them sidled up next to her and started to breathe sweet nothings—rather disgusting nothings, actually—in her ear. She looked at him. Just looked. He moved away.

None of the others gave her any trouble. As far as she could tell, they did not even notice her or give a damn who she was. No autograph hounds here.

Sometime later, around two in the morning, a cop unlocked the barred door of the cell to release one of the shadows imprisoned there. Billie sang to the cop.

282

She sang the song that hypnotized its listeners. She had no bold escape plan in mind. She simply wanted to see if the magic still worked.

It did not. The song had no effect. She felt nothing as she sang it. It was merely a strange, unmelodious tune. Whatever power it had once possessed had died when the Door was closed.

Past three A.M. she caught a snatch of news from somebody's radio down the hall. There were developments in Africa. Usu Ndamos had been overthrown in a coup. The new government had announced immediate plans to withdraw its troops and sue for peace.

Billie thought about that. If her powers were gone, then the same must be true of all the cultists. They would no longer be able to protect the tyrants whose careers they had nurtured. She wondered idly which other governments would fall in the weeks and months ahead. She wondered what kind of world mankind would build, now that its only enemies were human beings with human weaknesses.

She slept for a while. She awoke to the sound of the cell door squeaking open on rusty hinges. She looked up. Lieutenant Pratt of the Malibu Police Department was there.

Billie got to her feet, wondering why they would send him to interrogate her when all previous efforts had failed.

"Miss Kidd," said Pratt slowly, "please come with me."

He led her down the hall to a private room. He shut the door behind him, then turned to her. "I've just come from the hospital. There are some men in the emergency ward who survived the fire in the Hills." He studied her face. "You've heard about that, I assume?"

She said nothing. She wasn't going to talk. She had decided on that from the start. There was no use in talking, because nobody would ever believe her. Certainly not a hard-ass like Pratt.

Then she shrugged. She supposed she could not keep silent forever, not when she came equipped with a mouth the size of hers. And besides, she couldn't wade into any deeper shit than she was already in.

She met Pratt's eyes. "I didn't have to hear about it," she answered evenly. "I was there."

His eyebrows rose a fraction of an inch.

"I had a feeling you might have been," he said carefully. "You know, you were lucky to get out alive."

"No shit."

"There's no telling how many men died there. All men, too. No women. At least, not so far. We're still digging out the bodies. Anyway, a few of the poor bastards have made it as far as intensive care. I talked to them. They're saying some very interesting things. Things I wouldn't have believed. Correction. Things I didn't believe—when you told me yourself."

Billie swallowed, feeling an emotion so unexpected, under the circumstances, that she required a moment to identify it. It was hope.

"What things?" she asked quietly.

"They're all ranting and raving about a new world and a mystical prophecy and some sort of door. And about you, Miss Kidd." He paused, then said simply, "They were out to get you, all right. Just like you said. They wanted to hunt you down and kill you. They had this crazy theory that there was a new world on the way and you had the power to stop it."

Pratt spread his hands helplessly.

"What I'm trying to say is, I was wrong. I should have listened. If I had, I would have saved you all kinds of hell. I know that now. And, for whatever it's worth . . . I'm sorry."

Billie stared at him for a moment longer, trying to take in what he had just told her. Then she lowered her head, fighting back tears.

She was not under arrest anymore. She was free. She had a life again. Just like that, she had a life.

A gentle hand came to rest on her shoulder. "Miss Kidd?"

"I'm okay," she said with effort. She raised her head to face him. "Really."

He looked away, so as not to see her face.

"The strangest thing," he said, "is that one of the victims was a man I knew. You knew him too. You met him at the precinct, though you might not remember. Sergeant Drake."

Her voice was hushed. "I remember."

"He was burned almost beyond recognition. And he'd been . . . mutilated somehow. Nobody would have identified him for days, if they hadn't found his badge. He carried it in his wallet. It was in the ashes, right near . . . near the body." He shook his head. "I still can't believe he was mixed up in something like this. I can't believe he was one of them."

"He wasn't."

Pratt looked at her. Billie took a breath. She did not know how much she should reveal. But, dammit, she had to say something. Just had to.

"He was trying to help me," she whispered. "To save me. And, in a way, he did." Her voice dropped lower, to a breathless monotone that only she could hear. "He saved us all."

A beat of time passed in the room.

"We'll need a full statement from you later," said Pratt quietly. "But right now, I imagine you'd like some rest. I'll take you home, if you wish."

She nodded.

Pratt led her outside, into the night. She climbed into the passenger seat of the same unmarked car that had shuttled her, yesterday morning, to and from the Colony.

Wordlessly Pratt guided the car down Hollywood Boulevard, then veered south and pulled onto the Santa Monica Freeway. Billie sat beside him, grateful for his silence. Together they raced into the western sky.

To the east, the horizon was already brightening with the promise of dawn. Billie smiled, seeing the first pale streaks of sun rays. She had always hated the night. Hated it and feared it. She had been so afraid of the dark. But now she had nothing more to fear. The abyss would haunt her no longer. She had banished it forever. Finally, after a lifetime of fighting it, she had won.

Then, as the car pulled onto the coast highway and sped north, a memory floated back to her, unbidden but impossible to dispel—a memory of the old man in the desert, kneeling by the vision she had planted in his mind.

"Life always loses," she heard him whispering, his voice gentle and almost sad. "Death wins in the end."

And then she knew that she had not won, not really. She had gained for herself and the universe only a reprieve, a stay of execution, no more. That awful darkness which was more than night—call it death, or the dark gods, or the abyss—whatever it was that dwelled in shadows, was not to be denied. It was still out there, still hunched and waiting, as it always waited. It had claimed Drake as its victim, and someday it would claim her as well, and all the others who played in the sunlight and laughed and sang, all the living and those yet unborn. Someday the world would see its last dawn, and then the night would fall and rule forever. Someday the sun would flicker like a dying light bulb and wink out, and this earth would freeze in darkness. Someday the universe itself would go dark with the death of its last star. Someday.

The old man had seen that much of the truth, at least—the truth that had driven him mad. Yes. Death always wins in the end.

But life, thought Billie with a faint touch of pride, can sure put up one *hell* of a fight.

She lifted her face to the rising sun. The wind off the ocean kissed her hair. She smiled.

A nice enough sentiment, she supposed. Poetic, almost.

You know, it might not be such a bad idea for a song.

ABOUT THE AUTHOR

Born and raised in New Jersey, Douglas Borton now works as a screenwriter and journalist in Los Angeles, California. He wrote the original screenplay for the action-adventure film *Counterforce*, and is the author of the horror novels *Manstopper* and *Dreamhouse* (both available in Onyx editions).